accidental
PRIVATE EYE

OTHER BOOKS AND AUDIO BOOKS
BY CLAIR M. POULSON

I'll Find You

Relentless

Lost and Found

Conflict of Interest

Runaway

Coverup

Mirror Image

Blind Side

Evidence

Don't Cry Wolf

Dead Wrong

Deadline

Vengeance

Hunted

Switchback

accidental
PRIVATE EYE

a novel

Clair M. Poulson

Covenant Communications, Inc.

To my oldest grandson, Austin, whose involvement in demolition derbies was instrumental in my coming up with the basic theme of this book. Good luck on your mission, Austin.

chapter ONE

I HAD EXACTLY ONE DOLLAR and fifty-seven cents to my name. At least I wasn't starving anymore, although I was still a little bit hungry. Just a few minutes earlier I'd spent five dollars and sixty-five cents on a cheeseburger and fries. Prior to that huge expenditure I'd been as hungry as I'd ever been in my life, and in a few hours I'd be very hungry again. Hard times had hit me right between the eyes, put me to my knees, and they were, it seemed, about to grind me into the dirt. Those hard times had begun when my apartment had been burglarized and my bank account cleaned out before I realized that the burglars had stolen and used my identity.

I was leaning gloomily against the wall of a business on Center Street in downtown Provo on an overcast Sunday afternoon in early September, wondering what to do with myself. I had left the army in July, just a few months after returning from my second tour in Afghanistan. They'd tried to get me to reenlist and even offered me a cash incentive, but I'd had all the war I cared for. I'd already spent nine years in the service. Having enlisted at age seventeen, I'd served three years and then reenlisted for six more. But now, after the thieves had cleaned me out, I was down to my last dollar, and the army didn't look so bad anymore. I'd been looking for a job for weeks and had failed miserably. Maybe I should enlist again. At least I'd have a place to sleep and food to eat. And maybe, if I was lucky, I'd be able to get my staff sergeant rank back before too long. After all, I'd only been a free man for a couple of months—surely they'd treat me well.

Of course, I'd have to thumb a ride to Salt Lake City. My Dodge pickup, the only home I had now, was nearly out of gas, and a dollar fifty-seven wouldn't do much to change that. It sure wouldn't get me to Salt Lake. I could sell it, but I didn't want to do that. Even if I reenlisted in the army, I'd need my truck, and anyway, I liked it. It was one of the few things the burglars didn't take—probably because I'd been in it and away from my apartment at the time. I pushed away from the wall, ready to leave my truck at a pawnshop in exchange for a few bucks, hoping to get it back soon. I was also ready to stick my thumb out and head for the army recruiting center in Salt Lake to reenlist, like I should have done before ever leaving the army in the first place, when a small, elderly lady approached me. Her short gray hair was frizzled, her wrinkled face pale, and her light blue eyes sad. She was stooped with age. "I need your help," she said, looking up at me, her voice sounding desperate. "I have money. I'll pay whatever it costs to get you to help me. Please, sir."

She had money. I didn't. She needed help. I wasn't doing anything. Maybe that thumbing idea could take a breather. I smiled at her. "Of course, ma'am," I said politely, envisioning a leaky roof or a cluttered backyard or some such mundane task that needed to be done and being more than willing to do it. "How can I help you?"

"My grandson was murdered, and I want to know who did it. The police aren't making much progress. Maybe you can."

I was only three or four sentences into this conversation and was already in way over my head, and that was saying something since I stood six-foot-four in my stocking feet. "Uh, ma'am," I stammered, warming my thumb up again. "That's not something I do."

"Of course you do," she said, her face stern. "Your advertisement in the yellow pages says you do all kinds of investigations. That's what I want you to do—investigate my grandson's untimely death."

As she spoke, she was opening her purse. "Here, I don't know what your usual retainer is, but take this." She withdrew her hand with a fistful of green bills in it. I couldn't help but think of that cheeseburger and how much I'd like another one just like it. She was thrusting the whole works toward me. My hands began to tremble. I held one of them toward her and, almost without conscious thought, allowed her to deposit the money in my hand.

"Thank you," she said as I closed my fist. "Let's go in your office, and I'll sign whatever you need me to sign."

She was looking beyond me—at a door. I followed her eyes and nearly choked. A brass plate announced to whomever cared to look that inside was the office of the Pierce Investigation Agency. *She's mistaken me for someone who does business from beyond that door.* Guilt flooded over me, and I said, "Why don't you take this back? I don't think I am who—"

She cut me off before I could explain that I didn't work for the agency as she assumed. "Please," she begged. "Let's go inside, and I'll tell you what I know. You weren't just leaving, were you? I know it's Sunday, but your ad says you are available seven days a week."

"I . . . I . . . was—" I began as my eyes again followed the direction of hers and saw the Closed sign in the window.

"Can we go in, then?" she interrupted persistently.

"I, uh—I don't have the key," I said. "I can't unlock the door." That was all true enough, but I felt guilty anyway.

"Is your secretary inside?" she asked. "Or doesn't she work Sundays?"

"I don't have a secretary," I said honestly. I didn't even have a daily planner.

"Then let's go down the street. We can sit in a booth in the corner and have a soft drink while I explain what I need you to do," she said, undeterred. "Now you put that money in your pocket. I know that's only a retainer. I'll give you more later. You just tell me how much you need."

I looked dumbly at the money in my hand. "Let's go," she said urgently, tugging at the sleeve of my jacket.

I followed her as she walked back the way I'd come not ten minutes earlier. I was trying to decide how to explain to her that I was not a private investigator, that I'd just happened to be standing in front of that office when she came to retain competent help. I also studied and then counted the money she'd handed me. They were hundred dollar bills, I discovered—a dozen of them! I shoved them out of sight in a pocket of my jeans. As I struggled with my conscience, she turned into the very Wendy's restaurant where I'd finally broken down and parted with most of my precious money in order to tame the unruly pangs of hunger in my stomach.

She selected a booth and opened her purse again. She handed me a five-dollar bill. "I'd like a Sprite," she said. "Get whatever you want for yourself."

Feeling like a total idiot, if not a crook, I ordered her a Sprite and me a cup of coffee and returned a minute later to the booth, drinks in hand. She took hers and began to sip before I got seated opposite her. I tried my coffee, wishing I had another cheeseburger to go with it. "Did you count the money?" she asked a moment later, her voice businesslike now but her previously sad eyes glaring disapprovingly at my coffee cup.

"Twelve hundred dollars," I said.

"Is that enough to get started?" she asked.

I wasn't an investigator, but I supposed that much money could persuade me to become one. I had read lots of mysteries over the years, and I loved them. I was pretty good at figuring out the whodunits. Perhaps that was all the background I needed. Anyway, I wasn't stupid. In fact, I liked to think I was quite bright, just down on my luck. "That'll be fine," I said. "Would you like to tell me what happened to your, uh, grandson?"

"Don't we need to sign a contract first?" she asked.

"I don't have one with me," I said. "I'm not having a good day, I'm afraid."

"I'm sorry to hear that," she said flatly as she set her soda on the table and once again dug into her purse. I didn't have any idea what she was after this time, and I was surprised when she pulled out a small notebook and pen. "Why don't you write one on this?" she asked. "We'll both sign it, and it will be official."

It would be deceptive, I was thinking, as I felt the pressure of the wad of large bills in my pocket. I felt like a thief, and for a moment, I just looked at the notebook and pen. "I prayed this morning before I went to church," she said. I looked across the table at her, wondering where that totally unexpected statement was leading. Those old blue eyes became misty. "I felt that I needed to look for an investigator today, despite it being the Sabbath. You are the answer to my prayer," she said so sincerely that I felt goose bumps on my arms. "When I saw you standing there leaning against the wall, I got this strong feeling that you could help me. I know that my feelings are not misguided. The Lord will help both of us—even though you drink coffee."

I wasn't so sure about that. After all, despite my early LDS upbringing, I not only drank coffee, I didn't even go to church. To make it worse, God and I, well, we hadn't talked much lately. Now don't get me wrong, I believed in God, and at times, when things were desperate in the war, I tried to pray, and I suppose I got an answer—I was alive, after all. That wasn't true of many of my army buddies. My grandmother, the only grandparent I ever knew, had taken me to church as a boy, but I hadn't been in years. My folks, who had died in an accident when I was only nine, were never active, and when my grandmother died a few years later and I went to live with a distant relative, I just quit going. I was fourteen at the time.

"That's good," I finally said uneasily, leaving the coffee on the table, feeling a twinge of guilt each time her eyes strayed to it.

"My name is Ellen Grady," she said as I sat with pen and notebook in hand, not sure what to write or even if I should write anything. If I wrote a contract, crude and unprofessional as it might be, I would be obligated to go looking for a killer. That was heavy stuff. I didn't even know where to begin. "And your name is?" she asked, scrunching her wrinkled brows. "Are you Mr. Pierce?"

She was asking me a question. My name? That was easy. "No, I'm not Mr. Pierce. I am Dallas Rowen," I said. Until a few weeks ago, I'd been Sergeant Dallas Rowen, and unless I pulled out a miracle for this little old lady, I would probably soon be Private Dallas Rowen, starting a military career all over again. The idea of having to do that got me writing. I hoped that the simple contract I wrote between me and Ellen Grady wouldn't one day land me in jail and make me Inmate Dallas Rowen. With that thought in mind, I didn't make any mention in the document of me being a private investigator, for I wasn't. When I had finished, she scanned the document briefly and said, "So you work for Mr. Pierce." It was a simple statement, not a question or an accusation of any kind. She went on in the same businesslike tone. "It looks good to me except that it doesn't mention your financial terms."

"Let's just work that out as we go," I said awkwardly. "The retainer you've given me is sufficient for now."

She nodded agreeably. "My dear departed husband left me with plenty of money, so I can pay whatever you feel is fair," she said. "All I want is justice for my grandson."

"Let's see how it goes," I said, becoming increasingly uncomfortable over being paid to do something I had no experience with and certainly wasn't licensed to do. She asked me to write the contract a second time so we could each have a signed copy; then she asked, "How do I get ahold of you when I need to? Should I just call your office?"

"No, the best way to reach me is on my cell phone. I'll give you the number," I said and recited the number of the phone that had been turned off just a couple of days ago when I couldn't pay my bill. With the help of that wad of money in my pocket, I'd rectify that little matter before the afternoon was over.

She gave me the number of her phone, saying, "I don't have one of those fancy new phones like you young people use, but I'm usually at home. At my age I can't get out a lot."

"That will do," I said as I wrote down her number and address on a borrowed page of her notebook.

I looked up as I finished writing, and she said, "Why don't I give you my granddaughter's cell phone number too. If for some reason you can't reach me, you can call her and she will find me. She's a sweet girl—solid and steady—unlike her brother Jerry."

I assumed, as tears began anew, that the not-so-steady brother was the deceased person whose killer she was expecting me to find. My stomach began to churn. What did I think I was doing?

Finding a way to eat, I reminded myself. A dollar fifty-seven wouldn't go far, especially for a big man like me.

"My granddaughter's name is Alexandra," she said. "But she usually goes by Alex."

"What's her last name?"

"Oh, I'm sorry. It's Grady, the same as mine. Her father is my only child. He was a career soldier, didn't marry until he was over thirty. He died in Iraq several years ago, and Alexandra's mother, who is almost ten years younger than he was, remarried. She's a good woman, but my grandson didn't take his father's death well, and he never got along with his stepfather or stepbrother. His stepbrother is older than he and Alexandra. He is a badly spoiled child."

"Where does he live?" I asked.

"St. George, I think. We never see him. He's really not part of our family."

"What's his name?" I asked.

"Kade Squire," she replied.

"Thanks. Now, you were saying that Jerry didn't take his father's death well," I prodded.

"That's right. He was bitter. I think that having a hard time with his stepfather and with Kade didn't help. Alexandra, on the other hand, turned out okay despite the trials the kids went through. Jerry didn't, I'm afraid." She paused, caught my eye, and went on. "Don't get me wrong. Jerry worked hard and all that. He talked a lot about going into the military like his father had, but his mother and I talked him out of it. Neither of us wanted to lose another loved one to the war. We should have kept our thoughts to ourselves." She choked, wiped her eyes, and then added, "Jerry was killed anyway, and he wasn't living like he should when he died. He just, well you know, he . . ."

When her voice trailed off, I rescued her. "He slipped from church activity, just like I did," I said. "It happens, you know."

"Yes, that's it. I'm sorry. I don't mean to offend you, Mr. Rowen."

I smiled at her. "No offense, Mrs. Grady. Now, I know this is hard, but tell me about what happened to Jerry."

chapter TWO

As soon as she began, between tears and sobs, I remembered seeing the story on the news. It was back when I still had an apartment and a TV. Jerry Grady had died during the demolition derby at the Duchesne County Fair in Northeastern Utah. That was the second week of August, about a month ago. "I was there just so I could support Jerry," she said. "Alexandra drove me out from my home here in Provo."

"What exactly happened?" I asked. "Was there an illegal hit by another driver?"

"Oh no!" she exclaimed. "He was shot."

I shuddered in astonishment. I bit back a comment as to how that seemed farfetched. How could someone have shot him, I wondered, with thousands of spectators looking on? But I didn't ask her that. Instead, I said, "Did you and Alexandra see it happen?"

"We don't know," she said tearfully. "Cars were crashing into each other and knocking one another about like they do in demolition derbies. The sounds of the cars crashing and the cheering of the crowd were so loud they were giving me a headache."

"I can imagine," I said sympathetically when she paused for a moment.

She began speaking again, her eyes focused somewhere beyond my right shoulder. I kept mine focused on her anguished face as she said, "His car had been hit quite hard, and he was just sitting there, trying to get the engine running again, according to his sister. He finally got it going, and when he did, he drove directly into the rear of another car. The two of them, his car and the other fellow's, got stuck together. Jerry was slumped forward on his steering wheel. It was like he was tired of trying, which wasn't like him at all. He claimed to be a champion derby driver. That's why he was out there. He was apparently really good at it. At least Alexandra thinks he was."

"I'm sure that's true," I said, trying to prod her out of another pause. Her thin shoulders were drooping and her eyes downcast.

She finally looked up and said, "The other car got unstuck from his and went on racing. Several minutes passed. Jerry just sat there, not moving. Some guy right behind me said something about him taking a catnap. But I knew he wasn't sleeping. A minute later, when he still hadn't moved, the announcer warned him that he had one minute to hit another car. He still didn't do anything. The guy behind me said something about a catnap again. Alex—she can be a real fireball—turned around and told him to be quiet, or words to that effect. I was feeling sick. My stomach was rolling. At that point I knew something was seriously wrong."

"Couldn't the officials see that?" I asked.

"I guess not. He was on our side of the arena, close to the stands. There was a lot of crashing and banging going on all around him. It was horrid. All I could do was watch my grandson. Alexandra had grabbed my arm and was gripping it so tightly that I looked over at her to ask her to let go. But when I saw her face, I didn't say a thing. She was white, her eyes were wide, and she was biting her lip so hard it was bleeding." Mrs. Grady took a deep breath then said, "Finally, Alex looked at me and said, 'Grandma, something's wrong with Jerry. I think he's unconscious. They need to stop the race and get him an ambulance.'"

"Did Alex try to do anything?" I asked.

"Yes, she called 911 on her cell phone and told them that someone needed to stop the race and why," she said, her watery eyes meeting mine. "The dispatcher promised to notify an officer. A minute later, an officer appeared, and he crossed the fence and climbed onto the big pile of dirt that surrounded the arena. He was waving his hands, and the official with the flag across the arena saw him and signaled with his flag for everyone to stop. The announcer also shouted at the drivers to stop their cars."

Mrs. Grady took a deep breath. I asked what the officer did then, although I was pretty sure that she was about to tell me without my prodding. She looked past my shoulder again and said, "He ran over to Jerry's car. Alexandra—she's an impetuous girl, a fiery redhead like I was as a girl—she jumped up and said, 'Stay here, Grandma. I'll be back.' Before I could say anything she was fighting her way down the stands. She climbed the fence, just like the officer had, and then she ran across the berm of dirt and reached the car just as the officer pulled his head out of the window and straightened up.

"He told Alex to move away. When she told him she was the driver's sister, he was even more insistent. But my Alexandra isn't the sort of girl that gives up easily. She just rushed past him. He grabbed her, but by then she'd gotten close enough to see the blood all over Jerry's shoulder. And she also spotted a small hole in the side of his helmet. The officer and other men who had reached Jerry's car carried her away from it. She was screaming and struggling. I was feeling faint, and the man next to me asked me if I was okay. I told him that it was my grandson in that car, and he and several other people were very kind to me," she concluded.

I gave her a moment while she wiped her eyes and blew her nose. Then I asked, even though I was quite certain of her answer, "Was he dead?"

She nodded. "It was horrible. I thought that somehow he'd been injured badly in one of the collisions, but that wasn't what had happened."

She grew silent, cleared her throat, and then said, "He'd been shot right through his crash helmet. Someone murdered him." Her eyes narrowed until I could barely see her pupils. "I want whoever shot him brought to justice. I don't care what it costs me. Just find out for me and I won't let the authorities rest until Jerry's killer is locked up forever."

Wow! What should I do now? I wondered to myself. This was surely not something I could help her with. I shifted nervously, and then I said, "I'm not sure I'm the right person to help you, Mrs. Grady."

She looked at me for a long time, her eyes still narrowed. Then she said firmly, "You are the right one. Please, help us."

"Us?" I asked with a cocked eyebrow.

"Alexandra and me," she said. "She kept thinking that Jerry would come around and straighten up his life. She was not willing to give up on him, even though they argued a lot. They were only a year apart in age, and since she was the oldest, she seemed to feel responsible for him. She says she won't rest now until his killer is brought to justice. If you don't do this for us, she might try to do it herself, and that scares me. She's the only one I have left."

"Okay," I said hopelessly. "I'll do my best."

I borrowed her notebook again and wrote down as much information as she could give me. Her grandson's full name was Jerry Owen Grady, age twenty-two. She told me that he was about five-foot-six and weighed one hundred thirty pounds. His hair, like his sister's, she told me, was bright red. And his eyes were green, also like Alexandra's.

Jerry had held a job as a mechanic, and she gave me the address of the garage in Provo where he had worked. As for his friends, she had no idea who they were. "Alexandra might know. You'll have to ask her," she said. I wrote down Alexandra's address and cell phone number. If, despite my better sense, I was going to attempt this, I needed to get to work. But where in the world should I begin?

Ellen Grady had scarcely disappeared down the street to where she had parked her car when I decided where to begin. It had to do with my stomach. I ordered a bacon cheeseburger meal. While I ate, I planned my next moves: First, gas up my pickup; second, pay my cell phone bill and get my phone turned back on; third, buy a notebook to keep track of the case as it developed and to keep track of my expenses; fourth, decide what to do after I'd finished with one, two, and three, and jot it down in the new notebook.

One, two, and three went well. Four went nowhere, so I put it off and washed my clothes at a Laundromat and looked up a listing of available apartments. I couldn't very well continue living in my truck if I was going to be a workingman again. By the time I'd found a small, lightly furnished studio apartment in Orem that had seen better days and hauled my newly cleaned clothes and few other belongings into it, it was evening, and I was hungry again.

I considered my cash. The twelve hundred dollars was sadly dwindling already. I decided I'd better not eat out again that evening, so I went to a grocery store, bought a few basic items, and ate a simple dinner in my small apartment. After cleaning up my dinner mess, I took a shower, shaved, and then sat down with the notebook.

After five minutes of head scratching and deep thought, I finally figured out what my first *official* move would be. I was still in the process of jotting down, *Look up news reports on the death of victim*, when my newly activated cell phone rang. "Hello, this is Dallas," I said without looking at the number. I didn't have a lot of people interested in me with my parents and grandparents having passed away when I was young. My only sibling, a brother ten years my senior, lived in Japan where he made a ton of money managing a branch office for some big California software firm. We had very little to talk about, so we didn't try more than once or twice a year.

"Mr. Rowen, this is Ellen Grady."

At least I now knew who was calling, but it was kind of soon to be requesting a progress report, I thought. So I offered nothing, which was all I had. Instead, I said, "What can I do for you, Mrs. Grady?"

"I just got threatened," she said in a matter-of-fact tone.

That brought me to my feet. "You got what?" I asked in astonishment.

"I got threatened," she repeated.

"Who threatened you?"

"I have no idea. The voice on the phone was very muffled, but whoever it was said that if I continued trying to discover who had put the bullet into my grandson's head, I would regret it," she said, seeming not terribly worried—if the tone of her voice was any indication.

"This is serious," I said, and truly it was. If she couldn't see that, then I was terribly worried. I wondered just how far over my six-foot-four I was.

"You must have already made someone nervous," she suggested.

Not unless the killer was worried about my having a place to lay my head and a cell phone to take calls from threatened old women. Of course, I didn't share those thoughts with my elderly employer. Instead, I asked, "Are you calling to tell me not to investigate?"

"Heavens, no!" she exclaimed. "You are making progress. I just wanted you to know so you would be careful. I'll be praying for you."

"Thank you. I'll watch my back, and you do the same," I said.

The call ended a minute later, and I sat scratching my blond head again. If I hadn't done anything to tip anyone off that the murder was receiving attention from someone other than the police, and I clearly hadn't, then who had? A name popped into my head. Alexandra Grady, fiery redheaded sister of the victim. I made another notation in my new notebook. Right after looking up news reports, I wrote that I would attempt to contact the young lady.

I had no laptop, that having been one of the items the burglars had stolen from me. As I headed out the door to find a public library that was open on a Sunday afternoon, where I could use a computer, I made a mental note to look for the burglars who had ripped me off if I succeeded in finding Jerry Grady's killer (very unlikely, I admitted).

I spent the next hour reading every article I could find about the murder of Jerry Grady. As his grandmother had already told me, he was killed by a bullet that struck him in the head as he was driving in the demolition derby in Duchesne, about one hundred miles east of Provo. Due to the noise of the race and the cheering of the crowd, no one heard the shot. According to the Duchesne County sheriff, Lee Rutger, the shot had been fired from beside a small cedar tree at the top of the tall hill that overlooked the fair grounds. They'd found footprints there and tire tracks nearby. There were no empty shells that they could find; however, a ballistics test taken with the bullet removed from the victim's head identified the murder weapon as a 30-06 rifle.

Beyond that I learned very little that I hadn't already heard from Mrs. Grady. His place of employment was listed, but even though Detective Milt Wakefield of the Duchesne County Sheriff's Office had questioned every person who worked in the garage, apparently no one had shared any information that helped in the investigation—unless the officers were keeping some things to themselves. I wasn't sure what I could do to find out those things, if they existed.

I had a couple of pages full of notes when I left the library. Darkness had crept over the area, and I looked at my watch. It was eight thirty. Was that too late to contact Miss Alexandra Grady? I hoped not and headed the old truck toward her apartment down in Spanish Fork. She wasn't home, so I called her cell phone. It rang several times before she answered. "I don't know who you are," she said the moment she spoke into the phone. "Anyway, I don't have time to talk until I go off duty. Sorry."

"Your grandmother hired me," I said quickly, hoping she wouldn't cut me off before I could at least tell her what I wanted. "I need to talk to you for a few minutes."

"Who are you?" she asked sharply.

"My name is Dallas Rowen. Is there a time we could meet?" I asked.

"Why would I want to do that?" she asked, sounding more like a fiery redhead than a sweet girl.

"Like I said, Ellen Grady, your grandmother, has hired me to look into the murder of your brother, Jerry," I said.

"I am working a twelve-hour shift," she responded slowly. "I have a break in about forty-five minutes. I'll give you ten minutes of my break."

"Great," I said. "Where do you work?"

"I'm a nurse," she said. "I work at the Mountain View Hospital in Payson. It's at Tenth East and First North—it's easy to find. I'm in the maternity unit, and you can't come in here, so meet me at the front of the hospital by the main entrance in exactly forty-five minutes."

"How will I know you?" I asked.

She chuckled. "I'll be the cute redhead in blue scrubs." She ended the call on that intriguing note. Maybe *sweet girl* was a more accurate description than *fiery redhead* after all. That would be nice.

I arrived at the hospital, found a parking spot, and loped to the main entrance just as a redheaded nurse in blue scrubs was coming out the door.

She had been right. She was indeed a cute redhead—a very cute redhead. I couldn't tear my eyes away as she approached me, her skin lightly tanned and her red hair cut short and combed forward. She was much taller than her grandmother. I judged her to be about five-ten. She was slender and yet curvy in all the right places. As eye-catching as she was in her blue scrubs, I couldn't help but wonder what she would look like in jeans or a dress.

"You must be the guy I'm here to meet," she said.

"If you're the cute redhead, then I am," I said with a grin.

She grinned back and said as the grin faded, "I haven't got much time. What can I do for you?"

"Your grandmother asked me to look into the murder of your brother," I reminded her. "I was hoping you could give me some information."

Her dark green eyes suddenly shot fire. "I'll do whatever I can. I want to have whoever did this to Jerry caught and sent to prison—or worse," she said, practically spitting the words out.

I opened my notebook and prepared to write. "I know what the press says about what happened, and I have your grandmother's account of it. Now I need yours."

She gave it to me, short and succinct, but it didn't vary from what I already knew. After she'd finished, she said, "Sorry if I haven't been much help."

"Actually, there are some things I wanted to ask you that could be very helpful."

She glanced at her watch. "I need to be getting back inside," she said. "But quickly, what do you have to ask?"

"For starters," I said, "I need to know who you've talked to about Jerry's murder. You seem to have touched a nerve somewhere."

"How did you know I've been talking to people?" she asked angrily. "And what business is it of yours if I have been?"

Rather than try to justify why it was my business, I simply said, "Your grandmother has been threatened."

Alexandra went pale. "What are you talking about?" she asked.

"Someone called your grandmother and told her that if she continued to try to find out who put a bullet into her grandson's head she would regret it," I said bluntly, hoping to shake her up.

Either I succeeded or she was a good actress. The color came back to her face, and she frowned. "I just asked his coworkers a few questions, like a cop from Duchesne had already done," she said, her voice firm.

"I didn't know that would make someone threaten my grandmother. I'd better make sure she's okay. I need to call her."

"She's fine, and she doesn't appear to be too shaken up," I told her. "Your grandmother has a lot of pluck."

"Yes, she does, and she loved my brother, even though he was a jerk to her. I only went down to his work and talked to those people because I felt like I needed to do something to help if I could," she said, her shoulders square and her fists clenched.

"That's where I come in," I informed her. "I need to know who you've talked to and what kind of questions you asked and what the responses were."

"Okay, I guess I can tell you that, but I don't have time right now," she said, glancing at her watch. "I've got to get back inside."

"Then let me meet you when you get off work," I said.

"That will be at midnight," she said. "Can't it wait until morning?"

"Midnight will be fine," I told her since I wanted to learn what she knew sooner rather than later. I might not be an experienced investigator, but I was a soldier, and this matter was shaping up to be a battle. That was familiar territory for me, and in war, the time of day was not always material. "Where would you like to meet me?" I asked.

"You'll have to buy me dinner," she said with a sly grin on her lightly freckled face.

"I wouldn't mind that at all," I said as I thought about what that might cost. An expensive restaurant wasn't in my slim budget but sitting in a booth across from this fetching redhead would be nice.

"It doesn't need to be fancy," she said. "I like Arby's. Can we meet there?"

I thankfully agreed and made a note of the location she recited in my busy little notebook.

"See you there about ten minutes after midnight. If I'm a little late, don't leave," she said, and with that she turned and hurried back into the hospital. I couldn't help but watch. She was quite intriguing.

Alex's departure left me with some time on my hands. I didn't want to waste gas driving all the way back to my apartment in Orem, so I killed some time walking around Payson, thinking about what I'd gotten myself into. I got another call from Ellen Grady at about ten o'clock. She sounded a lot more troubled than she had before.

"Mr. Rowen," she began, "I am worried about Alexandra."

"She's fine," I assured her quickly. "I just talked to her a little while ago. She and I are going to meet when she gets off shift at midnight."

"That's a relief," she said. "She's a good girl. I'm sure she'd like to help you, but I don't know if that's such a good idea. I don't want her life in danger. That's what I'm worried about. I'm afraid she's already been talking to people about Jerry's murder. She must leave that up to you. I don't want any harm coming to her."

"I'll warn her, but I'm not sure I can keep her from helping in her own way. She's seems like a girl who has a mind of her own," I said. *Much like her grandmother*, I didn't say.

"She does at that," Mrs. Grady agreed. "But Mr. Rowen, you will have to control her. Tell her I hired you to figure this terrible thing out and that I want her to leave it up to you."

"I'll try," I promised. "And by the way, you can just call me Dallas. I don't usually go by Mr. Rowen."

"Then you must call me Ellen," she countered. "I may be an old lady, but 'Mrs. Grady' makes me feel stiff."

"Very well," I told her.

We spoke for a minute or two more, and she reminded me before hanging up to keep her granddaughter out of the investigation. I made no promises beyond my pledge to try because I had a feeling that Alex Grady would do as she pleased despite what I might say.

chapter THREE

I ARRIVED AT THE DESIGNATED Arby's well before Alex did. I waited in my truck in the parking lot and watched for her. She drove up in a shiny, lime green, late-model Volkswagen Beetle. I exited my truck after watching her get out of the Beetle. She looked around and smiled when she spotted me walking toward her.

"Remember, you're buying," she said by way of greeting.

"Whatever you say," I told her easily. "Shall we?" I opened the door for her and waved her past me.

She ordered a Reuben sandwich, and I did the same. "You like Reuben sandwiches too?" she asked, like it was surprising.

"It's the sauerkraut," I answered. "I love the stuff, even though you can't get it here in the states like you can in Germany. I spent a couple of years there, and I must have eaten it at least two or three times a week."

"Lucky you. Did you serve a mission there?" she asked as we filled our drink cups.

"No, no, not me. No mission," I said. "I was in the army. I served in a lot of places overseas. I quite enjoyed Germany. Not so much some of the other countries."

"So you've been a soldier. Did you fight in Iraq or Afghanistan?" she asked, her dark green eyes watching me intently.

I squirmed under her penetrating gaze. "Both," I replied. "Most recently in Afghanistan."

"How brave of you," she said.

"Not so much brave as just doing one's duty," I told her. I had never thought of myself as particularly brave, although I did not consider myself a coward by any means.

Our meals were ready. After we'd begun eating, I placed my notebook on the table beside me, looked across at Alexandra, and said, "I'd like to make a few notes as we talk." She nodded in agreement, so I said, "First, would you tell me who Jerry's friends were, at least those you know about?"

"He didn't have many," she said. "He mostly just worked and went to the derbies."

"Did he have a girlfriend?" I asked.

"I don't think so, but I'm not sure. He didn't talk to me about that part of his life," she said. "We mostly talked, when he would take the time for me, about his work and his driving. Jerry loved cars, and that's what we talked about. I know this may sound silly, but he considered himself a professional when it came to driving in demolition derbies. He also had plans to do some real professional racing. He used to dream of NASCAR when we were kids. But as far as I know, he never did anything that would lead him in that direction. He just liked to talk about it." She looked at me, shaking her head. "He even wore a NASCAR coat and cap."

"I suppose that professional racing wouldn't be something easy to get into. Do you know the names of any drivers who regularly competed with him in the derbies?" I asked.

She closed her eyes for a moment. When she opened them, she said, "One of them is a guy that I think is over forty. His name, if I remember correctly, is Jake. That's his first name, but I don't know what his last name is. And another one is a guy about Jerry's age. He was twenty-two and very competitive. Again, I don't know the guy's last name or even where he's from, but his first name is Lyle."

"Where does Jake live?" I asked.

"I think he's from somewhere here in Utah County," she answered after a moment's thought.

"Can you describe him?"

"Oh yeah, I've seen him quite a few times. He's a bit shorter than you, maybe six-one or so. I suppose he weighs around two hundred pounds. He's got dark skin and black hair that grows over his ears and collar." She was thoughtful for a moment, and then she said, "He has long sideburns and a mustache. I think his eyes are brown, but I can't say for sure."

"What about Lyle?" I asked next.

"He's just a little guy, like Jerry was, but he has a big ego. He and Jerry definitely grated on each other."

"How little?" I pressed.

"He's probably somewhere around five-five to five-seven. He's skinny and dirty." She wrinkled her pert nose in disgust. "He doesn't really grow a beard, but whenever I saw him, it looked like he hadn't shaved for a week."

"Hair?"

"It's long and greasy, often in a ponytail. It's brown, I think. His eyes are hazel or green if I remember correctly. I don't really like to even look at him. He gives me the creeps," she said with a shudder.

"Are there any others you can think of?" I asked.

"Not that many people travel around to the derbies like these guys," Alex responded. "Most drivers are young men from the local areas where the races are held. It's not a professional sport. To drive in many of them would take a lot of cars. I honestly don't know where Jerry came up with all his cars, but he always had one when he needed it. I'm sure there's more who like to think they are pros, like Jerry did, but I don't know them."

I wrote for a moment, and then I looked across the booth at her and asked, "Alex, were either of these guys, Jake or Lyle, driving the night Jerry was killed?"

"They were both there. Neither one of them drove in the particular round he was in when he was shot, but I know they were there that night," she said with a firm nod.

Again I wrote for a moment, and then I reviewed what I'd written so far. I hadn't asked about coworkers, I realized, so I asked her about Jerry's employment—where he worked and who he worked with.

She recited the name of the place as Jim's Garage and the owner, Jerry's boss, as Jim Ralsen. She told me that she didn't know him very well, even though she'd been to the garage a few times, but she had seen him there. "He seems like an okay guy. I mostly remember that he doesn't have much hair, although what little he has is brown. The first thing you notice about him is his huge stomach," she said. "I don't think he could ever slide under a car on one of those flat little rolling things Jerry used."

"Age?" I asked.

"Late fifties or early sixties would be my best guess."

"Do you know any of the others who worked there?"

"Oh yeah, the woman who runs the office is probably about fifty. She's almost as big as the boss, maybe an inch or two shorter, but almost as heavy. Jerry clashed with her a lot. He didn't like her at all. Her name," she said just as I was about to ask for it, "is Alice Berryman."

I urged Alex on, and as she talked, I wrote down the names Kelsey Glazer, Kanon Storm, and Randy Faulk, all mechanics who had worked with Jerry. *Kelsey,* I wrote, *is probably in his early thirties. Near six feet and something in the neighborhood of two hundred pounds. Longish, light brown hair.* Alex was unsure of the eye color. She knew that Jerry didn't like him, but she didn't know why.

I made note of Kanon's description as well. Alex assumed he was nineteen or twenty. She described him as medium height and fairly skinny. He wore his dark brown hair fairly short. "About the length you wear yours," she said. Of all the employees in the garage, she thought that he was the one who Jerry related to most closely. "In fact," she said, "Kanon was in what Jerry called his pit crew. He helped with his car at the derbies."

"Great, who else was in the pit crew?" I asked.

"A guy they call Razorback. It was mostly just Kanon and Razorback, as far as I know," she added. "I might have seen a girl there a time or two, a very pretty girl with black hair. I'm not sure if she was helping or if she was just someone that knew them or something. She didn't look like their kind of girl, but you never know."

Alex was pretty sure that Razorback's last name was Jones. She supposed he had a first name, but she had never heard it. She described him as skinny but strong. She said he was taller than her, but not by a lot. "His name has nothing to do with hogs," she said. "Jerry told me that he got cut in the back by some guy with a straight razor. It happened in a bar fight before Jerry ever knew him. The other guy apparently liked to cut people. I remember Jerry telling me that Razorback told him the guy had gone to prison. Anyway, they started calling Jerry's buddy Razorback, and the name stuck."

"How old is Razorback?" I asked.

Alexandra thought for a moment before saying, "Probably a little older than me. Maybe twenty-five—I'm not sure."

"Were there other mechanics he worked with at Jim's Garage?" I asked.

"Yeah, there was Randy Faulk, the foreman. He's quite a bit older than the other mechanics. He's probably somewhere around fifty. He is close to six feet tall and probably weighs two hundred pounds or a little more," she said as I wrote. "He wears his hair short."

"What color is it?" I asked.

"Blond," she replied. "But it's turning gray. Randy seemed to like Jerry. He sort of took him under his wing and taught him a lot about his job."

"What can you tell me about your family?" I queried.

"My family?" she asked, sounding a little irritated that I would ask. "There's only my mother, my grandmother, and me."

"And stepfather?" I pressed.

"Well, yes, but I don't count him or his son. They never took to Jerry and me very well."

"Do you ever see them?" I asked.

"Yes, but not very often," she said. "Mom and her husband live in Arizona. It's hard to get down there much. And Kade, my stepbrother, lives in St. George."

"What's he like?" I asked.

"He doesn't like us much, although he's civil to us. He called me when Jerry was killed. Said he was sorry to hear it and asked if he could help. I said I didn't think he could," she told me. "He was only saying that. He wouldn't have done anything for me if he could. He never really claimed me or Jerry."

She said she couldn't think of anyone else, so I set my pen and notebook down on the table and concentrated on finishing my meal as I mulled over what I'd already learned.

"I need to get home," Alex said after a few minutes.

I wasn't so sure she couldn't tell me more, so as we gathered our trays up, I asked, "Which of these people you've mentioned have you talked to about Jerry's death?"

She looked at me sharply. "You mentioned some of his coworkers," I reminded her. "You said you talked to some of the guys at the garage. Which ones?"

For a moment, as we emptied our trays in the trash bin, I didn't think I was going to get a response. But as I held the door open for her she paused and said, "Yes, I went to the garage and talked to all of them. I wasn't pushy, and no one seemed offended or angry or anything like that. In fact, they all said they hoped whoever did it gets caught."

She passed on through the door. I followed her to her little lime green Volkswagen and held the door for her as she got in. "One more question," I said. "Did your grandmother tell you she was going to hire me?"

She looked up at me, her face neutral in expression. "Not you specifically," she said, "but she did tell me she was going to hire someone to investigate."

"Did you think that was a good idea?"

"No, and I still don't see what good it will do," she said frankly. "I think I could learn as much as anyone else, but it's her money to waste." She stuck the key in the ignition. "Good luck," she said with a bit of a frown just before I shut the door for her.

I stood watching her as she drove away, thinking about what she'd told me. I was puzzled. Why would anyone threaten Ellen Grady if all Alex had done was talk to the people at Jerry's work? Maybe one of them was guilty of the crime, I thought. Or else one of them knew who was guilty and was protecting the killer. Or maybe Alex had mentioned to someone that Ellen had planned to hire an investigator. Maybe that was all it had taken. I shook my head, watched the taillights of Alex's Beetle disappear, and turned toward my truck as a light rain shower began. It had been cloudy all day, but this was the first it had rained.

I drove toward my new quarters in an increasingly strong storm. By the time I entered the parking area adjacent to the apartment complex, the storm had become a downpour. I pulled toward the spot the manager had told me was reserved for apartment ten, which was my number. A black sports car was parked there. I stopped and looked through the deluge, angry that someone had parked where they shouldn't. The rest of the spaces were also filled. Assuming that someone had a guest and they had taken my spot, I finally found a place to park on the street nearly a block away.

I ran toward the apartments, getting a good soaking in the process. I climbed the stairs two steps at a time and ran right to my apartment, slipped the key into the lock, and turned the knob. As I entered, intent on getting dry as quick as I could, I flipped on the light and gasped. They say lightning never strikes in the same place twice, but I don't recall anyone ever saying that it didn't ever strike someone, if they survived the first time, again at a different location. I had been burglarized—*again*. The tiny apartment was a mess. Everything was turned over. The bathroom door was shut. The hair on my neck stood up.

The bathroom door suddenly flew open, and a dark-clad figure with a nylon sock pulled over his face rushed out and barreled toward me. Caught off guard, I couldn't get out of his way before he slammed into me, and I fell over backward and cracked my head against the door. For a moment, stars swam before my eyes. During that moment, the bank robber look-alike made his escape. It took me a minute to get my feet under me, and by the time I got out my door and to the second-floor balcony the black sports car was exiting my parking space. I was too dizzy from the hit I'd taken to run down the stairs. So I did the only thing I could under the circumstances—I watched him drive away in the pouring rain. As I did, I thought I recalled seeing a black sports car pass on the street in front of the agency where Ellen had found me. Had someone been following her? Could that person be the one who threatened her? I had no way of knowing.

Back at the door a moment later, I checked the doorknob and the lock. Everything seemed fine. I stepped inside and picked up the key that I had dropped when I was attacked. I experimented for a minute with the lock and discovered that whether the door was locked or unlocked, it felt normal when I slipped the key in and turned. Since nothing was broken, I assumed the burglar had either picked the lock or had a key. I wondered if it was a former renter who had kept his key and come back to get something he'd left hidden in the apartment—wearing a nylon sock over his head? Not likely.

When I shut the door and looked around, surveying the damage, the idea of a former occupant was totally dismissed. My suitcase was open and the contents, which I had not yet put in the dresser, were scattered across the room. The mattress was off the bed, the sheets and blankets thrown to the floor. I spent a few minutes cleaning up the mess in my soaked clothing. As near as I could tell, nothing was missing. Not that I had much to steal after what the last burglary had cost me.

My clothes were still wet and I had not yet changed when I thought about my truck. I decided to brave the storm again and bring it to the parking area where it would be off the street and closer to my apartment. I walked quickly through the rain, dismayed to learn when I reached the truck that it was going to have to spend the night where it was. Both tires on the street side had been slashed. I literally shook with anger.

The driving rain gradually cooled my rage, and as I stood with it pounding down on me, I engaged my brain. Finally, I started back. By the time I reached the apartment building, I had also reached some conclusions. Whoever I had surprised in my apartment had not chosen my apartment by chance. It seemed logical that that same *whoever* knew that I drove the black pickup. He must also have known that I was not at home at the time he'd broken in, as evidenced by his having used my parking space. He had also known that I might come back before he was through looking for whatever it was that he was trying to find—hence the stocking mask he'd had handy when I entered. He clearly hadn't wanted to be recognized. I had been singled out for some reason, the question being what that reason was.

Chilled from the cold, and with my head throbbing from where I had cracked it on the door when I fell, I changed my clothes, ending up in a pair of dry, warm pajamas. I took a couple of Excedrin for my aching head and stretched out on the bed—which was newly restored to order. As I lay thinking about the guy in the mask and dark clothing, I realized that I didn't know for certain that it was a man, although it seemed to me like that was most likely the case, the speed and power of the body that had struck me seeming to me to have been too much for a woman, at least for most women.

I couldn't imagine that the attack had had anything to do with my investigation into Jerry Grady's death. The only people I had discussed him with were his sister and his grandmother. There was no way that anyone else could possibly know that I had agreed to look into the young man's death unless one of those ladies had mentioned it to someone else. And that didn't seem likely. I finally fell asleep, with that mystery unresolved, sometime between three and four in the morning.

My phone went off, waking me earlier than I had planned when I'd gone to bed about four hours before. It was seven o'clock. I groaned and reached for it where I'd left it on my nightstand. I recognized the number this time. Ellen Grady sounded wide awake, certainly much more awake than I was. "How did your meeting with Alexandra go?" she asked brightly.

"It went fine," I said groggily. "She gave me some names of acquaintances of Jerry's that I hope to find and interview."

"Mr. Rowen, are you okay? You don't sound right," she said.

"I've had kind of a rough night," I admitted.

"What happened? Surely it didn't have anything to do with the work you are doing for me."

"I don't know for sure," I said. "When I got back from meeting with Alex, someone was in my apartment. Whoever it was caught me by surprise."

"Are you hurt?" she asked anxiously.

"Not seriously. I've got a lump on my head, but that's all. I'll be fine."

"Have you been to a doctor?" she asked.

"Oh, goodness, no, it's nothing that serious," I told her. "I cleaned up the mess the guy made and then went to bed. I'll be as good as new in a few hours."

"I need to call Alexandra and make sure she's safe," the old lady said with worry in her voice. "Whoever killed my grandson has a great fear of being caught, and it seems like the rest of us are in danger."

I thought about telling her that Alex would probably be asleep like I was, but I refrained, knowing she was a woman who wasn't likely to be deterred by a little thing like that when the safety of her family was in jeopardy.

"Mr. Rowen," Ellen suddenly said, "why don't you drive over to my house and let me take a look at that bump on your head. I get the feeling you are not admitting how bad it really is."

"I'm okay," I said. "Anyway, my truck has two flat tires, and I can't drive anywhere until they are replaced."

"How did you get two flat tires?" she asked.

"They met the sharp blade of someone's knife," I said, bringing a gasp from Mrs. Grady. "I'll need to get new tires before I go anywhere." As I told her that, I thought morosely about the twelve hundred dollars she'd given me. Two new tires, even of poor grade, would about exhaust what I had left of that supply of money.

"Mr. Rowen, give me your address, and I'll come there right away," she said. "I feel responsible for what has happened to you. I'll buy you some new tires."

I felt like a real moocher, but unless I let her do that, I wouldn't be doing anything. So I reluctantly gave her my address, and she again promised to be right on her way. I hurriedly showered and dressed. I had barely finished but hadn't had time to get my razor out when she knocked on my door.

"Oh, Dallas," she said the moment she saw me. "You don't look like you feel well."

In all honesty, I didn't. Between a hard knock on the head and only four or so hours of sleep, I felt like a walking corpse. I guess I looked like one as well. "I'll be fine," I managed to say unconvincingly. "I just need to shave."

"You sit down right now and let me see that head of yours," she ordered. I did as she said, and a moment later, after prodding and poking through my short blond hair, she pronounced me fit to go with her to her house, where I was to get some rest under her strict supervision. I didn't argue, knowing it would do little good. She was a woman who didn't like her decisions to be challenged, it seemed.

I grabbed my notebook and pen, the only tools of my new trade, as she looked around the apartment. When I stepped to the door, she said, "Dallas, this place isn't fit for a man to live in. Your work must be slow lately."

She had *no* idea, but I wasn't about to tell her now. "I have lots of room in that big old house of mine. Why don't you stay there for a while, at least until things pick up for you? We'll come back later and bring some boxes. You can pack your things and move into my basement. I insist."

Little did she know that packing up was nothing more than putting things into a suitcase. I didn't bother to tell her that. I wasn't feeling well at all, and I needed to either get back on my bed here or get to her house and rest there. Either way, I wasn't good for much longer on my feet. One thing

I was firm on, I thought, was that I wouldn't move into her basement. But for now, I was too weak to argue.

She asked about my truck as we went down the stairs. I explained where it was parked and why I had left it there rather than in my designated parking space. She drove me by it and uttered several "oh mys" when she saw the sliced tires. "We'll call someone to get it taken care of and delivered to my house as soon as the shops begin to open up," she announced.

"How is Alex?" I asked as we rode, watching her sitting up straight in order to see over the top of the steering wheel, me with my head against the headrest, which was not at all comfortable considering the location of my lump.

"I haven't called her yet. After talking to you, I realized she would still be sleeping. I'll call her a little later."

Calling her a little later proved unnecessary. Alex's lime green VW was parked in front of Ellen's house when we arrived and pulled into her driveway. "Alex is here," my elderly chauffer announced. "That's good."

Alexandra met us at the door. "Grandma, you scared me to death," she fumed. "I'm going to buy you a cell phone whether you like it or not, and you better keep it with you. I had no way to get ahold of you, and with the threat and all, I was worried. I called your house, and you didn't answer. So I drove over. Then when I got here, you weren't even home."

It was almost like she had barely registered that I was with her grand-mother. Her attention shifted to me, but it was her grandmother she asked, "What is he doing here?"

"He was attacked right in his apartment when he got home from meeting with you, and someone sliced the tires on his truck. He needs to be doctored, fed, and made to rest," Mrs. Grady announced. "I'm glad you're here, because you can help me. Let's have you begin by looking at the back of Dallas's head."

Alex's eyes grew wide, and she mumbled something as she took my hand and led me to a large sofa in her grandmother's living room. "What happened here?" she asked as she did an uncomfortable repeat of the poking and prodding I'd undergone a few minutes earlier.

"I bumped my head on the door," I said, trying to downplay the scene in my apartment.

"I can see that," she said grumpily. "I mean, how did you come to hit the door? Grandma said you were attacked."

I quickly weighed my options and then decided to tell her exactly what had happened. It would be the easiest thing since I was feeling so awful. I spoke slowly, as I felt like my tired brain was slipping into a black hole. I honestly don't know if I lost consciousness or if I just simply fell asleep at that point. At any rate, when I awoke, I was stretched out on the sofa with a soft, clean pillow beneath my head and a brightly colored afghan covering me. Alex was sitting on a hard-backed chair beside me.

"You're still alive," she said with a little grin as I opened my eyes.

"What happened?" I asked.

"I guess you didn't want to tell me what happened to you, so you closed your eyes and went to sleep." She grinned again as she spoke, and the thought ran through my still-tired brain that it would be nice to someday wake up each morning to a smile that pretty. But I quickly banished that thought to the recycle bin of my brain. It was not something I should even be thinking about.

"I'm sorry," I said sheepishly. "I wasn't feeling so good. If you'd like, I'll tell you now."

"That would be great," she agreed.

When I had finished, she said, "Grandma had me call the garage where Jerry used to work. Jim, Jerry's old boss, promised to get tires on your truck and deliver it here. It's parked out front now."

"That's great, but she didn't tell them who I am and what I'm doing, did she?" I asked.

"No, we're smarter than that," she said, looking offended. "I had her tell them that you were a friend of Jerry's that just got out of the army, that you have some experience as a mechanic, and that you are looking for work. I said you'd been robbed and that as soon as you could, you'd like to talk to him about a job."

"You did what?" I asked incredulously.

Her face dropped. "You need to talk to them. I thought that would be a good way to get in there and learn something about what happened to Jerry, if any of them know anything."

"Great idea," I said as my foggy brain slowly realized that she had in fact arrived at a creative way to begin my official investigation. "I did work on cars a lot as a teenager, and I still do most of my own work on my truck. I guess that counts as experience. Thanks, Alex. I'll go down and talk to him today."

"It's a little late for that," she said. "They close at five, and it's already five thirty." I must have looked puzzled, and indeed I was, for she added, "You've been asleep all day."

"I'm sorry. I didn't mean to—" I began.

Alex waggled a finger at me. "You got hurt. Grandma almost called a doctor, but we decided that I could take tonight off at the hospital and stay here and take care of you myself."

"Thank you," I said lamely. "I need to get back to my apartment now."

Just then Mrs. Grady entered the room. "You will be staying here, Mr. Rowen," she said firmly. "Alex will go with you after you've had something to eat and help you pack your belongings."

"That won't be necessary," I said. The last thing I needed was for the two of them to discover how meager my personal belongings were.

As it turned out, I wasn't in control. My truck, with the ruined tires replaced, had been delivered to Ellen Grady's house. Alexandra took me by the arm and escorted me to it. "I'll drive," she announced. "You still don't look so good."

"Thank you," I murmured with a hint of sarcasm.

"You took that wrong," she said, punching me lightly on the shoulder. "I meant that you look like you might still be a little dizzy."

I made no further comment, and as she drove my pickup back to my apartment, I worried about how I was going to explain why I had so little of this world's goods. Surprisingly, Alex didn't say much as I gathered my things. I thought I saw surprise register on her face at first, but all she said was, "Is that all?" as I finished packing.

"I'm afraid so," I said, my face burning. "I seem to attract burglars. Virtually everything I own was taken a few weeks ago. They even stole my identity and cleaned out my bank accounts."

She looked at me with what I interpreted as disbelief on her face. "That's awful," she said, but her voice matched her facial expression. I had a feeling she suspected I wasn't being truthful. The ride back to her grandmother's home was both quiet and uncomfortable.

chapter FOUR

ELLEN GRADY SHOWED ME TO the rooms she wanted me to occupy in the basement, a bedroom and family room. They were large and well furnished—luxurious when compared to what I had known in both recent days and recent months. There was even a fireplace in the family room, not something I was likely to use, but it gave the room a homey feeling.

Ellen was kind and concerned, but I got the idea that her feelings might not mirror those of her granddaughter, who seemed to view me with distrust following the visit to my shabby little apartment. I made up my mind that I would stay the night but that come morning, I would carry my meager belongings back to my truck and resume residence at the apartment. Then I would get seriously to work on doing the impossible—finding the killer of Jerry Grady.

I slept fitfully, but by five in the morning I got out of bed feeling good enough to go about my duties. I showered, shaved, dressed, and took my suitcase out to my truck. I had intended to slip away without drawing attention to myself, but I had barely placed the suitcase in the truck when Mrs. Grady called out my name. She was standing on her front porch, dressed in a long blue terrycloth robe, her hair disheveled, her face looking very concerned.

I walked back up the walk and said, "Good morning, Mrs. Grady. I didn't mean to disturb you so early."

"You can't leave without breakfast," she said sternly. "I'll fix you some bacon and eggs. It won't take me long."

"You don't need to do that," I began. "It's very early."

She insisted, and I finally surrendered. We ate together, and I have to admit, it both tasted good and gave me some much-needed strength. As I finished the last bite of toast, she said wistfully, "You will be staying here with me again, won't you?"

She must have seen me take my suitcase out. "I appreciate your hospitality," I said. "But I will be fine at my apartment. I don't like to impose."

She frowned. "Alexandra said that you didn't have much there. She said you told her you'd been robbed before."

"A little run of bad luck," I said. "But I'll be fine." She argued, but I'd given in last night. I was feeling better this morning, and I wasn't about to give up my independence again.

"All right," she finally agreed. "But at least you can let me pack you a lunch, just in case you get busy working and don't have time to stop."

Thinking about my dwindling funds, I once again gave in. I sat down in her living room and jotted a few notes in my notebook while I waited. It was only a few minutes before she came in with a paper bag, which she handed me. "Don't let the lunch meat spoil," she said. "And remember, you are welcome to stay here. Your rooms will be ready if you change your mind."

I stopped at a convenience store and bought a small roll of cellophane tape on my way to my apartment. I didn't plan to be brutally surprised again if I could help it. I remembered a trick I'd read about in a detective magazine. A strip of clear tape applied over the crack at the top of the door was a sure way to determine if someone had opened that door. It was unlikely that anyone would notice it there, so if they entered illegally, the tape would break and I would be able to see it and be duly alerted.

Once I was inside the apartment, I opened the paper bag and emptied its contents on my small table. There were two large sandwiches, an apple, a banana, a small bag of carrot sticks, a piece of chocolate cake, and a white envelope. I put everything but the banana and envelope in my refrigerator. I placed the banana on the counter and then opened the envelope with curiosity.

Ellen Grady must keep a large supply of hundred dollar bills in her house. There were ten of them, along with a note, in the envelope. The note explained that it was a further advance on my work. "Get yourself a few things to make up for what was stolen," she had written. "And please reconsider staying in that dangerous apartment."

I felt guilty as I tucked the money into my pocket. But I was also more determined than ever to do my best to earn it. I was parked at the garage where Jerry had worked and where my new tires had been obtained and paid for by Mrs. Grady before it opened. At eight o'clock sharp, a heavyset, gray-haired woman opened the door and flipped the sign around that announced the place was now open. Alice Berryman, I assumed, the bookkeeper/secretary.

Not a full minute later, a bald-headed man about the same size as the woman but with his weight distributed differently, much of it in the form of a large belly, walked in. From Alex's description, I knew it had to be Jim Ralsen, the owner. I supposed that the others would all be showing up shortly, but Mr. Ralsen was the person I had come to see this morning.

"You can start right now," Jim said ten minutes later, even though I'd admitted that it had been some time since I'd done mechanic work on anything other than my own truck. "The guys will help you when needed," he said with a shrug. It was the fastest and easiest job interview I'd ever had. Alex had paved the way for me very effectively. After all the interviews I'd had the past few weeks without any success, I almost went into shock.

Alice took down my name and other important information for payroll purposes, and then she gave me a pair of coveralls and some gloves. She showed me a locker where I could store them and any personal belongings I wanted when I went off shift. She seemed nice, chatting with me like we were old friends. From my first impression, I wondered why Jerry hadn't gotten along with her. Perhaps he was not an easy person to get along with.

One by one the mechanics arrived. Jim introduced me to each one. They all greeted me with varying degrees of indifference except for Randy Faulk, the foreman. He pumped my hand with some enthusiasm and said he was glad to see me. "We've been shorthanded here since we lost Jerry Grady. I'm glad Jim finally decided we needed help. He's drug his feet. I can put you right to work."

My first job was to put new brake pads on a Jeep Cherokee. It was an older model, and I didn't need any help, but with an unearned twenty-four hundred dollars eating at my conscience, I asked for advice from the mechanic in the next bay, hoping to strike up a conversation. Kanon Storm was the youngest of the mechanics and the one I was most anxious to get to know. I remembered that he was the one who had not only been a colleague of Jerry's at the shop but also a member of his pit crew. His hands were black, like mine were quickly becoming, and he was a skinny guy, but he seemed like a decent kid. After he'd given me a couple of pointers, he asked, "Are you the friend of Alex Grady's that she talked to Jim about?"

"Yup, that's me," I said.

"Too bad she's so old," Kanon said with a lewd grin. I didn't think of twenty-three as being old, but maybe to a nineteen-year-old, which was about what Kanon appeared to be, it was. "She's hot," he added. "If I ever get sick, I hope she's my nurse."

I didn't mention that she'd sort of been my nurse last night. I did agree that she was hot, but I didn't say exactly that. "She's very attractive," was the way I phrased it. "She seems like a nice girl."

"I don't think Jerry appreciated her like he should have," Kanon said. "He was rude to her and about her. But then, he was rude to a lot of people."

"He must have been good to you," I ventured.

"Oh yeah, I guess so. We got along, but I just didn't let his orneriness bother me." He looked at me quizzically and asked, "Is she your girlfriend?"

"No, just a friend," I said. "Sure too bad about her brother."

"Yeah, I'll say," Kanon said. "We better get back to work."

"Do you have any idea who did Jerry in?" I asked as Kanon turned back to the car he was working on.

"If I did, I'd do to him what he did to Jerry," he said fiercely. "I'm going to have to drive his car now in the next derby, and I'm not as good a driver as he is."

Kanon had turned away from me before he spoke, and I didn't get to see his eyes, which I had noticed earlier were dark brown. Eyes are the windows to the soul, they say. I could almost picture Kanon's shooting fire at the thought of Jerry's murder. Then again, was he only talking? Had he wanted to take over the driving but Jerry had been in his way? I wish I could have seen his eyes when he'd spoken those two sentences. I might have learned something. He didn't seem like the kind that would murder someone, but I remembered from all the detective stories I'd read that one should never be too quick to rule anyone out as a suspect.

After I'd finished working on the Jeep, Randy asked me to help Kelsey Glazer pull an engine from an old Ford Bronco. Kelsey was a well-built, muscular man in his early thirties. I soon discovered that he was an easy man to dislike. He grumbled and complained incessantly as we worked. Some of the words that came out of his mouth shocked me, and I'd been around soldiers for nine years. They were nothing compared to Kelsey. At one point, when I was steadying the engine and he was working a wrench, I asked him what it had been like working with Jerry Grady.

"He thought he was pretty hot stuff," Kelsey growled. "We're better off around here having him gone."

Now that had been a cold-blooded thing to say. I made a mental note to learn more about this guy and to try to figure out what he had against Jerry besides the kid thinking he was "hot stuff." I tried to get Kelsey to say more, but he clammed up after that.

By the time most of the others had left that evening, I had managed only one more conversation about Jerry. That was with the foreman, Randy Faulk. Randy was a friendly fellow in his early fifties. He brought Jerry's name up just before we left for the day. "It's good to have you here, Dallas," he said. "We've missed Jerry, although I must say you will get a lot more done than he ever did. The kid seemed to have other things on his mind. Racing and driving in derbies was all he talked about. I tried to help and encourage him, but frankly, I didn't get far. Jerry could be sullen and hard to talk to at times."

"Did the others like him?" I asked.

"I wouldn't say that anyone here was exactly fond of him," Randy responded, rubbing his chin and leaving a black streak across it. "Kelsey complained about him a lot, even suggested several times that Jim should fire him. Kanon helped him with his derby car this past season. The two of them got along, but I wouldn't say they were particularly close friends. I sort of think that Jerry used Kanon because he let him." He added another black streak to his face before saying, "I can't imagine anyone here hating him bad enough to kill him. I doubt the cops will ever figure out who shot him."

"It sure has upset his sister," I said, watching him closely for a reaction.

He swung his eyes toward me, and I thought I detected sadness there. "She came around a few times, but I got the feeling that the kid resented her. It might have been because she was taller than him. He was defensive about his height. I feel bad for her. She's a cute gal." He left his analysis at that.

What I had earlier suspected seemed to be very much the case. Jerry Grady hadn't been a very nice guy. But was he *not* nice enough that someone would want to kill him? It appeared that might have been the case, although I thought there had to be more to it than that. At some point he must have done something to really anger someone.

I asked Randy, "Did Alex come here asking about Jerry after Jerry was killed?"

The foreman looked at me curiously. "Sort of like you are," he said. "But I didn't get the feeling that she expected anyone here to really tell her anything helpful."

I didn't want to seem too pushy, so I dropped the subject. There would be other days, although I hoped not too many. I had dreams of actually getting this matter cleared up soon. Actually, I was hoping the cops would clear it up. I intended to make some calls to the Duchesne County sheriff. I just wasn't sure how I would approach that since I was not acting in a legal or official capacity.

Jim hollered at me as I headed for the door after leaving my coveralls in the locker. "Rowen, hang on a minute."

"See you tomorrow," Randy said, and I headed toward Jim's office. He was standing just outside his door when I reached him.

"It seems you did okay today," Jim said with a smile, his arms folded across the top of his ponderous stomach. "It's good to have you here. I'd been going to advertise for a new mechanic. The guys have been telling me Jerry needed replaced. You've saved me the trouble."

"I'm just glad for the job," I said.

"I'm glad you came along when you did. I guess you knew Jerry," he said.

"Yes, and his sister is a friend. So is his grandmother."

"It's too bad about the kid, but he had a way of getting on people's nerves. He was rude to Alice all the time. She really disliked him. It's actually relieved some tension with him gone, although I would rather he'd have quit than to go and get himself killed. It's tragic, but these things happen."

"I'm afraid so," I agreed, wondering what he'd called me over for. It surely wasn't just so we could chat.

"I have a favor to ask," he said. Now we were getting to it.

"What's that?" I asked.

"Jerry had a small toolbox that he left in his locker. I haven't looked in it because there is a little padlock on it, but I suppose it contains some small tools. I'm not sure why he'd have them. I provide everything the men need. He brought it in several times over the past month or so. The last time was a day or so before he was killed. I don't even remember seeing him use anything out of it. Anyway, he left it in his locker the day before he was killed. I was wondering if you'd give it to his sister or at least ask her what she wants done with it," he said. "I didn't think about it when she was in here the other day. It was a bit uncomfortable. She seemed like she was trying to figure out if any of us killed her brother, or at least if we might have known who did. I'd just as soon she doesn't come around again, although I do appreciate her sending you to me."

"She did me a favor too. Sure, I'll take it to her," I said as I wondered just how pushy she'd been. She didn't seem to think she'd said anything that would have caused someone to threaten her grandmother, but then, if someone here was somehow involved in the murder, they might be kind of jumpy.

"I'll get it, then," Jim said. "Oh, and he also left a couple of other things in his locker—a hat and a coat. I have them in my office."

"I'll take them to his sister," I said.

The toolbox was small, red, and looked quite new. The hat and coat had been stuffed in a large black garbage bag. I threw the bag in the backseat of my truck and placed the toolbox in front of it on the floorboard. I took them up to my apartment when I got there. I just wanted to have a look before I delivered them to Alex. I checked the tape on my door. I was relieved to see that no one had intruded while I'd been gone. I pulled it off, unlocked the door, and carried the bag and the toolbox inside. I opened the bag and pulled its contents out. The hat said NASCAR across the front, and the coat had the same lettering on the back—the coat and hat Alex had mentioned. They were nothing but evidence of the guy's dreams. It would probably make Alex cry, I thought.

On an impulse, I checked the pockets of the coat, not really expecting to find anything. I was right until it came to one on the inside. I pulled a folded piece of paper from it. I opened it and read what was written there in quite neat handwriting. It read: *Jerry, don't go to the demolition derby in Duchesne. You aren't welcome there.* It was unsigned.

I held it in my hand, knowing that I'd discovered a piece of evidence the cops would want. It might have been written by, or at least with the knowledge of, the killer. The handwriting could prove very important if and when the cops or I developed any suspects. It gave me an excuse to call the police in Duchesne without giving away what I was doing for Ellen Grady, having come by the note quite innocently. I laid the incriminating piece of paper on my table and checked the coat over again. For all I knew, the cops would want it too. Finding nothing else, I turned my attention to the toolbox. The padlock that held it shut was small, but I had no way to remove it without doing damage to the box itself. But after finding the note, I really wanted to see what was inside. I needed a hacksaw to accomplish that.

Leaving a piece of tape on my door again and taking Jerry's stuff with me to make sure it didn't fall into the wrong hands, I drove to a nearby hardware store where I purchased a small hacksaw. I passed several fast-food places on my way back to the apartment, but remembering the lunch Mrs. Grady had packed and that I had left in my refrigerator, I drove straight home. The lunch would be my dinner.

A small, lime green Volkswagen was parked on the street near where my truck had been when the tires had been slashed. I suspected it was Alex's and wondered if she would still be as cool toward me as she had been after discovering how little I had in my apartment. I could see her standing in front of my door as I pulled into the parking area. She saw me and started toward the stairs. I parked and got out before she reached me.

Alex was still a cute redhead, but the anger on her face nearly made me choke. I left Jerry's things in my truck along with the hacksaw. Now wasn't the time to be turning anything over to her. I'd let the cops decide what to do with it, I decided. "Hi, Alex," I called out as I moved apprehensively toward her.

"You fraud," she hissed. "You nasty liar!"

I stopped in my tracks, stunned. "What are you talking about?" I asked.

She stalked toward me, pointing a waggling finger in my direction. When she reached me, she poked it right in my face, almost stabbing an eye with her long pink fingernail. "How could you?" she demanded.

I took a step back, putting a hand up to keep her finger from blinding me. "What did I do?"

"I'm not stupid," she said angrily. "Did you actually think you'd get away with pretending to be something you're not?"

She took a step forward, and I took one back. "You are wrong, you know," I said. "I'm exactly who I say I am."

She laughed without mirth, throwing her head back and then forward again. She dropped both hands to her hips. "Sure you are! You have no belongings, and you live in a dump. Just answer me this, Mr. Rowen, or whoever you are. How long have you been out of prison?"

That one caught me totally off guard. "I can't believe this, Alex," I said, feeling anger swelling in me. "I have not lied to you."

She angrily shook her head, making her short red hair bounce. "You made me believe you were a soldier. I don't believe a word of it now. And to think you'd play on my sympathies and my poor old grandmother's by saying you'd been robbed. To think that you'd actually move in with her—unbelievable."

"I'm living here. Apparently you haven't talked to your grandma today," I began defensively.

She was crowding me again, and I stepped back until I bumped into the tailgate of my truck. The finger once again poked at me. "I'm going to her house now to tell her I fired you."

Now she'd gone too far. "You didn't hire me, and you can't fire me," I said angrily. "Would you like to tell me why you are so mad at me?"

"I was getting to it," she hissed. "I've been to your so-called office. They've never heard of you there. You are not a private investigator. You are a fraud. I don't know how much Grandma paid you, but you better give every dime back. Then you better never talk to her again."

My anger began to fade away, and I said meekly, "Why don't we both go see her. Maybe we can work this out. I have not lied to her. I never told her I was a PI. She may have assumed it, but when I told her I wasn't, she wouldn't listen."

Alex was glaring at me with so much venom I finally decided there was no use talking to her alone anymore. "You lead the way," I said. "I'll follow you."

"You better," she said starkly, and she turned and headed for her car.

Following her for the next few minutes, I couldn't help but think that my work for her grandmother would be ended as soon as Alex had a chance to tell Mrs. Grady what she believed she should do. I had spent a lot of the money already, but the rest was in my pockets. I'd give it back and agree to pay the balance from my checks at Jim's Garage—if Alex didn't get me fired. I wouldn't put it past her to try, as angry as she was.

Alex pulled into Mrs. Grady's driveway. I parked on the street, exited my truck, and followed her meekly to the door. I felt like the world's biggest heel. Alex knocked on the door, waited a moment, then opened it before her grandmother had reached it. She stepped inside, slamming the door behind her—right in my face. I waited on the porch like a naughty puppy.

At least five minutes passed before the door again opened, and Mrs. Grady said, "Please come in, Dallas. Alex tells me that you and I need to talk."

Alex, with a smirk on her face, slid past me, "See you later, Grandma. I need to go now." Her eyes caught mine before she went out the door. They conveyed her disdain for me. "And I won't see you, Mr. Con Artist," she said. "At least I better not."

After the door had closed, I stood like a dummy, facing my stooped, aged employer, feeling every bit the fool I was. My impulse was to begin talking, to attempt to explain to Mrs. Grady that my intentions had never been evil, that I fully intended to try to find the killer of her grandson. But the hurt in her blue eyes kept my tongue in check.

"Please, come in and sit down, Dallas," she said.

"Yes, ma'am," I said meekly as I followed her into her living room. I took a seat on the sofa where she pointed.

She looked at me for a moment, and then she herself sat down. A smile crossed her wrinkled face, and she asked, "Do you have any idea who killed my grandson, or is it too early in your investigation for that?"

"Mrs. Grady," I began uneasily. "I'm sure Alex told you about me."

"I love my granddaughter," she said, shaking her head sadly. "She reminds me of myself when I was younger. Well, maybe even the current me. She is headstrong, quick to form opinions, and slow to change them, even in the face of good evidence. Sometimes I wish she wasn't so much like me."

I nodded. "She's right, you know," I said after a moment of uneasy silence.

"Partly," she said. "You aren't a licensed private investigator."

"I never actually told you I was," I said as I felt my face get hot.

"Dallas, I thought at first that you worked for the agency where I found you standing when I asked you to look into this matter for me. In looking back, I realized that you tried to correct my wrong perception. But I pushed you, and you finally agreed to do what I wanted," she said.

"I should have made you listen to me," I said. "I'm sorry. I've spent—"

She cut me off sharply. "Dallas, I realized my error within hours of hiring you. I called the agency first thing Monday morning, and they said they'd never heard of you."

"Then why didn't you tell me that?" I asked.

"I wanted you to look into this matter for me. I told you before, I prayed about it, and the Lord led me to you. Please, I hope you will continue to look into Jerry's death."

I must have looked stupid to her, my mouth hanging open and all. But I finally spoke. "I thought you were firing me. Alex said—"

Once again she cut me off midsentence. "She told me I had to," she said with a slowly forming grin. "But as much as I love Alexandra, she's not the boss of me."

"What did she say when you told her you wanted me to continue?" I asked, choking back a chuckle at her childlike expression.

"I didn't tell her." Ellen Grady grinned again, mischievously this time. "She'll sputter and fume when she figures it out, then she'll let it alone."

"I hope so," I said, shifting nervously on the sofa at the thought of Alex's anger. "She is awfully mad at me."

"I know her, Dallas. It'll all be okay with her in a few days. I want you to continue, if you will."

"I'd be glad to do that," I said as I thought about the money I wouldn't have to be paying back after all. "I just hope you're right about Alex because I don't want to cause you further problems or tension with her."

"Why don't you get your things again and stay here?" she asked in a sudden shift of subject. "I would feel safer having you here. Please."

Her eyes were pleading. There was no doubt that she sincerely wanted me to live in her basement. I felt myself wavering. That apartment really was the pits. "I'll think about it," I said, not at all sure what I'd do in the end. "For now, however, there is something I need to do," I told her. I didn't mention the toolbox, the hat, or the coat. That would all be included in a report when I felt the time was right.

I got to my feet. "I better get to work."

At the door, she once again said, "Please, come back tonight, Dallas. I'm afraid."

I took a closer look at her face and realized that she meant it. I could feel the fear coming from her. I could also see it in her eyes. I wondered if she'd had another call, one that had gotten her attention more than the first one. But I didn't ask her. I caved once again and said, "You need to keep the doors locked. I might be late."

"I'll get you a key," she said, her eyes getting misty. She turned and hurried into her kitchen. When she came back, she said, "This is to the front door. I don't know what I did with the one to the back door. I guess I misplaced it. But when you come, why don't you park back there. It might be well if you kept your truck off the street where passersby can't see it."

"I'll do that," I agreed, actually liking the idea. Maybe I could keep the new tires knife free if I didn't leave my Ram in plain view.

I accepted the key and slipped it onto my key ring, right with the ones to my apartment and truck, wondering what Alex would say. I didn't actually wonder long. I knew what she'd say, but I decided it didn't matter. Like Mrs. Grady had said, Alex wasn't "the boss" of her. I was working for and at the request of the sweet old lady, and I would give her my best effort.

"If I'm late, I'll let myself in," I said. "And thank you for understanding."

A tear found its way down her wrinkled cheeks. "Thank you for helping me. I know you can do it."

chapter FIVE

I DROVE BACK TO MY apartment and carried the hacksaw, garbage bag, and toolbox inside. There I cut the padlock off and peered inside Jerry's shiny little red box. I don't know exactly what I expected to see. I'd suspected that it didn't contain tools, but what I saw when I opened the top was a total surprise. The toolbox contained a mix of car keys attached to key chains, each in turn attached to a variety of good luck charms! I examined them, discovering that all the keys were for older model cars— Fords, Chevys, Dodges, Chryslers, even a Cadillac. The charms they were attached to included two rabbit feet, three tiny horseshoes, two metallic copies of the number seven, a silver wishbone, a shiny penny, and what I took to be a shark's tooth. That made a total of ten keys and ten charms.

I had no idea why Jerry would have kept these keys and charm key chains in a locked box. I assumed he had had a reason and I wondered who, if anyone, could enlighten me. The first thing I decided to do was try to determine if Jerry owned cars that the keys fit, and if so, where those ten cars were stored. Perhaps Mrs. Grady would know. Alex might too, but I didn't think I'd approach the subject with her right now, or any subject, for that matter.

I called Ellen Grady and, without telling her about the keys, asked if Jerry had any cars, not only ones he might have driven on the street but ones he might have been planning to alter so they could be used in future demolition derbies. "He drove a shiny Trans Am," she said. "It was blue, what Alexandra called metallic blue."

As she spoke, I examined the keys again. There was nothing in the box that would fit a Pontiac. "Where is the Trans Am?" I asked her.

I thought I detected a huff. "His stepfather came up from Arizona and took it, for Jerry's mother, he said. I don't believe that. He always did like

Jerry's car. My daughter-in-law said it seemed fitting that they take the car since they were the next of kin. I think Alex would have liked to have it, but she didn't argue over it. And of course, I would never drive such a flashy car as that. I thought it should go to Alex, but she let her folks take it."

"I guess that's their choice," I said, although I thought Alex would have looked cute in it. Of course, she looked cute in the lime green Beetle. Not that it mattered. "Do you know of other cars?" I asked.

"No, but Alexandra might."

"What about the car he was killed in?" I asked. "The one he was driving in the derby in Duchesne? Do you know what make it was?"

She shook her head. "No, just something big and old is all I know."

"Do the cops there have it?"

"I suppose they do," she agreed. "Why do you need to know?"

"I'm just trying to be thorough," I told her evasively. "Do you think Alex might know?"

"She might. You can ask her," she said, but then she gave a small gasp. "I'll ask her," she amended. "I forgot that she's mad at you. I'll call you back."

She did call me back, but she sounded hurt. "Alex said that she wouldn't tell you if she knew and that I was being stupid for letting you continue to investigate for me."

"So she doesn't know?" I asked, feeling Ellen's hurt at her beloved grand-daughter calling her stupid and knowing it was my fault.

"I guess not. So that answers your question?" Ellen asked.

It did, and I thanked her. "I'm sorry I've caused you problems with Alex," I added. "Are you sure you—" I began, but she cut me off.

"Alexandra is a good girl. She'll come around. I'm grateful to you for what you're doing. You just keep doing it."

The rest of the evening was not at all fruitful, and I got very tired, finally eating my dinner, the lunch Ellen Grady had fixed for me. I thought about retiring to my bed right after finishing with it. Then I remembered the fear I'd seen in the eyes of that sweet old lady and the promise I'd made. So despite how angry I knew it would make Alex, I packed my suitcase, stepped outside, put a small strip of tape above the door, and drove to Mrs. Grady's house. After parking behind the house like she'd asked me to, I walked around to the front door and let myself in with the key Ellen had given me. Despite the lateness of the hour, Mrs. Grady greeted me, clad in her blue terrycloth robe with matching slippers.

"I'm so glad you returned," she greeted me, smiling. "Would you like something to eat?"

I told her I was fine, that all I needed was rest. What I didn't get was as much rest as I'd hoped for. I fell asleep okay. The hard physical labor at the garage, coupled with the stress of the other work I was doing, had made me very tired. However, my years of sleeping in war zones had made me a light sleeper. When some sound or other woke me, I sat up in the bed, instantly alert. After listening for a moment, I heard something outside the basement window across the room from me. I slipped from under the covers and put my jeans and shirt on, followed by my shoes. I mentally reviewed the room as I'd seen it with the lights on. I recalled the fireplace in the adjoining room. If I remembered correctly, there was a poker there, a solid steel affair with a very sharp end.

After retrieving it in the darkness, I began to walk silently up the stairs, intent on going outside and trying to find out who or what was prowling around. I was mostly thinking about my truck, hoping it was not about to receive more damage. As I tiptoed silently upward on the carpeted steps, my ears were tuned to the sounds of the house, and I gripped the fireplace poker tightly in my right hand. I heard the refrigerator come on where it stood only a few feet from the top of the stairway. There was a creak from somewhere undefined, the kind of creak all houses seemed to have. When it was followed by another, I discounted it as an ordinary sound and continued at a slightly faster pace up the stairs.

When I got to the door at the top, I reached out with my left hand and grasped the doorknob, but I paused before turning it and listened for whatever sounds might come from beyond it. The sound I heard sped my already rapidly pounding heart. Unless I was mistaken, it was the front door opening. I recalled the peculiar squeak of the hinges and was sure that was what I heard. It could mean only one of two things. Either someone was coming in or someone was going out.

I turned the knob and eased the stairway door open, hoping this door wouldn't also squeak. It was silent as a mouse, and so was I as I slipped through the opening and into the hallway between the kitchen and living room just as the front door was eased shut—by someone who had just exited the house. That didn't seem like something Mrs. Grady would do in the middle of the night.

Abandoning stealth, I ran to the front room window, parted the blinds, and looked out. Ellen Grady, in a worn nightgown, was moving down the walk in her bare feet, being propelled by someone holding a gun tightly against the small of her back. There was a black van parked on the street in front of the house next door. I could only assume that was where they were headed.

My heart pounding, I rushed through the house and out the back door, leaving it swinging open so the sound of it slamming wouldn't alert the abductor. I ran through Ellen's backyard, vaulted a fence that separated hers from the neighbors, and then ran as fast as I could go around the neighbor's house. There was not a fence in the front, but there were a lot of shrubs growing along the edges of the lawn as well as bordering the sidewalk. I could see the black-clad person, a man, I was quite certain, still pushing Ellen, who was resisting just enough to make progress slow. I dropped to my knees and crawled along the east edge of the lawn, hoping to blend in with the plants in the darkness. Then I continued on, the shrubs between me and the sidewalk giving me excellent cover.

Peering through the hedge, I could see them as they reached the van. The abductor had his back to me as he struggled to open the rear door of the vehicle. He was still holding the weapon against his elderly victim's back. Acting almost automatically, I leaped the short hedge and brought the fireplace poker downward with all my strength as the man in black swung the gun my way. My aim was lucky, and when it connected with his wrist, I heard it crack and the gun flew in my direction. The elderly Mrs. Grady jumped back onto the sidewalk, moving almost as quickly as a cheerleader. I swung again, catching the man on his left shoulder as he attempted to escape around the van to the driver's side. He jumped in the door as I swung again, breaking the glass out of the door.

The key had apparently been left in the ignition for a quick getaway. And that was what the man in black did, broken wrist and all. The engine started up as I grabbed the door, attempting to open it. Then it squealed away from the curb, sending me hurtling onto my back on the pavement. I was slow getting up, but my dear landlady offered me a hand, and with her aid, I was soon upright again. "You saved my life, Mr. Rowen," she said tearfully.

"Dallas," I said. "I'm just Dallas."

I looked about us to see if we had any spectators, and not surprisingly, we did. The man of the house through whose backyard I'd trespassed was running down his walk toward us. "I called the police," he said in one breath, and then in the next, he added, "Mrs. Grady, are you okay?"

"I'm fine, thanks to Dallas here," she said, sounding anything but fine. She was a brave old girl, I'd give her that.

Other doors were open both on our side of the street and across it. I glanced at the pistol lying on the sidewalk and thought about picking it up. I thought better of it and let it lie, figuring it would be in my best interest for the police to find it there rather than in my hand. A siren sounded in the distance. A police car appeared a minute later as neighbors, clad mostly in pajamas and robes, gathered around my landlady. I stepped discreetly away, keeping my eye on the pistol, which I didn't want anyone touching until the police collected it.

The police car sped up the block toward us and slid to a stop. Two officers jumped out and did what cops would be expected to do in such circumstances. There were questions asked and answers given. The gun was duly collected, as was the fireplace poker I had used to whack the abductor in my rescue of Mrs. Grady. She and I both gave a description of the black van, including the freshly shattered driver's side window and what description we could of the abductor, a male person in black—not unlike the one I'd surprised in my apartment. Statements were taken from neighbors as I was allowed to escort Ellen back to her house, where she promptly put her robe and slippers on.

The officers soon joined us there, and we were asked to provide written statements. The responding officers and a pair of plainclothes detectives who joined them naturally wanted to know what motive there might be for such a horrendous crime to be perpetrated against Mrs. Grady. I took the lead without explaining my own role in assisting her and told them that she wanted to learn who'd killed her grandson. I advised them of the threat she had received. The only questions they asked about me had to do with why I was living in her basement. Ellen explained that I was a military veteran who had been robbed of virtually everything I owned and was homeless and that she had taken me in. They all looked at me with suspicion, and one of them, a detective by the name of Pete Richards, slipped from the room with his cell phone to his ear. When he returned a few minutes later, he said with a smile, "This guy is okay." He went on to report to the others that it was true that I had been the victim of a burglary and of identity theft. He also confirmed my status as an army veteran with an honorable discharge. After that, Detective Richards treated me with respect. I felt like he was someone I could work with if I needed to in the future.

When the police officers finally left, Mrs. Grady prepared to go to bed again, but despite her assurances to the contrary, I could see that she was very much afraid that the attack might be repeated. To reassure her, I slept on the living room couch, fully dressed, with a lever action 30-30 rifle she had asked me to retrieve from her late husband's gun cabinet in the basement—one I hadn't known existed. With it loaded on the floor beside me, we both finally retired, hoping for at least some of the rest we'd so far been cheated of.

The rest of the night, unfortunately, was very short, and neither of us was much rested as we ate breakfast. I had to get to Jim's Garage, where I would spend the day with an assortment of wrenches in place of the fireplace poker and hunting rifle. I was worried about leaving Ellen home alone. Though she promised to keep the rifle nearby and assured me that she knew how to use it, she was clearly worried about being left alone. That problem was solved for us when someone knocked on the locked front door.

Alexandra came in, totally unaware of the night's dramatic events. When she spotted me, her pretty face darkened, and she stalked toward me, again threatening my eyes with a sharp pink fingernail. "How dare you come back here?" She demanded. "And where have you hidden your truck? You thought I wouldn't figure out that you were still sponging off my grandmother by parking where I couldn't see it."

Mrs. Grady moved to intercede, but I raised a hand and smiled at her. To the angry granddaughter, I said, "I'm just leaving. And you need to calm down and listen to your grandmother. She has some things to say, some things you need to hear."

Alex started in on me again, but I simply walked away. I went downstairs and got my belongings, including the toolbox and bag that contained Jerry's things—all of which I intended to give to the police, not to Alex. As I headed out the door, Alex was glaring at me. I smiled at her and then said to Ellen, "Keep that rifle close by and see if your spitfire of a granddaughter will keep you safe for the day. I have to get to Jim's Garage."

The look on the young lady's face was priceless. She was stunned by what I'd said and must have wondered, at the same time, what it was all about. I left the house, leaving further explanation up to Ellen. On my way to my new, likely very temporary job, I attempted to contact the sheriff of Duchesne County, Sheriff Lee Rutger. I finally reached him on his cell phone.

I explained who I was and that, at my new place of employment, I had come into possession of some things that had belonged to the late Jerry Grady. "What do you have exactly, and why were they given to you?" he demanded.

I said, "Among other things, there is a threatening note. I think it would be best if I could turn them over to you today, and then you can do what you need with them. They were given to me to give to Jerry's sister, who is a friend of mine." That was a stretch, but I had hope that perhaps we could at least be on speaking terms again someday. "But I thought you should have them."

Sheriff Rutger said, "I'll send Detective Milt Wakefield out today. It will probably be this afternoon. Where can he find you?"

I gave him the address of the garage, thinking how awkward it might be to have a cop contact me there. I didn't want to give up that job just yet, if at all. I also gave him Mrs. Grady's address. Then I gave the sheriff my cell phone number and said, "It would be best if he calls me when he gets in town. Maybe my boss will give me a few minutes off so we won't have to talk at my place of employment. I'd rather they don't know that I am giving an officer the property that was entrusted to me instead of to the family like I had promised."

The sheriff agreed, and I closed my phone. There was something else I wanted to do that day, something that could be very awkward, but my mind was made up. I hoped to get some time off for lunch to do what I felt I should do without letting Jim know that there was evidence in the toolbox and jacket likely important to the investigation into Jerry's murder. I thought Jim could be trusted, but at this point I wasn't willing to trust anyone Jerry had known. I wasn't a student of detective novels for nothing.

When I arrived at the garage, the other mechanics were also getting there, all but one. Kelsey Glazer didn't show up. Nor did he call in. Jim Ralsen wasn't happy. "He has work to do," he said angrily. To the shop foreman, Randy Faulk, he said, "The owner of the Bronco wanted that engine rebuilt and put back in *yesterday*. He's getting cranky. You'll need to have someone else finish the job. I'll have Alice call Kelsey's home to find out what's going on with him."

Randy asked me to take over on his project, promising to help me if I needed it, which I assured him that I would. I set to work, hoping Detective Wakefield didn't arrive in town until late afternoon or, better yet, in the evening. I really wanted to take care of the other matter of business I had in mind before I spoke to him. I got a lucky break. I needed a part for the engine Kelsey and I had taken out of the Bronco the day before. Jim called around and found one at an auto parts store in town. He said to me, "Dallas, they can't deliver it here. Their driver called in sick this morning. You'll need to go pick it up."

"Sure thing," I said agreeably. "And if you don't mind, maybe I could take my lunch break before I get back, and then I can concentrate on the engine the rest of the day." *Uninterrupted by a deputy,* I did not add but certainly thought.

"That would be fine. Just don't be too long," he said.

I picked up the part first, and then I drove to the street where I had first met Mrs. Grady. I parked in the parking lot of the Wendy's restaurant where I had worked out our arrangements, hoping I could complete my other business and still have time to buy a cheeseburger. I walked up the street with butterflies in my stomach. The detective agency was open, and both a secretary and the owner of the business were in—my good fortune, I hoped.

I introduced myself to the large fiftyish-looking woman at the desk and asked for a private meeting with Hank Pierce. She looked up from her typing and waved at the private office behind her. "He's in there." I took that as an invitation to step in. So I did.

The man behind the desk appeared to be between fifty and sixty. He was almost as tall as my six-foot-four frame but probably had my two hundred twenty pounds beat by at least ten or fifteen. He rubbed his hand across his thin gray hair as I stood in front of the cluttered desk and said, "I'm Dallas Rowen. I'd like a few moments of your time, if possible."

"Your name sounds familiar," he said, adjusting his silver-rimmed glasses as he peered at me from the dark blue eyes behind them.

"I expect it would," I began. "A young woman by the name of Alexandra—"

Hank cut me off midsentence. "Oh yes, fiery young redhead," he said with a grin. "She doesn't seem to like you very much. Your loss. She's a great-looking girl. Her grandmother, on the other hand, thinks you are the cat's meow. At any rate, what can I do for you? And please, sit down."

"I came to apologize and ask for your help, if possible," I said as I took a seat on the hard-backed chair he'd indicated.

The investigator leaned back in his chair, making it creak. His dark blue eyes looked at me appraisingly. He frowned thoughtfully, and then he smiled. "Actually, *I* could use some help. I'm having some health issues lately. My wife, the woman in there typing," he said, "insists that I not work so hard." He grinned broadly. "She says she can't afford to lose me. I don't know if it would be as big a loss as she thinks."

"I hope you're going to be okay," I said.

"I'm sure I'll be fine, but I can't carry on like I have been. I hate to admit that, but it's reality. So, I guess what I'm thinking is that if you would be interested, and if you pass my little background check, I'd offer you a job as an apprentice investigator."

"You'd do that?" I asked, totally shocked. I'd come to ask for advice and even to hire him to do some of what Mrs. Grady had asked me to do. I'd never dreamed that he'd suggest I might be able to work for him.

"If you fit the bill, I would," he answered. "I already know you are an honorably discharged veteran. That means a lot to me. Are you interested? Or would you prefer to keep working on cars?"

"How did you know what I was doing?" I asked, surprised again.

"Miss Alexandra told me. What a pistol that girl is." He grinned broadly.

"Yeah, she is," I agreed. "And no, I don't actually want to mechanic any longer than necessary. What do I have to do to be an apprentice to you?"

"There's an application that needs to be sent to the Department of Public Safety, but for an apprentice it really isn't much more than a formality. I'll take care of that. In the meantime, I'll do a quick background check on you. If I don't find any surprises, I'll probably take you on."

"You won't find any surprises, I can promise you that. And I'd love to work for you if you decide you want me to," I said.

The fellow grinned again. "If I do decide I want you here, and if you don't go around identifying yourself as an investigator until the approval comes in, I wouldn't care if you continued to do what Miss Grady claims you're doing, very unofficial like. I might even be able to give you some help. So let me get some personal information from you, and I'll get to work."

For the next few minutes, I told him what he wanted to know and gave him several references from my army days. Then I quickly filled him in on the work I'd done regarding Jerry's murder. I looked at my watch. I wasn't going to have time to eat, I realized, as my lunch hour was almost used up. I stood and asked, "When will I know?"

"Hopefully, I can be ready today. Why don't you come by after you get off at the garage? I should know by then what I'm going to do."

"You'll still be open?" I asked.

Hank's grin covered his face again. I was fast learning to like the guy. "I'll make sure I am," he said. "If the door's locked, it'll mean Shirley's gone. Just knock. I'll be here."

chapter SIX

THE DUCHESNE COUNTY DETECTIVE CALLED my cell phone as I was leaving the garage shortly after five. "I'll be there," he said. "I've had a hard time getting away from here. I'm just barely leaving my office in Duchesne."

"So what time can I expect you?" I asked.

"Let's say around seven. Maybe we could talk over dinner somewhere."

"That would be fine," I said, assuming that I would have to pay from my diminishing funds. "Call me when you get to the mouth of the canyon, and we'll arrange a place to meet."

He agreed and then asked, "You'll have the evidence with you?"

I assured him that I would.

Hank's wife was gone and the door was locked when I reached the investigator's office. So I knocked, and Hank opened the door and invited me in. He still seemed to be in a good mood, if his grin was any indication. I hoped that was a good sign for my future. "Come in, and let's get down to business," he said.

I again sat in his office, and he shuffled some papers on the desk in front of him. When he looked up, he said, "Everything checks out just fine. Your military record is impressive. And I couldn't find anyone who would say anything bad about you. I took the liberty to begin the approval process on you from the Department of Public Safety."

"Does that mean you are offering me a job?"

"It does at that. Are you agreeable?"

I was, and I was grateful for the opportunity, excited even. "I accept, sir," I concluded, trying to keep my excitement contained.

"We are not in the military here," he said as he adjusted his glasses. "You won't need to call me sir. To you I'm just Hank."

"Got it," I said, barely suppressing another "sir."

"Now that you've accepted, maybe you'd like to hear what arrangements I have in mind as far as pay, working hours, and so forth." He grinned again.

"That'll be great. While we're at it, I need to talk about what Mrs. Grady has already given me."

"I've been on the phone with her. She says you saved her life last night. From the sound of it you did so at considerable risk to yourself. Anyway, she has agreed to my fees and says that you are to keep what she's given you."

"I'll bet Alex will like that," I mumbled.

"Her granddaughter wasn't there when I called. She was expecting her back shortly though. We need to discuss what to do to keep the lady safe. This sounds like a dangerous case," he told me.

I couldn't have agreed more. He grinned and said, "Much of the time what us PIs do is boring stuff. But there are times like this where it's anything but boring. You have started off right in this case. I have no doubt you'll be good at this job. Now, about pay, here's what I'd like to do."

He then laid out a plan where we would split the fees that came in, less the costs of running the office and paying his wife. He'd keep 60 percent, and I'd get 40. "That will change after you get more experience," he assured me.

"You're being very generous, Mr. Pierce," I said, flattered at the proposed arrangements.

"Call me Hank," he insisted. We worked out a few more things, with me receiving a clear understanding that my hours would vary widely depending on the jobs we had. "There will be a lot of night work. And speaking of nights, what do you plan to do this evening?"

"I have a dinner meeting with Detective Milt Wakefield of the Duchesne County Sheriff's Office at seven," I said. I'd told Hank about the coat, hat, and toolbox when I reviewed the case with him at noon.

"That's good," he said. "One of the things I try to do is keep good relations with the cops. It isn't always possible, but it usually works out. Where are the items you mentioned?"

"They're out in my truck," I told him. "Would you like to see them?"

"I guess I better since I'm going to be in charge of this case as soon as you get this agreement signed by Mrs. Grady." He waved a paper in the air as he spoke. "I'll be filling this out while you retrieve the evidence."

I almost skipped to the truck. To think that just days ago I was homeless and hopelessly broke. Now I had a job—two jobs, that is. But I wasn't sure how long my new boss would want me to keep working at Jim's Garage.

I hoped it wouldn't have to be too long. My knuckles hurt from banging around on the old Bronco today.

Hank looked over the note with a great deal of interest when I handed it to him. "This is definitely critical evidence for the cops," he said. One by one, he examined the car keys and the good luck key chains they were attached to. When he looked up, he said, "Somewhere, there are cars that these keys fit. As soon as we can, we need to find out where they are."

He got up from his desk and left the room, signaling for me to follow. We entered another room, one filled with shelves. On them was a variety of things. "Tools of the trade," he said as I looked around the room. "Somewhere in here I have some of that stuff a dentist uses when he takes an impression so he can make a crown for a bad tooth."

I'd never had such a thing done to me. My teeth were still in very good shape. "Ah, here it is," he said and pulled a box from a shelf. "I want to make impressions of those keys before the deputy takes them."

"I never thought of that," I said.

He grinned that big grin of his and said, "That's because you are still a trainee. You'll learn quickly."

A few minutes later we had good impressions of each key. "Don't bother to mention this to the deputy unless he asks," Hank said. "Another little bit of your training here—cooperate with the cops, but don't volunteer too much. After all, the reason guys like me and you get hired on cases like this one is because someone feels like the cops aren't moving as quickly or as efficiently as they should."

It was almost seven when Hank said, "You better get on your way and meet with Detective Wakefield. Come by in the morning, if you can, before you go to the garage, and bring me this contract."

I took the sheet he'd filled out for Mrs. Grady's signature and started for the front door of the office. "One more thing," Hank called out, and I turned back and looked through his office door. "You won't need to keep beating those knuckles up much longer. Get all the information you can from the people at the garage and then quit. You'll have all you can do working for me, both on this case and others."

"Yes—uh, Hank," I said. I had almost called him sir again.

"Oh, and keep track of your expenses. Our clients cover the costs of such things. I expect the cop will let you buy dinner. If he does, it will be on Mrs. Grady. By the way, when you meet with this detective, it will be okay for you to tell him that you work for me. In fact, I think it would be a good idea. I would come with you, but I promised Shirley we would have a quiet dinner at home and that I'd let you take care of things this evening. And by the way, she's excited that I hired you. That's a good sign, because my Shirley is a great judge of character."

I called Ellen on the way to meet Milt just to let her know that I'd be in as soon as I finished up with some work I was doing. I told her I had the contract for her to sign, and I also informed her that we would then talk about the money she had already given me. She let me know in no uncertain terms that it was mine to keep for all I'd done for her. I told her we'd talk about it. She told me we already had. I also asked her if Alex was still there, and she told me that she planned to spend the night. "But that doesn't mean I don't want you here too," she was quick to add. "I think Alexandra is impressed with the way you dealt with that awful man last night." I wasn't so sure Ellen was right, but I hoped.

A few minutes later I was seated in an Arby's with Detective Milt Wakefield. Milt hadn't wanted to take time to sit down in a restaurant, as he said he had to get back before it got too late. He suggested fast food, and that was fine with me. It would cost Ellen Grady less. He looked to be in his midthirties and impressed me that he was both smart and efficient. He was about six feet tall and must have weighed near two hundred pounds, but none of it was excess fat. He was in very good shape. I wasn't sure what I had expected, but as I assessed him while we were waiting for our order to be filled, I felt like he would be good to work with.

Milt had a lot of questions about what I'd done and who I'd talked to. I filled him in. He seemed to be impressed that I was working at Jim's Garage. He asked me a lot about the people who worked there. He was concerned when I told him about the incident with the would-be grandma-napper during the night. "You need to be really careful, Dallas," he warned me. "Sheriff Rutger isn't going to be happy about this development. It raises this investigation to a whole new level."

By the time we'd finished our dinner, I had told him everything Hank had instructed me to. I hadn't mentioned that Kelsey Glazer hadn't come to work that day and that Alice and Jim had been unable to reach him. Hank wanted me to try to learn more about the guy before letting the cops know we were suspicious of him. We sat in his Ford Expedition while I showed him the hat, coat, threatening note, and small toolbox with its assortment of keys and good luck charms.

"Oh boy," he said with a groan. "Looks like I've got a lot of work to do." Then, as he gathered the evidence I'd handed him, he looked at me with what I interpreted as a hopeful look. "You'll let me know if you turn anything up, won't you?"

"Sure thing," I said.

"I'll keep in touch," he said as I got out of his vehicle. "And keep a sharp eye behind you, Dallas. Whoever killed our young demolition driver doesn't want to get caught."

That, I thought, was an understatement.

I stopped at my apartment after leaving Arby's. My stomach began to churn when I saw that the tape at the top of the door had been broken. I looked up and down the street, wondering if there was a car parked there somewhere that shouldn't be. Not that I'd know it if I saw one. I didn't see the black sports car parked anywhere this time or a black van with a shattered window. I hoped there wasn't someone inside. I was not particularly anxious for another fight, even less for on outright ambush.

Hank had told me he was going to help me get a concealed weapons permit, but that would take a little time. In the meantime, he had told me to be very, very careful. Part of being careful was going back to my truck and grabbing the heavy flashlight I kept under the front seat. With that in one hand, I opened the door, flipped on the light, and surveyed the room. Satisfied that I was alone a few seconds later, I picked up a piece of paper lying on my bed. It had only four words scribbled on it, but those four words made goose bumps break out all over me. In very neat handwriting that looked like that on the note I'd found in the pocket of Jerry's jacket it read: *Back off or die.* I didn't plan on doing either one.

It was after eight before I got to Mrs. Grady's home and parked my truck behind the house again—beside a lime green VW Beetle. Alex was there. This should be fun, I thought as I circled back to the front door and knocked.

Ellen Grady answered the door. "You don't have to knock," she scolded. "This is your home now."

"Thanks," I said. "How are you doing?"

"I'm a tough old bird," she said unconvincingly. "I'm fine."

Her voice didn't sound as strong as it had been. She wasn't fine, and I knew it, despite the fact that I knew she didn't want me to. "You are probably tired," I said.

"Not as tired as you," she answered with a weak smile. "I had a nap this afternoon. And I bet you're hungry. Come in the kitchen and let's get you something."

She headed that way, but I said, "I've eaten already. But we can go in there and I'll let you look over this contract Hank Pierce sent with me."

"Did he hire you?" she asked.

"He did."

"Fine, then I'll sign it," she responded resolutely. "As long as I know that you are on the job, I have no objection."

We were sitting at the table with the contract in front of us when Alex entered the kitchen. "You again," she said coldly. "I guess I should thank you for taking care of Grandma last night, but you don't need to stay tonight. I can protect her. Anyway, I can't imagine that whoever that was will come again."

"Don't kid yourself, Alex," I said, the anger in me rising way too fast. "Besides, this is Ellen's decision, not yours."

As we argued, she'd approached the table. "What's that?" she asked, stooping over and peering at the paper her grandmother was reading through. "Surely you aren't trying to stiff Grandma for more money."

"Alexandra, please, Dallas is trying to help us. This is a contract with his boss, Detective Pierce. I believe you've met him," Mrs. Grady said with sadness in her voice.

By then Alex had no doubt confirmed what the paper was. She stepped back from the table. "You don't work for him," she said, but her voice lacked confidence. "He told me he didn't know you."

"I went to him to apologize today," I said, trying to control my temper while being totally honest with Alex. "I asked him to help your grandmother. He agreed to do so, but he also asked me to work for him. We'll be working on the case together now."

"He doesn't even know your background," she said with a sneer.

"You don't, you mean," I answered, getting tired of arguing with the girl. "He spent the afternoon checking me out, and then he asked me to go to work for him."

"Oh," she said, and without saying anything further, she left the room.

Ellen and I completed the business of the contract, and she gave me a check made out to Pierce Investigation Agency. I promised to give it to Hank first thing in the morning. Ellen asked if I'd been able to learn anything that day. "I'm afraid I haven't had much time. I did meet with a detective from Duchesne. That's who I was with for dinner. I believe he is going to be good to work with. Between him and his boss and my new boss, maybe we can get to the bottom of this thing."

Alex reappeared. I assumed she had been eavesdropping. "What is his name?" she asked without looking at me.

"Milt Wakefield," I said, still angry enough that I didn't want to spend a lot of breath answering Alex's questions.

"I met him," she said. "Why did he call you?"

"He didn't," I said, trying very hard to be patient. "I called his boss, Sheriff Rutger. At my request, he sent Milt out to talk to me."

"Does that mean you actually had something to tell them, or are you just trying to act like you're not the fraud you really are?" Ooh, that girl could be nasty. I wasn't sure now what I'd seen in her at first.

"I had some evidence I felt they needed. I called to tell the sheriff about it. I knew he'd want it." I was speaking to Ellen, really, not Alex. A terrible thought occurred to me as I spoke. Did Alex really want whoever had killed Jerry caught? Though it was an appalling thought, I couldn't discard it. I had to look objectively at everyone who was acquainted with Jerry, even his sister. But I kept that to myself for the time being. I might mention my concerns to Hank when we met in the morning. But I wondered how much I should say to her grandmother in front of her.

Unfortunately, I had already said too much. Ellen looked with sad eyes at Alexandra and then leaned toward me and asked, "What was the evidence?"

"Just some things of Jerry's Jim Ralsen gave me. I thought the sheriff should look at them in case there was anything useful," I said evasively.

"If they were Jerry's, shouldn't you have given them to me?" Alex asked. She wasn't giving up. She really didn't like me.

"When they are through with them, I suppose the sheriff will let you have them," I said, conscious of the pain in her grandmother's face and hoping to somehow cool things a little.

"What was it that you gave them?" she asked.

"A small toolbox, a coat, and a hat." I didn't mention the note I'd found in the coat.

"That's all? What would the cops want with them?"

"I guess you'll have to ask them," I said. I was really getting tired of her attitude. I hoped she wouldn't ask what was in the toolbox, that she would just assume it had tools in it, because I really had no intention of telling her about the keys and good luck charms or the note.

As we were talking, Alex had moved around the small kitchen table to sit across from me. I decided to ask her about Kelsey Glazer while she was where I could see her reaction when I brought him up.

"You know the guys at Jim's Garage," I began. "What can you tell me about Kelsey Glazer?"

"Why do you ask about him?" she asked, furrowing her brow.

"He didn't come to work today, and he didn't even call in. Jim says that's not like him. I just wondered what you thought of him."

"He didn't like Jerry," she said. "Nor did Jerry like him. Other than that, I couldn't tell you much. I didn't go there that often when Jerry was alive. And when I went in asking questions the other day, he was quite rude. Not that it matters what he thinks of me since you have so *expertly* taken over the investigation."

Her words came out with a bite. She didn't give me any indication, through body language or with her eyes, that told me anything other than what she'd said. I dropped the matter. I'd about had it with Alex tonight. I stood up and Ellen said, "Why don't we all have a dish of ice cream and some cookies."

"Thanks, I'm fine. I think I'll go to bed," I said. "I hope to catch up on the rest I didn't get last night. Would you like me to sleep on the sofa, Ellen?"

"Why would you do that?" Alex demanded.

I gave her a look of disgust. "Some of us are still worried about the guy who tried to kidnap your grandmother last night."

"I'll sleep there, Grandma," she said. "Dallas needs his beauty rest."

"Neither of you has to do that. I'm sure I'll be fine tonight," she said. Her eyes told me a different tale.

"I'll sleep there," I said with finality. "I'll be back up in a few minutes."

Alex sort of snorted and then said, "I'll have some ice cream, Grandma."

"Are you sure you don't want some, Dallas?" Ellen asked.

"I'm fine," I said and headed for the stairway.

When I came back up in a few minutes, still fully dressed, I retrieved Alex's late grandpa's rifle from where Ellen had left it in the kitchen. "Do you know how to use that thing?" Alex asked facetiously.

"I know you don't believe it, but I was a soldier for nine years. Yes, I know how to use it. In fact, I'm really quite good with weapons of all kinds."

"Probably killed lots of people with them," she said with her now-familiar sneer.

"I did what I had to do," I answered, refusing to meet her eyes. I didn't like to dwell on all the fighting I'd seen. I'd killed more of the enemy than I liked to admit. I'd also seen my own buddies and comrades die beside me, some of them in my arms. Those weren't things I liked to think about, let alone discuss with others.

A change came over Alex that threw me for a loop. "Sorry," she said. "It was probably awful."

I nodded, not daring to speak right then, as the memories she'd conjured up in my mind still caused me to choke up. War was a terrible thing.

I stepped over to the sofa and laid the gun on the floor where I'd left it the night before. Alex followed me. Her grandmother was standing by the kitchen sink looking terribly wounded in spirit, and yet her eyes were on her granddaughter, I noticed a moment later.

Alex sat down near the sofa. She seemed contrite now. I hoped she truly was. And I hoped my suspicions of her were unfounded. Suddenly, a question popped into my head. Without revealing what I knew about the contents of Jerry's little red toolbox, I asked Alex, "Do you collect good luck charms?"

My question clearly startled her. Her eyes grew wide, and one hand came toward her mouth, like she was trying to cover her astonishment. "How . . . how did you know that?" she asked after an awkward, silent moment.

"I will take that as a yes," I said. "What are your favorites?"

"What does this have to do with anything?" she asked, the fire building in her eyes again.

"Don't worry about it. I didn't mean to upset you."

"I'm not upset," she said, her feistiness almost fully restored. "I just can't figure out why you would ask that, because I have always liked good luck charms. You must have a reason for asking. I'd like to know what it is."

"Did Jerry collect them too?" I asked, ignoring her request.

"Dallas, what makes you ask? Tell me. I have a right to know." She was getting very angry.

I tried to ignore her anger. "Did he?" I pressed.

For a moment, she seemed to be struggling with her thoughts. Finally, she let out a breath and sank back in her chair. I noticed that Ellen had stepped near her and was watching her closely. "You liked four-leaf clovers," she said. "I remember the day you found one out on the lawn and how excited you were."

Alex nodded. Then so quietly that I could barely hear her, she said, "I had lots of good luck charms, but they disappeared. It was months before I suspected that Jerry had stolen them from my room. I demanded that he give them back, but he just laughed at me. I still remember him saying that they wouldn't bring me any luck. He asked why I cared that they were gone."

She looked up at me. "I was seventeen at the time. Jerry was sixteen. He didn't admit taking them, but I know he did. He could be really mean at times."

She pushed herself out of the chair. "I hated him that day," she said. After a moment, she added, "But I got over it. I didn't collect any charms after that."

"Alex, how big was your collection?" I asked, trying to sound sympathetic.

She turned her dark green eyes on me. The fire was gone again. She looked like a little kid at that moment. Her eyes filled with tears. "I had a hundred or so. There were key chains, lockets, bracelets, and so on. I still don't know why Jerry took them. I know he did. It was so mean of him. I suppose he threw them away. I don't know why he wanted to hurt me like that. It wasn't that way when we were younger."

"They were very close as children," Ellen added.

Alex gazed across the room for a moment. "This might sound silly," she said, "but we used to write each other notes and then hide them where we figured the other one would find them."

"What kind of notes?" I asked, intrigued.

"All kinds of stuff," she said. "We'd share secrets, tell something we did that we didn't think our parents would approve of, write something mean we did to a friend. You might say they were often little confessionals of sorts. But we eventually quit doing that. I don't remember the last time I wrote or received one. Although I'm sure it was sometime when we were young teenagers." She gave a mirthless chuckle. "I do remember thinking, after he stole the charms, that maybe I'd get a note from him. But I never did. That was some of the meanness, I think. He probably knew that I'd think he'd write a note and then laugh to himself that he didn't. I'm tired. I'm going to bed."

Ellen put an arm around her granddaughter. "We both love Jerry, we always did, but he did do some things that were just plain mean. I never could figure out what was going on in his head at times. He was a troubled boy. Probably losing his father at such a young age was harder on him than any of us imagined."

"I lost my father too!" Alex said with a snap. "Good night, Grandma." With that she fled, furiously wiping at her eyes.

"I'm sorry, Dallas. Alex isn't herself lately. She's not usually like this. In fact, I've never seen her so angry. She usually gets over it quickly. She and Jerry fought from time to time, but she adored him. Please forgive her for the way she's acting," she said.

"I understand," I said softly, not sure that I really did.

After lying down, I couldn't quit thinking about Alex and the anger she harbored. I wondered how she *really* felt about her brother. I was no longer convinced that she loved him like she claimed. I also wondered what she would say if I told her that several good luck charms were in

Jerry's small red toolbox. I suspected that they were some of the ones Jerry had stolen from her years before.

chapter SEVEN

I DISCUSSED ALEXANDRA GRADY WITH my new boss, Hank Pierce, the next morning after delivering the signed contract and check from Ellen Grady and discussing my meeting with Detective Wakefield. "She has a hot temper," I said of Alex, "but I don't see her as a killer. Anyway, she was sitting beside her grandmother when Jerry was killed and went over the fence and ran right out into the arena to get to him."

"Some people do hire others to do their dirty work," he reminded me. "She probably is innocent, but we can't count her out. You've obviously thought a lot about this. Be careful around her, Dallas."

"I'll do that," I promised.

"Good, now before you head to the garage, we should decide what else we need to do," he said. "I've given it a lot of thought. Shirley, when she comes in, will get some keys made from the impressions I made yesterday. I suspect that Detective Wakefield will be looking into the matter of those keys at some point, but they are a priority to me. It's also important that we talk to everyone on that list you got from Miss Grady, and soon. If you'd like, I could try to track some of them down today while you're at the garage."

"That would be great," I said, relieved that I now had competent, experienced help as I was the incompetent, inexperienced help. With that in mind, I asked, "What would you like me to do?"

"Well, for starters, I think you need to see what else you can find out from the people at Jim's Garage. By the end of the day, I think it would be well if you let Jim know that you and I are looking into Jerry's death in an official capacity. How much longer you work there will have to be determined by what you learn today and how cooperative Jim is after you let him know what's going on."

"Can we safely say he's not a suspect?" I asked.

"He's low on the list, let's put it that way. At some point we have to trust someone. But right now, I think our client is the only one we'll put in that category," he said.

I wasn't surprised when Kelsey Glazer didn't show up for work at the garage again that day. I didn't have to ask Jim about him because he spoke to all of us as we were getting ready to begin our assignments. "Alice finally talked to Kelsey's wife last night. It seems he has a broken wrist. He says it happened in a bar fight. That could very well be true," he said. "He does have a habit of spending too much time drinking."

My stomach lurched uncomfortably. The hard swing of a fireplace poker was more likely to have been the cause of his injury. I needed to go see the guy—maybe with a backup.

Jim was still talking. "It seems Kelsey went somewhere yesterday. His wife is worried because she hasn't seen him since."

I needed to talk to Hank. Kelsey was involved. If he wasn't the killer, he was very likely in league with that person. I also thought a call to Detective Wakefield was in order at this point. I'd have to see what Hank thought about that.

"I'm guessing we'll need another new mechanic," Jim was saying as I was thinking just that. "Dallas," he said, "I'm glad you're here. You, along with the rest, will have to do more if possible. In the meantime, I'll see about hiring someone else."

"Right away?" Randy asked, looking worried and stressed. "We have a lot of work right now."

That was true. I not only had to work on the Ford Bronco that was getting the rebuilt engine, but I also had to mount three sets of new tires Randy had sold that day. The other guys were also busy. I looked for an opportunity to talk to each of them. It simply didn't work out that morning. I decided I couldn't break the bad news to Jim tonight. While on a short break at noon, I stepped outside and called Hank. His wife answered the phone.

"Shirley," I said, "there has been a major development here at Jim's Garage. Is there some way I can get in touch with Hank?"

"He's out somewhere. Didn't he give you his cell number?"

"He was going to, but we both forgot," I explained.

She gave it to me, and I punched the number in on my phone. Just as I was ready to send the call through, Kanon strolled up. That killed any possibility of talking to Hank now. I closed my phone. "Hey, Kanon," I said. "Hard day, huh?"

"Not so unusual. You just as well get used to it," he said. "By the way, I've been hoping to talk to you."

"Sure thing," I said.

"Aren't you going to eat your lunch?" he asked.

"Uh, yeah, sure," I said. "It's in my locker."

"Why don't you grab it, and then maybe we can sit out here and eat while we talk," he said.

It was a nice day, so I thought, why not? After I'd retrieved the lunch my sweet landlady had fixed for me, we sat on the cement barrier that separated Jim's property from the business next door. "What do you have on your mind?" I asked after Kanon had started eating and hadn't yet broached whatever subject it was he wanted to talk about.

"Uh, you know Alexandra and all."

"That's right," I said. "Why?"

"There are things she doesn't know about Jerry," he said, fidgeting with his sandwich. "She thinks me and him were tight. We did do stuff together, but I don't think he liked me much. But then he didn't like many people, or trust them, for that matter."

"I think Alex understands that better than you think," I commented when he grew silent. "He hasn't always been nice to her, either."

"I'm not surprised. Jerry was a real jerk sometimes. But he let me help with his derby cars. Now I guess I'll need to drive in the race Saturday in Ogden."

"He has a car entered there?" I asked.

"Yeah, he entered it about a month ago, just a day or two before he was killed."

"But his car," I ventured. "Don't the cops in Duchesne have it? I mean, that seems likely, doesn't it?"

"They have the one he was killed in, but he has plenty more. He was planning on using the Chrysler we were working on," he said gloomily. "Razorback and I have been working on it a little. It's about ready to go, but with just him and me, I don't know if we can do it. I guess you don't know about Razorback, do you?"

"Actually, I do remember Alex mentioning a guy she called Razorback. She says he got cut by a guy with razor. He was part of the pit crew, wasn't he?" I asked. I knew it was the case, but I wanted to keep Kanon talking now.

Kanon took a bite of his sandwich. I also took one of mine while I waited. He chewed for a minute and then wiped his mouth with the back of his hand. Finally, he said, "Yeah, and this is the problem; it only seems right that one of us drive in the derby in Ogden. Razorback says it can't be him. That leaves me. I'll do it, but the problem is, it leaves us short in the pit crew."

"Then get someone else," I suggested, not having the vaguest idea that I was giving him the opening he was looking for.

I soon learned it. "That's why I wanted to talk to you. Would you help us?"

My first reaction was to say no, that I didn't have time or interest or aptitude. Then I realized he had just given me a break. What better way to get to talk to Razorback and perhaps some of the competitors Alex had named? Hank might be making contact with them now, but I still thought this could prove to be a great opportunity. So I said, "Sure, why not? But you'll have to tell me what I need to do."

"Can you weld?" he asked.

"I've done some," I said.

"Good. And I already know you can do mechanical stuff. Could you come down to my place after work?" he asked. "That's where the car is, and me and Razorback, we could show you what we do while we finish getting it ready."

"Sounds good to me," I said as my enthusiasm for the idea grew.

We ate companionably after that. Kanon's mood had lifted greatly. "Maybe you could drive sometime," he suggested a few minutes later.

"That might be fun," I agreed, although I had no desire to get beat around in a car in the middle of an arena while the crowd cheered for others to bash me up. Kanon didn't need to know that just yet.

We were just finishing our lunch when Kanon said, "By the way, Jerry has a small red toolbox. I know he had it here before he was killed. I need it, but when I asked Jim about it, he said he gave it to you to give to Jerry's sister."

My pulse quickened. "Yeah, he did," I admitted, not even remotely inclined to tell him what I'd actually done with it.

"I need it," Kanon said anxiously. "Do you think you could talk her out of it? She doesn't need it."

"But you do?" I asked. "Does it have some specialty tools of some kind in it? It's not very big, so there couldn't be anything big enough to do serious work on a car with."

"It has a padlock on it," he said.

"Yeah, I remember."

"So she can't open it, but I can," he said.

"Oh, so you have the key?"

"No, but I have a bolt cutter and a hacksaw," he said with a grin.

"What's in it, Kanon? I'm part of your crew now. You can tell me—if you know, that is."

"I know," he said. "You get it from Alex, and I'll tell you what's in it. We better get back to work."

We worked a little late that evening, but none of the guys complained as it meant overtime pay. However, I could see that Kanon was getting fidgety. When we finally closed the shop at six thirty, he said to me, "How quick can you get over to my place?"

"I don't even know where you live," I reminded him.

He gave me the address, and I said, "Give me a few minutes. I have a couple of things I've got to do first."

"Okay, but hurry. Razorback and I will be there."

I reached Hank at home and explained about Kelsey, and he agreed that the two of us should approach him together, if we could locate him. He also agreed that I had made the right decision in accepting a position on Kanon's pit crew. Further, he agreed that I'd better wait until I saw how things shook out at the race on Saturday evening before deciding when to quit the job at Jim's Garage.

For a guy who just days earlier had nothing to do but search for a job, I had more on my plate than I could have imagined. I pulled up in front of the address Kanon had given me. The house was white, old, and faded. The front yard looked neglected. A rutted dirt driveway led around the back like Kanon had told me. I drove around and got the first of several surprises in store for me that evening.

The backyard was huge and well kept, much better than the front. I had expected it to be full of junked cars and junk in general. Instead, there were several cars, but none of them were shells. They were all older models but also complete and neatly parked in front of a chain-link fence at the back of the yard. A large building stood in the far corner, the huge doors open. Unlike the house, the shop, which is what I assumed it was, had received a fresh coat of paint sometime in the past few years. Kanon's car, a red Camaro, was parked beside the building. The only shabby looking thing back there, if you didn't look at the back of the house, was a rusty old pickup truck parked next to the Camaro.

I stopped next to the two of them and got out of my truck. Kanon walked through one of the two large doors and said, "Thanks for coming, Dallas. We're working on the car in there." He pointed back the way he'd just come from.

I followed him inside, where I got the second surprise of the evening. The shop was not only large, but it was clean and exceptionally well equipped. "Wow, Kanon, this is a great shop. Is it yours?"

"Sort of. Actually, I guess technically it's my mother's, but she never comes out here. She just sits in the house and drinks. My dad built this shop, and he put every dime he could into both the shop and the equipment. He told me that he wouldn't put money into the house because Mom would just let it go to pot anyway. So he put his money in this place. Dad was a good mechanic and a great body man. He loved to restore antique cars. He made a lot of money doing it. This shop was his life," Kanon said. "He's dead now. He was killed in a car wreck. Can you believe it, a guy who spent his life making cars look great and run great was killed in a wreck that wasn't even his fault? And to make it worse, the car that hit him was a classic Chevy, one dad would've loved to have restored. The driver of the Chevy was as drunk as my mom."

What a sad commentary, I thought as Kanon waved an arm around the shop, inviting me to take a tour. We wandered around the shop for several minutes, admiring the equipment, the painting room, and the two hydraulic lifts. Finally, Kanon said, "I guess we better get to helping Razorback."

Razorback Jones was one of the thinnest men I'd ever met. He wasn't much short of six feet but couldn't have weighed an ounce over 120. He was working in the shop, bare from the waist up. Despite his build, he looked like he was strong. His arms were sinewy, and the muscles on his back stood out. So did the long white scar that ran from his right shoulder clear down to his belt line. He was leaning over the open engine area of the big blue-and-white Chrysler they were planning to race in the derby on Saturday. The hood of the car was leaning against the wall.

Razorback straightened up and turned around when Kanon said, "Hey, Razor, this is Dallas, the guy I told you about, the guy that's going to help us on Saturday night."

The thin man smiled at me and held out a greasy hand. "Good to meet you, my man. Kanon didn't tell me you were so tall. But you'll do." I judged him to be about my age, maybe a year or two younger. "Kanon says we got a lot to teach you tonight, so I guess we better get at it."

For the next hour, they gave me a crash course in demolition derby mechanics. I concentrated hard, trying to retain everything the guys told me. At the end of that hour I got the next surprise. "I've decided to tell you what's in that red toolbox of Jerry's," Kanon said. With a quick look at Razorback, who nodded, he went on. "It has some car keys in it. Each key is on a key chain, but not just any key chain. Jerry was into good luck charms." *Stolen ones*, I thought to myself.

He leaned across the driver's-side door, which was welded shut, and through the window, from which the glass had been removed, and pulled the key from the ignition. He held it out to me. The key was attached to a silver four-leaf clover. "Jerry wouldn't drive a car without a good luck charm."

"He must have had quite a collection of good luck key chains," I ventured, still thinking of Alexandra's stolen collection.

"He had a bunch of them. He kept them in a safety deposit box at a bank. I don't know where the key to that box is or even which bank it's at, but I do know that he had several keys in the toolbox," he said.

"What do they go to?"

"Three of them go to those cars over there," he said, pointing out the door in the direction of the cars lined up against the fence.

"And what about the rest of them, or are there only three in it?"

He glanced at Razorback. The two of them shared a secretive look. Then Kanon said, "They fit some cars Jerry bought that aren't here yet."

That was at least a partial lie. I was almost certain of it, but I didn't let on that I felt that way. I just said, "I hope I can get it back for you."

Razorback gave Kanon a dark look, and then he said, "She better give it back," in a threatening tone. I thoughtfully let it pass.

The last surprise of the evening walked through one of the large doors a few minutes later. I didn't see her until Kanon said brightly, "Hi, Sis."

I looked up from the brake line I'd been inspecting and grabbed my jaw to keep it from dropping. Clad in white slacks and a blue blouse, a young woman had just entered the shop—a drop-dead gorgeous young woman. She was curvaceous, had long brunette hair, dark brown eyes, and a huge smile. I judged her age, after the shock of seeing her, to be around twenty. Kanon confirmed it when he said with a grin, "Meet my big sister, Sophie. She's only a couple of years older than me, but somehow God made her taller. It's not fair. Oh, Sis, this is Dallas Rowen, the soldier I told you about."

I couldn't pull my eyes away from the vision in the doorway. She glided toward us as I said, "It's nice to meet you."

Razorback had been leaning over the engine. He straightened up and looked at Sophie. "Hi," he said.

"Hi, Razor," she responded, but she never even looked at him. She was watching me. When she reached us, she stopped in front of me. She looked me over for a moment while I tried not to be too obvious in doing the same to her. She was beautiful. I couldn't believe she was Kanon's sister. When her eyes finally ceased to assess me, she looked at her brother. "Mom said to tell you that you guys are on your own for dinner tonight. She burned the roast."

"What else is new?" Kanon said with a touch of bitterness to his voice. "She's a drunken old woman, that's all she is."

"And she's your mother, Kanon," Sophie said sharply. "Have some respect. How long before you're done here?"

"We've just been orienting Dallas," he said. "He's going to be in my pit crew Saturday."

"I'm glad you found someone. I really didn't want to have to help, although I would have if I had to," she said. "I'm a fair mechanic, you know." I think that comment was directed at me, but I said nothing.

"I know you are, Sophie," he said as I remembered Alex saying that a young woman had been with Jerry's crew a time or two. It had to be this young woman.

Razorback, who had been watching us closely, said, "You can help us anyway, if you'd like."

The big sister grinned at me. "Maybe I'll do that. Is that okay with you, Dallas?"

"Sure," I said, trying to dampen my enthusiasm. She was not only pretty, but she also seemed, at first blush, to be really nice.

"What are we going to do about dinner?" Kanon asked. "Unless you or Mom have been shopping, there's nothing in the house."

"Actually, maybe we could eat out tonight. Dallas could join us if he'd like. Razorback too," she said.

I was hungry, and dinner with Sophie and the gang was quite inviting. "It's up to you guys," I said.

"Sounds good to me," Razorback chimed.

"Then let's do it," Kanon agreed.

"When?" Sophie asked.

"How about right now?" Kanon said.

"That's fine. Let's go. You guys clean the grease off, and I'll be back in a second," Sophie said, and off she went.

Kanon grinned. "I think she likes you, Dallas. She's a looker, isn't she—like Alex?"

"She seems nice," I said neutrally. "How much more do we have to do here?"

"Not much. I think this old car is about ready. I just wish I was more confident about driving. Maybe you'd like to, Dallas," he suggested again.

"Nope, that's your job, wouldn't you say, Razorback?"

"Yep," the thin man said. He was not a man of many words, it appeared.

"Okay, I just wish Jerry would have let me drive more before he went and ticked somebody off and got himself killed," Kanon said gloomily.

Razorback added nothing. The three of us cleaned up the best we could before Sophie came back out.

chapter EIGHT

WHEN SOPHIE CAME BACK OUT a few minutes later, she walked quickly but gracefully toward us. She flashed me the kind of smile that made a bachelor's knees go weak. "Is this your truck?" she said, pointing to my black Dodge.

"Yes. Not much, I know, but I like it."

"It's fine. I'll ride with you. We'll meet you two at Chuck-A-Rama, Kanon. Is that okay, Dallas?"

"You bet," I said, trying not to sound as enthusiastic as I felt.

She stepped around to the passenger side and stood there. I hurried around and opened the door for her. She hopped in with a quick, "Thanks, Dallas. You're a real gentleman."

I was embarrassed. I probably wouldn't have opened the door if it hadn't been for her waiting for me. I got in, and as I did, Sophie fastened her seat belt. "Do you know where Chuck-A-Rama is? Or would you rather go someplace else?"

"It's fine. In fact, as hungry as I am tonight, it's more than fine," I said. She grinned at me, and my whole world seemed brighter.

On the ride to the restaurant, we talked quite a bit. I found her company very enjoyable. She asked me about the army and my time in the war zones. I told her the basics. She seemed impressed. She asked about my family. "I only have a brother. He manages a branch of a large software company," I said. "The branch is in Japan."

"I'd like to go to Japan someday," she said wistfully. "It's always been a country that intrigues me."

"I've never been there either," I said. "My brother and I aren't that close, but someday I need to surprise him with a visit."

"You should," she said. Then she changed the subject abruptly. "So is Jerry's sister, Alexandra, a close friend of yours?" she asked. "I mean, like are the two of you dating?"

"No to both questions," I said. "She is an acquaintance. Her grand-mother is my landlady."

"Oh, I see," she said. "Jerry was a creep. Is his sister one too?"

"She can be difficult," I said, "but I think she's probably a nice girl. She's a nurse."

"Oh, really? I didn't know that," Sophie said. "Jerry didn't mention that. In fact, when he talked about her, he was usually quite rude. It's too bad he was murdered, but I can imagine he brought it on himself. I'm surprised that Kanon and Razorback stuck with him. He wasn't appreciative at times."

I was getting a clear picture of Jerry Grady. I'm afraid it wasn't a pretty picture. "Do you have any idea who might have wanted to see him dead bad enough to shoot him?" I asked. "That seems pretty drastic to me."

"I don't know who would do that. Maybe it was some competitor of his in the derby business. But if so, I wouldn't know who. I didn't go to the derbies much. I helped Jerry and Kanon with their cars but usually only at our place. Kanon and I don't have much in common outside our interest in mechanics. Oh, sure, we have the same parents. Dad's dead. Did Kanon tell you that?" she asked abruptly.

"He mentioned it."

"He was a good dad. Mom is an alcoholic. I swear, Dallas, if she's taught me nothing else, she's taught me to avoid alcohol. I love her, but she's let drinking ruin her life. Dad drank some too, but not like Mom. Kanon, I don't know. I haven't seen him drink, but I suspect that he does some."

"I hope not. I don't drink myself," I said. "I've seen it ruin too many lives."

"I hope they catch whoever killed Jerry, even if he brought it on himself. It worries me for Kanon. I tried to talk him out of taking Jerry's place driving up in Ogden, but he doesn't listen to anything I say. He says he feels like he has to. But I think he actually wants to, and that's foolish. I'd sure hate for what happened to Jerry to happen to him," she said.

Having been given an opening, I decided to ask her about Kelsey, hoping my interest didn't appear to be anything more than mere curiosity. "One of the guys at Jim's Garage didn't come to work yesterday . . . or today either," I said, glancing over at her.

Our eyes locked for a moment, and then she said, "Which one? Kanon didn't mention it to me—not that he would."

"Kelsey Glazer," I said.

"No loss to the garage," she said with a shiver. Her eyes narrowed. "He's a louse. Now there's someone who could shoot somebody and never bat an eye," she said. "He gives me the creeps. He has the most awful tongue."

"I noticed that he's not very friendly. His language is horrible, like you say. I get the feeling that he didn't like Jerry at all."

"He doesn't like anyone. You guys would all be lucky if he doesn't come back to work," she said with more bitterness than seemed normal for someone who didn't have to work around the guy.

"I think Jim is expecting him not to," I said. "Alice, the bookkeeper—" I began.

"I know Alice. She's okay," she interrupted. "I'm sorry, I didn't mean to break in like that. It's a bad habit I have. I need to work on that."

"That's okay," I said. "Alice called his wife, and she—"

Her habit stepped in again. "Kelsey has a wife?" Sophie asked in shock. "He never told me he had a wife. I should have guessed."

"Really," I said, wondering why it would have mattered to her in the first place if he was such a louse.

She soon filled me in. "He took me out once, about a year ago, not long after Kanon went to work for Jim's Garage. I would never have gone with him had I known he was married. I shouldn't have gone with him anyway. He's not the kind of guy I normally date—not even close."

"Maybe he wasn't married at that time," I said casually.

"Maybe, but I'm betting he was. Anyway, he's not someone I would ever go out with again. I was stupid for accepting even that once." She looked over at me. "Believe me, Dallas, he's not my type. I only did it because Kanon said it might make things easier for him at work."

"I don't blame you for not wanting to go out with him again," I said, meaning it sincerely.

"He was awful that night. He kept trying to put his hands on me. I kept shoving them off. Then, after dinner and a movie, he pulled up to a motel! Can you believe that? I am not that kind of girl—at all! When he went to go inside, he told me to wait in his car, that he'd only be a minute," she said with a frown. The frown deepened. "At that point I was desperate. I didn't wait. I called a taxi after I'd made my escape. The next day, Kanon said he wanted to know why I wouldn't let Kelsey take me home. *Like he intended to.* I despise that man."

My suspicions of Kelsey Glazer were much deeper now. "I don't blame you," I said to her.

"He kept calling me for weeks after that. And he kept showing up at places I happened to be. He could never keep his eyes off of me," she said with a shudder.

"You do have a tendency to turn guys' heads," I said with a grin.

"Thanks, Dallas. I normally don't mind guys looking at me. What I object to is leering. That's what Kelsey did. He leered, and even worse, he stalked. It finally stopped, but not until Kanon said something to him. He said he told him that I might call the cops if he didn't leave me alone."

"Good for Kanon," I said.

"I would have done it too—called the cops, I mean. Now maybe you see why I think he would kill someone if he got it in his head to do so. I'll be honest with you, Dallas, that man frightens me," she said, and as she said it I could see goose bumps rise on her arms, and she shuddered. She looked at me. There was fear in her dark brown eyes.

"I'm sorry he put you through all that," I said.

"Thanks, so am I. Honestly, Dallas, I never did know he was married. I wonder if Kanon knew."

A minute later we pulled up to the restaurant. We waited outside until Kanon and Razorback showed up a minute or two later, then we all went in together.

The first thing Sophie said to Kanon when we were in line waiting to pay for our meals was about Kelsey. "Kanon, did you know that Kelsey was married?"

"Not until Jim mentioned it at the shop this morning," he said. The young man's face went dark, and his eyes narrowed. "Has he been bothering you again?"

"No, Dallas was just telling me that he didn't come to work yesterday and today," she answered.

"Yeah, and Alice said that his wife told her it was because he got his wrist broken in a bar fight. Now that could actually be true," he said. "I hope so. Actually, it would have been nice if it had been his neck."

The subject of Kelsey Glazer didn't come up again during dinner, nor did anyone mention Jerry Grady's murder. Dinner was a pleasant affair. I sat next to Sophie in a booth, across from the guys. I learned more about her as we ate. She was currently going to school at Utah Valley University, majoring in early childhood education. "I love little kids," she said when she was talking about it. She still lived at home, she explained, because she was trying to keep her living expenses down so she could pay for school. She also worked two or three evenings a week as a waitress to try to make ends meet.

By the time we had finished, I was stuffed. I wondered if Sophie was too. She ate more than I would have ever expected for a girl with such a perfect figure. When we were back in the truck, she asked me if we could stop at a hamburger place. "What for?" I asked in surprise.

"Not because I'm hungry," she said with a grin, punching me playfully on the arm. "I'd just like to get something for Mom. Do you mind?"

I not only didn't mind, I was impressed. I'm sure Kanon had no such generous thoughts. I went in with her, and when we were back in the truck, she said sadly, "Thanks. Mom needs something besides whiskey."

When we pulled up at the house, Sophie said, "Would you like to come in for a minute? I'd like you to meet my mother."

Surprised, I agreed. Kanon was in the living room watching TV when we entered. I got another surprise in that evening of surprises—the house was clean and orderly on the inside. I suspected that was Sophie's doing.

Kanon looked up and saw the sack of fast food in Sophie's hand. "Didn't you get enough to eat?" he asked. "I'm stuffed."

"This is for Mom," Sophie said. "She hasn't gone to bed already has she? I wanted to introduce Dallas to her."

"Why would you want to do that?" Kanon asked, turning back to the TV.

"Because she's my mother," Sophie said. "I know she's a drunk, but she's all we have, and I, for one, love her."

"She's in the kitchen," Kanon said without looking at his sister.

When I left the house a few minutes later after meeting the woman Sophie claimed as her mother, I decided to stop by my apartment, just to see if anyone had been there again. To my dismay, the tape I'd left above the door was broken once again. Fearing that might be the case, I had my heavy flashlight in my hand. I slipped the key in the door and slowly opened it. Once again, the place was empty, but signs of the intruder were all over the room. The place had been trashed.

I had had enough. I called the manager, who in turn called the police. He complained about who was going to pay for the damage. I pointed out that the door had not been forced. "Perhaps you didn't collect a key from a previous renter," I suggested.

That took the fire from his eyes. "I suppose someone could have used lock-picking keys to get in, but either way, I think that I'll live someplace else," I said. "I'm tired of this happening to me here."

"You don't get your money back," he said stubbornly.

I wasn't in the mood to argue. "Fine, then I'll keep the room until my rent runs out. But I'll expect you to clean it up." With that I left, the manager calling after me, but I ignored him. I was anxious now to get back to Ellen

Grady's house. That is where the danger lay, I was afraid. Somebody wanted to stop me and might use Ellen to do so.

When I got to the Grady house a few minutes later, I parked around back as usual. Alexandra's lime green VW was there. I parked beside it, locked my truck, and walked back around to the front door, glancing at my watch's illuminated dial. It was close to ten. I let myself in and, despite the lateness of the hour, was not surprised to see Ellen Grady sitting in her favorite chair in the living room. "There you are," she said. "I've been worrying about you."

Alex entered at that moment. She seemed to know when to enter and usually did so with a flourish. "He's been on a date," she announced snippily. "He was with a flashy brunette." The night of surprises wasn't over yet, apparently. I wondered how in the world she knew I'd been with a young woman.

"Well, dear, I suppose he does have the right to a personal life," Ellen said quickly, as if she had to defend me against her granddaughter.

Alex had a way of rubbing me wrong. "I'm sorry to disappoint you, Alex, but I've been working," I said, probably sounding defensive, but I couldn't just stand there and let her continue to belittle me in front of her grandmother.

"You left the garage late, but from there you went to Kanon Storm's house," she announced smugly. "Later, you took a very pretty brunette girl to dinner. And don't try to deny it."

"I went to dinner with Sophie Storm, Kanon's sister, that's true, and with Kanon, and with a guy you told me about yourself, Razorback Jones. And for your information, I learned a lot at dinner." I turned to Ellen. "I'm finally making headway," I said.

"What did you learn?" Alex demanded. She sounded a little defensive now, and I again wondered what secrets she might be hiding and why. I didn't trust her at all at this point.

"That's between me and your grandmother," I said. "I'm sorry, but I can't divulge anything to you. And by the way, how did you know where I've been tonight?"

"I have my ways," she said with a snip.

"I'll bet you do," I said. I then turned to her grandmother. "Are you all right?" I asked Ellen. "I didn't mean to worry you."

"I'm fine," she said wearily. "And like I was saying before Alexandra interrupted us, I was worried about you."

"I'm being careful," I said, even as I admitted to myself that she had reason to worry about me. She also had reason to worry about herself. I said to her, "You are the one I'm worried about. I'd like to move you out of your house for a few days. Hank agrees with me. We talked it over as I was driving here just now."

I expected an argument, but I got none from her. In fact, she surprised me when she said, "I'll do whatever you say. Where should I go?"

"We'll work something out. In fact, Hank is making some calls as we speak."

"I'll take care of Grandma," Alex said angrily. "You aren't going to move her anywhere."

"You will stay out of this," I said, angrily pumping my fist. "You are not helping at all. In fact, you are making the job harder for me and Hank."

"I don't trust you," she hissed.

"Then we're even," I countered hotly.

"Alexandra, please," poor old Mrs. Grady said, her eyes filling with tears. "Dallas is only trying to help. Please, don't make this tragic situation even worse."

"Fine!" she thundered, her pretty face dark with rage. "I'm going home. I hope nothing happens to you, but if it does, don't blame me." She whirled and stormed out of the room. A few moments later the back door slammed, and then her Beetle roared around the house and onto the street.

"This isn't like my Alexandra," Ellen said, sobbing softly. "She's hurting worse than I ever guessed. We have to catch whoever did this terrible thing to Jerry."

"We'll get whoever it is," I said. "Believe me, we're making progress. Now, about your safety; we'll move you out of here in the morning. For tonight, I'd like you to sleep downstairs. I'll stay up here with the rifle."

"Do you really think that guy will be back?" she asked, fluttering one hand feebly.

"Either he will be or someone else. I still have my apartment rented, and I checked it just before I came here. Someone broke in sometime after I was there last night. They tore it up pretty badly. There's a lot of anger in someone."

"Do have any idea who?" she asked.

"Yes, I do, but I don't think I should say right now. I need more evidence before I point fingers."

"I trust you, Dallas. You are such a dear," she said.

After my landlady was safely in bed in the basement, I took some extra precautions. I made sure all the windows, upstairs and down, were securely shut and locked. The ones in the basement were small, too small for a person to easily get through, if at all. Ellen's house had been built back when the building code was very lax. Upstairs, I propped a chair beneath the knob of both the front and back doors. If anyone came, even Alex with her key, entry would require force, and force meant noise, and noise would wake me. I set the alarm on my wristwatch and settled down on the sofa.

Long before my alarm was set to go off, I woke to the sound of someone shaking the front door. I grabbed the rifle from the floor beside the sofa and then sat up, swinging around to face the door. The shaking stopped as I moved quickly toward the door, holding the rifle ready. A hammering began after that. Then a voice, enraged and loud, demanded, "Let me in, Dallas."

I chuckled to myself. It was Alexandra Grady, angry as usual. I moved next to the door and paused. Was she alone? Maybe and maybe not. "What do you want?" I asked through the closed door.

"I want to make sure my grandmother is okay, what do you think?" she shouted.

"Who's with you?" I asked as I shifted silently from one side of the door to the other. I couldn't afford to be careless. I hadn't been given a single reason that made me want to trust Alex.

"I'm alone, you idiot. Why would I have someone with me?" she responded. "Now open up."

I jacked a shell into the rifle then, crouching, moved the chair. Then I stepped back into a dark corner and said, "You can come in now."

When she entered, I was relieved to see that she was by herself. She slammed the door behind her and reached for the light switch. The room was instantly filled with light. She spotted me at once. "You!" she hissed. "What do you think you're doing?"

"Keeping your grandmother safe until we get her someplace where she will be secure."

"I couldn't sleep, worrying about her here with you," she said, flouncing across the room and into the hallway. I waited, and a moment later, she was back. "What did you do with her? She isn't in her room."

"I know," I said. "She's safe. Why don't you sit down now, and you and I will have a talk."

"Where is she?" she demanded, her eyes piercing, her finger pointing dangerously.

"Sit down. There's something I need to talk to you about." I spoke firmly, and it brought more color to her cheeks.

"I hate you," she said. "Why can't you just be honest?"

"Why can't you?" I countered.

"What do you mean?" she asked, looking fairly confused.

"You not only hate me, you hated your brother, didn't you?" I said. "I've learned how badly he treated you."

"No, I didn't hate him. I didn't like him very well, but he was my brother, and I was doing all I could to try to help him turn his life around," she said defiantly.

"Were you really?" I asked

"What? You think I killed him, don't you? That's horrid. Grandma has to hear this, and then she'll know what a rotten, evil person you are." She paused, took a step toward me, stopped, and spoke again. "I was in the stands with Grandma when Jerry was shot. You know that. So how can you say I did it?"

"I said no such thing," I reminded her softly. "The idea seems to be yours."

She quickly dropped the subject. "Where is Grandma?" she demanded again.

"She's asleep in the basement, and I intend for her to stay that way, if you haven't already woken her up with all your shouting and pounding. Now, why don't you either go sleep in her room or go back to your apartment," I suggested, hoping she chose to leave. I didn't trust her, and if she stayed, I'd have to practically sleep on the rifle.

"You wanted to talk," she said. "What did you have to say?"

"Quit having me followed," I said.

She paused just long enough to convince me that I was right. "What are you talking about?" she asked, her eyes turned to the side.

"Don't deny it, Alex. Just call off your dog, whoever he is. You're making this whole thing much worse. Now either go to bed in your grandma's room or leave."

She stayed, and I slept with the rifle. Or at least I occasionally dozed with it tucked safely between me and the back of the sofa.

chapter NINE

My alarm went off, but I was already awake when it did. I groaned and sat up. I was afraid I had another long day ahead of me. The first thing on my agenda was to move Ellen Grady to wherever Hank suggested. And when I did that, I needed to do it without Alex knowing where I took her. That would mean dodging whomever she had hired to keep an eye on me. Now that I knew what she was up to, I was confident I could do that.

Mrs. Grady came up the stairs just moments after I'd gotten up and folded the blanket I'd slept under and moved the chairs from the front and back doors. "Good morning, Dallas," she said. "Did you get any rest?"

"Not very much," I said truthfully. "Did you?"

"I actually slept well," she said. "I guess I'm just so exhausted that I couldn't do anything else. I'm going to go in my bedroom and get dressed and pack a suitcase. Then I'll fix us some breakfast."

"Wait, Alex is in there," I said.

"She is in where?" Ellen asked, looking confused.

"She's in your bed. She came back at about two this morning."

"Bless her heart. She really is a good girl, Dallas. You'll see."

Yes, I thought, I *would* see. Either she was good or bad, but I would definitely see. I hoped that what I learned would not create more heartache for her sweet and trusting grandmother. We had eaten breakfast by the time Alex came out of the bedroom. She had already showered, and she looked really good. I couldn't help myself from mentally comparing her to Sophie. It was a toss-up, I decided. They were both beautiful women.

I shook off the pointless musings and stepped outside, where I called Hank on my cell phone. He announced that the arrangements were made and that as soon as I could get Mrs. Grady away from the house, he would help me get her settled into a hotel room. "There is a problem. I'm pretty sure that Alex is having me followed," I said.

"She's what?" he asked, sounding incredulous. "Why would she do that?"

"She doesn't trust me," I said. "She had me followed last night. We've got to find a way to avoid that happening today or Mrs. Grady will still be in danger."

"Okay, we can deal with that," Hank said with a chuckle. Then he laid out a simple plan that would keep Mrs. Grady's whereabouts secret. "So here's where you are to take her." He gave me a location.

"That will work," I said, again grateful to have a man with experience helping with this case. I was definitely in over my head before we began working together. I hoped his health would hold up for a long time.

An hour later, I pulled my truck up to the entrance of the Provo hotel Hank had specified. A small white car that I had noticed shortly after I pulled away from Ellen's house was parked across the street. I gave it another look now. The driver was slumped down in the seat, a baseball cap pulled low over his head. Whoever it was had followed me. But that didn't bother me too much at this point. I helped Ellen from the truck and up to the door. Then I went back and retrieved her suitcases. Together we went inside. Once we were in the lobby and out of sight of the white car's driver, we walked through the hotel and out a back door, where Hank was waiting. Mrs. Grady got in with him, and away they went.

I waited a reasonable amount of time before going back to my truck. When I did, the white car followed me again. The driver, I was quite sure, was confident that he could report Ellen's location to Alex. He stayed back a ways, but it was easy to keep track of him. Whoever the guy helping Alex was, he was far from professional. When I entered Jim's Garage for my shift a few minutes later, he parked a short distance away. An hour later, when I checked, the white car was gone, but I had a feeling that when I got off that evening it would be back.

When I got a short break midmorning, I called Hank from in front of the shop. "Mrs. Grady is safely stowed away," he reported. "But there is a hitch I hadn't anticipated. She says she is going to church on Sunday even if she has to call a neighbor to take her."

"That figures," I said. "It does present a problem."

"One that is easily solved," Hank said with mirth in his voice. "She will need a tall, strong bodyguard to take her there, to stay with her, and to take her back to the hotel."

It was no challenge reading my boss's mind. "I guess I'll be going to church on Sunday," I said.

"That's right. And after church, you will bring Ellen to my home for dinner. My wife thinks it's a great idea. Then we'll slip her back to her hotel without anyone being the wiser."

I shook my head. I had not anticipated this, although I suppose I should have. I determined to make the best of it, although I would have to find something to wear before Sunday. This being Friday, it didn't give me much time, especially considering the work I was committed to on Kanon's car. There was also the matter of the demolition derby the next evening as well as several contacts Hank and I needed to make during the weekend.

For the next couple of minutes, we made our plans. First we had to locate the missing mechanic, Kelsey Glazer, if we could. Hank was going to work on that today, but he felt like we both needed to be in on the interview if and when the mechanic was found. We also had to find and speak with Jake Frankland and Lyle Wertz, fellow drivers from the derby in Duchesne. I would try to find out if Kanon knew if they would be at the Ogden event the next evening. If so, I told Hank I would talk to them. On Sunday, Hank and Detective Wakefield planned to have a look at Jerry's apartment. They thought it would be good if I could be there too. It had been searched before, but Hank wasn't sure it shouldn't be searched again. The detective didn't argue with that, nor did I. I looked forward to snooping around.

The rest of the day was uneventful. Kelsey was nowhere to be found. Hank wasn't feeling well and had to go home and rest. He hadn't yet had any success on finding the cars the keys from the red toolbox fit, but he said that would have to wait. I checked on Mrs. Grady twice during the day and found that she was doing fine in the rather nice hotel room Hank had placed her in. She did complain about Alex not knowing where she was. As gently as I could, I explained that Alex wasn't trusting of me right now and that it would be best if we kept her location secret for a little while. She agreed, albeit reluctantly.

When I left the garage that evening, the small white car had reappeared. The driver was once again slumped in the seat, the baseball hat riding low on his forehead. I was not surprised to see him waiting there. Nor was I surprised when he followed me toward Kanon's place. Alex was being quite thorough, I decided. I really wished she would join my efforts instead of fighting them. My distrust of her grew.

As the man in the white car and I were proceeding to the Storm residence, I spoke with Hank again. He still wasn't feeling well, but he said he could come out if I needed him. I hoped I wouldn't have to bother him.

I worked alongside Kanon, Razorback, and Sophie for several hours that evening. Sophie had showed up wearing a pair of blue bib overalls, gloves on her hands, and her long dark hair tied back with a red bandana. She looked quite fetching. It was hard to imagine her not looking good.

She also worked hard and was as pleasant to be around as she was to look at. In addition, I learned that Sophie was actually a very good mechanic. I felt like a real novice working beside her.

We had everything in readiness, including the car loaded on a trailer and ready to be towed to Ogden Saturday afternoon. I headed for my truck, but Sophie caught my arm and said, "I have pizza inside. Please, won't you join us?"

That was an invitation that was hard to turn down. Sophie headed for the house to put the pizzas in the oven and, as she described it, "Make myself presentable." That couldn't be much of a job for her, I thought.

Kanon, Razor, and I cleaned up the best we could in the shop before heading for the house. Mrs. Storm was nowhere to be seen when we got inside. Sophie appeared from the kitchen, smiling and looking more than presentable in white pants, a red blouse, and with her dark hair neatly brushed and hanging down over her shoulders. "It won't be long," she announced.

I strolled over to the window and peered outside. It was too dark to see well. I wanted to know if the slouch in the white car was still waiting for me. Sophie joined me and didn't ask what I was doing but, glancing first at Kanon and Razorback, who were already glued to the TV, did say, "Would you like to step outside for a few minutes while we wait for the pizza to cook?"

That was exactly what I wanted. Once outside, she slipped an arm through mine and said, "Let's take a little walk. It's a nice evening."

It was at that. And the little white car was parked a short distance down the street. Alex would get a report about my stroll. Just to make sure, I purposely steered Sophie in that direction. The driver was slouched in the seat like before, the hat pulled down over his forehead again. He was parked on the far side of the narrow street, and as we passed by, I could see his head turn ever so slightly in our direction. We walked on, went around the block, and returned to the house a few minutes later. We talked very little, and I enjoyed being in the company of a girl who seemed to enjoy being with me.

The white car was still parked there. Sophie didn't seem to notice, and I didn't draw her attention to it. "The pizza should be about done," she announced when we reached the front door. "Thanks for walking with me."

"Thank you," I said. "I enjoyed it."

Mrs. Storm was sitting in the living room with Kanon and Razorback when we stepped inside. She looked marginally better than she had the night before. There was no doubt that she had once been a beautiful woman, but years and alcohol had stolen her looks.

"Good evening, Mrs. Storm," I said.

She looked my way, grunted, took a drink from the bottle she was holding, and turned her attention back to the TV. Sophie took my arm and said, "Let's check the pizza." Once we were in the kitchen, she said, "I'm sorry, Dallas."

"No, I'm sorry," I said. "I wish there was something we could do to help her."

Sophie, who was reaching for a hot pad, turned and looked sadly at me. "You mean that, don't you?" When I nodded, she said, "You are a good man, Dallas Rowen."

"I could be a lot better," I said as a tear found its way down one of her cheeks. I reached over and wiped it away with my finger. "Who knows, maybe we can figure something out."

"Like what?" she asked without rancor. "I've tried everything I know to convince her to give up the alcohol. If you have any ideas, I'd love to hear them. I want my mother back."

I took a deep breath. "Maybe she needs some in-house treatment," I suggested.

She smiled without humor. "I've thought of that," she said, "but even Kanon and I together can't afford it."

"There may be a way," I said. "Let me think on it."

"Will you?" she asked, stepping close to me and reaching up and touching my face.

"Give me a few days," I said. "I've got some personal things I'm dealing with. But I promise, I'll help if I can."

For a moment, Sophie looked at me, and then she moved closer still, reached up on her toes, and gently kissed my cheek. "I'm glad I met you," she said. Then she turned quickly back to her task.

I watched her. There was something special about her, I was thinking. Then I thought about the case I was working on. I needed to be careful not to get emotionally involved with anyone right now, I told myself. What if her brother turned out, despite my doubts, to somehow be involved in Jerry's death? What would she think of me if I ended up getting her brother arrested? I hoped that would not be the case, but in the meantime, I needed to be careful about my feelings.

The pizza was ready. Mrs. Storm accepted a piece and began eating as she watched the television. She washed it down with more whiskey from the bottle. Kanon and Razorback also ate while watching TV. That left the kitchen table to Sophie and me. I had no argument with that. We ate and talked and generally enjoyed being together. At least I enjoyed it, and she certainly gave me every indication that she did too.

I finally left, but it was quite late. It was after eleven when I pulled up and parked behind the Grady house. The white car had followed me right to the house. After I got out of my truck and walked around to the front of the house, the white car sped down the street. I watched until it was out of sight then turned back to Ellen's house.

It looked dark and empty and uninviting. I decided to go back to my apartment instead of staying in Ellen's house. I returned to my truck and drove away. I didn't see the white car, but I supposed its driver could have seen me. Back at my apartment, I found that the mess hadn't been cleaned up. I spoke for a few minutes with the manager and then again returned to Ellen's house. I drove around the block a couple of times, not sure if I should go in or not, but I finally decided that I would go in and get some rest. I planned to keep the rifle handy, just in case, but I hoped that with Mrs. Grady not being at home I wouldn't be disturbed. I trudged up to the door and pulled out my key.

I unlocked the door and stepped inside, turning to shut it before I flipped the light switch on. I hadn't expected a welcoming committee. I had barely registered the fact that someone was there when I was hit from behind by something solid and heavy. The blow to my back sent me smashing into the door, slamming it shut. Stunned, I tried to turn, putting my hands up to protect my head. I was too slow. The second blow hit the top of my head, and I felt myself sinking helplessly to the floor. I heard no voices, at least not that I could recall. Mostly what I remembered were boots connecting violently with my side, my legs, my shoulders, and my back. Then I recalled being jerked farther back into the room. At that point, something solid connected with the back of my head and blackness smothered me.

I awoke to sunlight on my face. I had no idea where I was or what I was doing there. The pain was acute from one end of me to the other. I was lying on my back, but when I tried to roll over, I gasped with pain and decided that wherever I was, it might be a good place to stay for a little longer. Several minutes passed, and I did, during those minutes, manage to move my arms and legs. All four seemed intact, and that was encouraging. However, I was still struggling with where I was and what I was doing there.

I figured out that I was inside a building, for I could see a ceiling above me. I turned my head and saw the window that was allowing the sunlight in, but I didn't recognize it. I heard something rumble by outside, and suddenly my brain remembered the sound of tanks and other armored vehicles. I thought I was in a war zone. Panic washed over me, and I felt the need to move. The enemy could be anywhere. My comrades in arms might be nearby, but then again, I might be alone, the only survivor of some kind of firefight.

I felt an overpowering urge to move, to seek greater cover, to find my weapon. It was the pain that shot through me when I rolled onto my side and then on over to my stomach that brought me to my senses. It wasn't a sudden flash of total recall, but it was a small fragment of memory. It was of opening a door and then being attacked but not by bullets or knives. I lay for a moment, my mind working feverishly. Slowly I remembered that I was not in a war zone but in Utah. Then I recalled the sweet but troubled face of Ellen Grady. Then my memory returned, and I knew where I was and why.

I also remembered that I was supposed to meet Hank that morning to do some work on the case and that later I was to help Kanon at the demolition derby in Ogden. Those responsibilities motivated me to get to my feet. Once there, I swayed and took a step toward the wall to steady myself. I never reached it.

The next time I woke up, I was on the floor again, but it only took me a minute or two to remember where I was. I realized that I must have fallen after getting to my feet, and I guessed that the fall had knocked me out again. I took several deep breaths and then started to sit up just as I heard the sound of the lock opening at the door. Even though my head was facing away from the door, I knew someone was there and that I had better prepare to defend myself, but when I tried to get up, my body refused. The door opened. I heard footsteps, then a loud gasp.

The next thing I knew was that someone who smelled very nice was kneeling beside me. "Dallas, what happened? Are you okay?"

There was no mistaking Alex's voice. And no, I was not okay, but I couldn't get my voice to work. Gentle hands touched my face. "Dallas, it's me, Alexandra. Wake up, please."

I was quite awake, just not moving so well. I tried to speak, but all I was able to get out was a grunt. That was enough to bring her around to the other side of me. She leaned down close to my face, and she actually looked worried.

For a moment, she just knelt there with her hand on my head—gently, I might add. Then, after a bit, I tried to move again, with more luck this time. "Let me help you to the sofa, then I'll call an ambulance," she said.

"No, don't," I managed to blurt.

"Okay, then I won't," she said softly. "I'll leave you right here, and the paramedics can move you."

As she was speaking, she was fumbling with her cell phone. "No, don't," I said again.

"Don't call an ambulance?" she asked, looking quite perplexed.

I nodded. For a minute, I thought she was going to disregard my wishes and summon help anyway. But after a moment, she put the phone away and said, "Let's get you to the sofa."

I didn't argue with that, and with her help, I finally managed to get to my feet and to stay there while we shuffled toward the sofa. Once I was lying on the soft comfort the sofa offered, Alex said, "Okay, if you don't want an ambulance, you'll have to at least let a nurse check you out. First, let's check for any broken bones."

Her fingers worked their way over my legs, arms, chest, etc. She finally said, "I think there's nothing broken, but you are going to have some bad bruises, and you have a couple of knots on the back of your head. What you need now is something for pain. Let's see what Grandma has in her medicine cabinet."

She found what she was looking for and helped me sit up to take some pills with a small amount of water. After I was lying down again, she said, "Okay, Dallas, out with it," she ordered. "What happened to you?"

"I think one of your goons got to me," I said.

She rocked back on the chair she'd pulled up next to the sofa. "What are you talking about? You don't think I had anything to do with this, do you?"

Talking was coming easier now, and even though the gentleness I'd just witnessed went against any guilt I might imagine on her part, I couldn't forget that she had had me followed. "A while before I came in the house, I saw a car I had seen following me before. I assume it was the guy you had follow me. It could have been him."

Alex folded her hands across her stomach, sitting ramrod straight in her chair. "Dallas, let's get some things straight," she said, the old familiar fire beginning to shoot from her eyes. "I don't like you very much. I don't think you can help us find out who killed my brother. You are right about one thing: my brother was a jerk. But he was my brother. I want whoever killed him to pay. But I don't think you are someone who can ever get that done."

"Thanks for being straight with me," I said when she stopped talking and stared at me. "But why are you having me followed?"

"I don't appreciate accusations like you are making," she said. However, a direct denial had not come. That worried me.

"If I'm wrong, then I apologize, but you did have me spied on last night, didn't you?" I asked.

For a moment, she said nothing, and I squirmed, trying to get in a more comfortable position. Finally, she responded. "Okay, you're right. I had someone follow you, but it wasn't last night. It was the night before," she said. "It was a friend of mine, a colleague from work. That person saw you with Kanon's sister. Sophie, I think you said her name is."

"That's right," I said. "Sophie."

"But after our little altercation in the night, I decided that since you were at least working with someone trustworthy, I'd stay out of it for now. I asked my friend not to follow you again, and I'm quite certain he didn't. He'd have had no reason to. I didn't even try to find out where you took Grandma, but I do wish you'd tell me. She needs me. And to be honest, I haven't given you much thought today. I only came here this morning to make sure everything was okay in Grandma's house. And what I found was you beaten half to death and lying on her carpet."

"Thanks for helping me," I said, "even if you don't like me."

She surprised me with a smile. "Dallas, how about if we call a truce?"

"That's fine with me," I said.

"But you still won't tell me where Grandma is?"

"Not yet," I said. "I don't want someone doing to you what they did to me, and that could happen if they knew you knew her location and wanted you to tell them."

She rocked back and forth for a minute, and then she said, "Okay, maybe you're right. I certainly don't want her to get hurt."

"Thanks," I said.

"I still think you need to go to the emergency room," she said, her fiery eyes filled with what appeared to me to be genuine concern.

"I'll have to pass. I've got to get back on my feet. I'm supposed to meet Hank in a little while so we can go talk to some folks," I told her.

"You aren't going anywhere," she said firmly, "unless it is to the emergency room. You may not have any broken bones, but you have been hurt."

"I've been hurt worse than this before," I told her. "I'll be okay. I need to call Hank and have him meet me here. Would you help me get moving around and maybe get some food in me after awhile?"

"I'll fix you something to eat, but can't you at least wait a few hours and make sure you really aren't hurt too badly before you call him?" she asked.

"I wish I could," I admitted as a spasm of pain made me shudder. "But I have to be in Ogden late this afternoon."

"What for?" she asked.

"I'm trying to catch a killer," I reminded her. "And some potential suspects will be at a demolition derby up there. I'll be helping Kanon with his car. He's in the derby."

"Is it one of Jerry's cars?" she asked, her head jerking back in surprise.

"I'm afraid so."

"Will Sophie be there?" she asked.

I couldn't help but smile. "I think so."

"No wonder you want to go," she said with a frown. "She's very pretty."

I made no comment. I didn't want to alienate my equally pretty nurse again. She looked at me for a moment, and then she reached out and touched my hand in what could only be described as tenderness, much opposed to what she said about not liking me. "For now, Mr. Tough Guy, you just lie still. I'll fix you something to eat."

I watched her walk out of the room, thinking about what she'd said and how she was acting toward me. I couldn't help wondering which girl was the real Alexandra Grady—the sweet, caring one or the one who shot fiery darts at me.

chapter TEN

I CALLED HANK WHILE ALEX was in the kitchen. He said he was feeling much better and was going to be able to work that day. I told him it would be helpful if he could pick me up at our client's house. "Actually, I'm with Deputy Wakefield right now," he reported. "We were just heading for the office. It would save us some time if you could meet us there."

I hesitated in answering. I wasn't sure I was up to driving just yet. Maybe in a few hours, I thought. "Dallas, what's going on?" he asked when I didn't respond right away. "Are you okay?"

"I'll be fine in a little while," I said. "But I don't think I better drive just yet."

"Okay, out with it, Dallas. What happened?" he demanded.

As I was telling him, Alex came into the room with a glass of juice I suspected she was going to make me drink. I knew I needed it, but I wasn't sure I was ready for it just yet. "Is that Hank?" she asked as her eyes looked at my phone.

I nodded, and she abruptly reached for it with her free hand. "Hey," I said, but she only smiled at me and held my phone up to her ear.

"Mr. Pierce, this is Alex Grady," she said, backing away from the sofa and shaking her head at me. "Dallas got beat up pretty badly. When I found him this morning, he couldn't even move. He was lying on the floor when I came in the door. He about gave me a heart attack. I thought he was dead."

She stopped talking and listened for a moment, nodding her head at whatever Hank was saying. Then she began shaking it. "No, he refuses to go to the emergency room." She listened and began nodding again. Finally, she said, "That will be great."

She gave me back my phone with a triumphant grin. "Mr. Pierce and Deputy Wakefield are coming here right now. He thinks the two of them can manage without you for the day. Hank says he's feeling better than he was yesterday. And there will be no argument."

I was actually quite relieved, but I had to be fit enough to go to Ogden. That was a must. I was anxious to meet some of the other people Jerry knew and may have made angry at the demolition derby that fateful evening in Duchesne—or sometime prior.

Alex again helped me sit up and made me drink the juice. I found it hard to swallow, and I embarrassed myself by slobbering a bit. She wiped my face with a washcloth she retrieved from the linen closet in the hallway. I did manage to get most of the juice down my throat, as opposed to down my front, by the time the doorbell rang.

Hank and Milt hurried across the room when Alex let them in. "You look pretty rough," Hank said. "Would you like to tell us what happened in a little more detail?"

"I think we need to get the local officials here," Milt Wakefield, the Duchesne County deputy said after listening to my story.

I shook my head. "Better not," I said. "It would only be a distraction."

Hank agreed, and to my surprise, so did Alexandra. She said, "It seems to me like Dallas has stirred a hornet's nest. He must be getting close to whoever killed Jerry. You guys need to keep working on this. Even if the local police came, they wouldn't be able to do any more than the three of you are doing, would they?"

"Probably not," Milt agreed. He turned to Hank. "Dallas clearly needs to rest. Why don't you and I go see if we can find Mr. Kelsey Glazer?"

"Let me know if you find him," I said. "And tell me if he has a broken wrist. I honestly think it was him that tried to abduct Mrs. Grady. And it could have been him again that did this to me last night. He wouldn't have needed both wrists because I mostly got kicked."

Alex fixed some hot cereal and toast for me. My stomach was weak, but I knew that if I were to appear in Ogden and not only help Kanon but do some investigating on the side, I had to build my strength and do so quickly. It took awhile, but I managed, and as I did, I felt my strength begin to return. "Is there anything else I can get for you?" my pretty nurse asked.

"Yeah, but I know you won't let me have any," I said.

She grinned at me. "Coffee?" she said.

"Please," I wheedled, thinking how pretty she was when she smiled.

"Not in my grandma's house," she said firmly. Her smile faded. "You need to quit drinking that stuff."

I didn't tell her that I'd actually been trying to do that the past few days, that I hadn't had any since Wednesday morning at Jim's Garage, but that it was very hard. I had decided that for Ellen's sake as well as my own I'd break the habit. But right now, I craved a hot cup. Had I been where I could have gotten one, I'm afraid I would have done so. "I owe you one," I said to Alex.

"For what?" she asked.

"For not letting me get my way," I said.

She gave me a funny look. "You're welcome," she said.

"When do you have to go to work?" I asked.

"I'm off until midnight. Then I have a twelve-hour shift. I'll have to miss church tomorrow. That's one drawback to my job. I sometimes can't make it."

I found that I believed her. In doing so, I was having a difficult time keeping her on my list of suspects. I struggled with that, but deep down, as I recalled some of our more difficult moments the past few days, I decided that I had to do so. I couldn't rule her out just yet. I was grateful, nevertheless, for the tender nursing she was administering.

* * *

Hank and Milt found Kelsey Glazer.

When they stopped by to report to me, Alex and I both stared at them, dumbfounded. He had told them nothing. Nor would he ever tell any of us anything. They had found him in the morgue. He had made his appearance there during the night—after he had beaten me up, I presumed. His next stop was the cemetery. Whatever secrets he had harbored would soon be resting beneath six feet of dirt.

"What did he die of?" Alex asked, her dark freckles standing out on her now pasty-white face.

Hank shook his head. "Lead poisoning," he said.

She looked at him blankly.

"He was shot," I clarified. She still looked puzzled. "Bullets are made of lead," I added.

Both men nodded as understanding shone in her eyes. "He was brought into the emergency room sometime after midnight," Milt said. "No one knows who brought him there. An anonymous call to the hospital announced that he was lying near the emergency room door. He was still alive then, but he died shortly after, in surgery. He had a bullet lodged in his spine."

"Did you see his body?" I asked.

"Yes," Hank said. "And yes again, he had a broken wrist. It seems that he got that several days ago. We have no idea why he was killed or who did it, but I suspect he was the one who tried to abduct our client."

Even though Alex and I discussed the matter of Kelsey's murder after Hank and Milt had left, neither of us could come up with a good idea as to who might have done it or why. I was convinced that he had in some way been involved in Jerry's murder. I did get one good idea though. I got my cell phone out and told Hank what I was thinking. I could hear his chuckle over the phone. He said, "You will be good at this business. You are thinking just like the deputy and me. With the help of a local detective, we are in the process of getting a search warrant for both Kelsey's car, if we can find it, and his house right now. We'll let you know how it goes."

"Good," I said, wishing I was with them.

"Are you feeling better?" he asked.

"I have a good nurse," I said, glancing at Alex as I spoke. She smiled. Boy, was her smile ever an improvement over her frown. If only I knew what thoughts were residing deep inside her mind.

"Does that mean you are feeling better?" Hank asked.

"Yes. I think I'll live," I responded. I didn't think it was wise to add that I was going to Ogden that night regardless of how I felt.

Kanon called my cell phone at about three in the afternoon. By then I was up and walking around. I'd taken all the pain pills Alex would let me, but the ones I had taken had helped. I actually felt like I had finally rejoined the living. "What's happening?" the young mechanic asked.

"Not much," I said.

"Have you seen the news?" he asked.

"No," I said slowly. "I've been sort of, uh, occupied."

"Sophie saw it. She came out to the shop shouting about what she saw." Kanon was going to drag this out, it appeared.

"What did she see?" I asked impatiently.

"Kelsey is dead. He got shot in the back!" he announced almost gleefully.

"Really," I said, surprised that it was already on the news.

"He was left in front of the emergency room at the hospital. They don't know how he got there. I guess I shouldn't say this, but he probably had it coming. After the way he treated Sophie, I'm afraid he was bound to end up like this sooner or later."

"Unbelievable," I said, trying to sound surprised. "I guess he definitely won't be coming back to work again."

"Guess not," Kanon said with a chuckle. "Me and Razor are going to head for Ogden in a few minutes. Would you mind picking Sophie up, Dallas? She isn't ready to go yet, and we need to get up there now."

I glanced at the pretty redhead who was currently sitting on a chair on the far side of the room reading a book. Then I said, "Sure," to Kanon. Actually, I wanted to pick up the pretty brunette but wondered if I could keep my pain from showing. I didn't need any distractions tonight. "I'll try to get on my way by four," I finished.

As I ended the call, Alex looked up from her book and said, "You don't really plan to go to Ogden, do you?"

"I have to, Alex. People are counting on me, and I really do want to meet some of the other drivers. Someone killed your brother. I want to know who," I said firmly. "They've made this kind of personal now."

"I'll say, Dallas. And I want them caught too. But you are hurt. You need to stay here and rest. I'm serious, Dallas."

"I'll make it."

"I wish you wouldn't, but since you so foolishly insist, please call me when you get back here," she said. "I want to make sure you're okay."

"Thanks, Alex, but I don't think I'll come back here tonight."

She threw her hand to her mouth and gasped. "Oh, I wasn't thinking. Of course you can't come here. Whoever did this to you is still out there."

"Yeah, unless he's in the morgue," I said, my mind still on the late Kelsey Glazer. But I couldn't be sure it had been him. "At any rate, I'll just take my suitcase with me. I'll catch a hotel somewhere or do like I did until I met your grandma," I said.

"What was that?"

"I slept in my truck," I said, chuckling at the shocked look on her face.

"You can't do that in your condition," she said. "I won't be home tonight. You can stay at my place if you want to. Nobody will bother you there."

I suppose I was the one with the shocked face now. "Don't look so surprised," she said. "You can sleep on the sofa there. It's as soft as the one you've been lounging on here."

There was no way I was taking her up on her offer, as sweet as it was. A hotel room would be fine. Suddenly, I remembered something I'd nearly forgotten. I had promised to take Ellen Grady to church the next day. And I still didn't have any proper church apparel. I had to get to a store and buy a white shirt and tie, some black dress shoes, and a pair of slacks. I could do without a sports coat. That was stretching my budget way too far.

"Well, don't say I didn't offer," Alex said, interrupting my thoughts. "But if you were smart, you'd let me help you to a hotel now, and then you'd stay there until you got well."

"Thanks," I said. "But I'll be fine."

"If you are so set on going to Ogden, then I better fix something else for you to eat," she said. "You need all the energy you can get. You haven't eaten much so far today."

She had a point, and I said, "I really appreciate that, Alex. I'll go get my suitcase while you fix us something."

"I'll help you with the suitcase," she said.

"I think I can do it. If I can't go down the stairs and carry a suitcase back up, then I'll know I can't make it tonight," I said.

She smiled. "You have a point. But please don't fall down the stairs."

It was not fun, but I made it downstairs and even carried a full suitcase back up. Unless Alex's current fixings did me wonders, I was in for a long, hard evening. "Dallas," she said after I'd taken the suitcase out the back door to my truck and returned to the kitchen, "please—you can't go tonight. I wish I'd taken you to the emergency room."

"Do I really look that bad?" I said as I sat weakly on a kitchen chair.

"Yes, you do. I insist. You are not going anywhere tonight but to a hotel room." She had one hand on her hip, looking as serious as she sounded. Looking quite cute, to be honest.

"Alex, I can't do that," I said. "But you're right about food. That will help me a bunch, I'm sure."

She shrugged and set a pair of plates on the table. I was finally able to eat, and Alex's frown slowly lifted as she watched me. I offered to help clean up, but she wouldn't hear of it, so I went back to the comfort of the sofa, wishing I could just stay there and not have to move again for a long time. I looked at my watch and groaned. I had to leave pretty soon.

When Alex finished the dishes, she came in and said, "One last chance. Will you let me help you find a hotel room and get settled in?"

I shook my head.

She frowned. "Then I guess I better get going. I don't want to be here alone. And you better go now too because I don't think you should be here alone either."

It was time, so I dragged myself from the sofa, trying not to appear to be in too much pain. But Alex wasn't fooled. "Take these," she said, holding out a bottle of painkillers. "Just don't overdo."

"Thanks, Alex. You've been great."

She looked away, headed for the door, then stopped and looked back as I followed her. "I misjudged you, Dallas. I'm sorry. Take care of yourself and don't forget to call before I go on shift at midnight."

I nodded but made no promise. I'd see what happened and decide later whether to call her or not.

We left together. I looked up the street and couldn't suppress a groan. "What is it, Dallas?" Alex asked, grabbing my arm.

I subtly pointed up the street. She looked where I was indicating. Her face went totally pale, a reaction I didn't believe could possibly be faked. She turned back to me. "That's the white car?"

"I'm afraid so," I said.

"I swear that it's not anyone I asked to watch you. That was only Wednesday night, and my friend from work doesn't have a white car," she said. I believed her. She had nothing to do with whoever had been following me so boldly.

We walked together around the back of the house. When we were out of sight, she said, her voice trembling, "Dallas, what are we going to do?"

"Call in the troops," I said lightly. I was quite serious though. I dialed Hank's cell phone. To my relief, he answered. Even better, he was within ten minutes of my location. "The white car is here. Alex and I were just going to leave. I can't stay here tonight," I said.

"Where will you stay?" he asked.

"A hotel," I told him, deliberately leaving out the fact that I would be going to the derby in Ogden first.

"Both of you go back inside like you forgot something," Hank said. "I'll take care of your tail."

"Is Detective Wakefield still with you?"

"He's at the courthouse getting the search warrant for Kelsey's place. I had to stop by the office for a little while. We will meet up in an hour," Hank said. "Don't worry, Dallas, I can take care of whoever the guy in the white car is. Who knows, I might even learn something from him. I'll call you when I'm in position and you guys can leave safely."

"Hank will create a diversion so we can leave without that guy following either one of us," I explained to Alex as we went back to the front door and into the house again. We watched the street through parted blinds. As promised, Hank showed up in his blue Chevrolet sedan. He pulled directly in front of the white car and got out. My cell phone rang. It was Hank. All he said was, "Go!"

We went—me in pain, Alex looking worried. I looked toward the white car and Hank as I followed Alex and her little green Volkswagen onto the street. The driver of the white car was standing on the edge of the roadway. From the way his arms were flapping, I gathered that he was speaking angrily to Hank. Hoping that Hank didn't get hurt, I quickly drove out of sight.

I stopped at a store, and after painfully extricating myself from the truck, I walked inside. Before I'd even had a chance to look for clothes, my cell phone rang, and I was glad to find it was Hank calling. "How did it go?" I asked.

"Fine. The guy was a jerk," he said.

"Did he say what his name is?"

"No, he refused. He denied doing anything but taking a break while getting his bearings. He showed me a map, and he claimed to be trying to find an address."

"I suppose you got his license plate number," I said.

"Sure did. Detective Wakefield is going to run it for me."

"He's definitely been following me," I said.

"After we serve the search warrant on Kelsey's home and vehicles, if they are there, we'll see what we can learn about the driver of the white car. In the meantime," Hank said sternly, "watch yourself. I didn't like the looks of the guy."

"Can you describe him for me?" I asked.

"He looks to me like he's around thirty or so. He's probably about five-ten, but he's very stocky. His eyes are brown, and there is a look in them I don't like at all," he said.

"Like what?" I asked.

"Full of hate, I'd say. Also, he has brown hair, about shoulder length but thinning. He was dressed in tan slacks and a yellow polo shirt. He looks like he probably works out a lot. If I'm a judge of character, I'd say he could definitely be dangerous."

"I'll be careful," I said.

"The car is white, as you already know. It's a Chevy Cavalier. Not real new. And here's the plate number," he said. I wrote it down in my notebook, but I also memorized it. "Call me later, when you are free to talk. I'll let you know what we learn," he promised.

After Hank rang off, I walked unsteadily to the men's section of the store. I bought the clothes I needed for church. Several people looked at me with suspicion, with pity, or simply out of curiosity. But no one said anything to me. I made it back to the truck without falling down, and after leaning on my door for a minute, I dropped my purchases in the backseat and dragged myself behind the steering wheel.

Out of sheer nervousness, I took a roundabout route to the Storms' home from the store. Exercising an abundance of caution, I parked my car behind the house. I sat for a moment, trying to acquire the courage to get out of the car and walk as normally as possible to the front door.

I'd hoped Sophie would show up at my pickup so I wouldn't have to get out, but she must not have seen me drive into the yard, or else she wasn't ready yet. I opened the door and slid from the seat. When my feet hit the ground, it jarred me clear to the top of my head. Gritting my teeth, I steadied myself against the truck for a moment, and then I stepped away from it. After a few steps I felt much steadier, better than I had at the store. By the time I reached the back door of Sophie's house, I was moving much better.

I can do this, I thought to myself as I knocked on the door. I waited. Then I waited some more. I knocked again. Finally, Mrs. Storm appeared at the door. She peered through the glass at me before her rheumy eyes registered recognition. Then she pulled it open. "Dallas, isn't it?" she asked.

"Yes, Dallas Rowen. I'm here to pick up Sophie. She's riding to the demolition derby in Ogden with me," I said.

"Yes, of course," she said, the alcohol from her breath hitting me like a thick mist, almost making me choke. "Come in. She'll be ready in a minute or two."

She stepped back, and I entered. Already queasy because of my injuries, I had to swallow hard, fighting back a wave of nausea. I followed her through the kitchen and to the front room. She took her place beside her bottle in front of the TV. I said, "Do you mind if I help myself to a glass of water while I wait?"

She waved her hand at me, and I took that as permission. I stepped back to the kitchen and took a deep breath of the less-alcohol-saturated air I found there. Then I got a glass of water. I sat at the kitchen table and sipped it. In a couple of minutes, my stomach had settled down.

I heard footsteps from a hallway that led toward the home's bedrooms, and I looked up as Sophie entered, looking absolutely gorgeous in blue jeans and a red blouse. "Hi, Dallas," she said brightly. "Sorry to keep you waiting."

"Not a problem," I said, wishing I could continue to sit at the table and sip cool water.

"I just need to grab a jacket and we can go," she said, smiling at me.

"I'm parked in the back," I said as she started toward the living room. I already knew there was a coat closet by the front door.

"I'll grab it and be right back," she said.

I used her short absence to get my battered body up from the table. By the time she came back, slipping a blue Levi jacket on and, with a dainty flip of her head, throwing her long black hair over her shoulders, I was on my feet and had stepped to the back door. I took a deep breath and opened it. She stepped past me, the fragrance of her perfume wafting its way to my nose. She smelled almost as wonderful as she looked.

Not wanting to appear to be anything other than a gentleman, I opened the door to my truck for her, waited while she slipped in, and closed it. I walked around the back of the truck so she wouldn't see me sway on my feet and then got in. She smiled at me again and said, "Thanks for picking me up, Dallas."

"My pleasure," I said sincerely. That was the only thing about this trip to Ogden that felt like it could be pleasurable.

Nothing more was said until we were on the street and headed east. "Dallas," she said softly.

I looked over at her. She was watching me with those soft, dark brown eyes of hers. "You're hurt. Are you going to tell me what happened?" she asked, her voice even and without a hint of inflection.

chapter ELEVEN

"What do you mean, Sophie?" I asked after a long hesitation.

"I mean, how did you get hurt?" she asked. "And don't tell me you aren't in pain." She smiled that bewitching smile of hers.

"I'm okay," I said.

"That's what I asked you not to say," she scolded mildly. Before I could think of how else I might deny my injuries, she went on. "I heard your truck when you drove behind the house. I looked out the window to make sure it was you. I was brushing my hair, but I held the blind back while I brushed and watched you. I saw you get out, Dallas. I almost dropped my brush. I thought you were going to fall down. Please, whatever happened, you can tell me. I'm your friend. You can trust me, Dallas."

I glanced at her again. I supposed that I could tell her a limited version of the attack without revealing the fact that I was investigating Jerry's murder. I believed I trusted her, but again, I wondered if I could be sure. "I ran into a little trouble last night when I stepped into the house where I'm staying," I said. "I apparently surprised a burglar."

"Were you . . . were you ambushed by the guy?" she asked, her eyes growing wide.

"That about sums it up," I said.

Either I was a sucker and Sophie a great actor, or she was genuinely concerned. She certainly expressed concern through gasps, groans, misty eyes, and lots of body language. It certainly seemed real. It was hard not to believe that she really was shocked by what had happened to me. And all she had received from me was a bare bones version of the attack. Alex knew more of what happened, and she had been sympathetic as well. The difference was that Alex at least had some idea about why I was attacked, but Sophie had been misled.

I was new to this investigation business, and despite what I had been told, it was certainly difficult to keep personal feelings in check and not eliminate folks like Alex and Sophie from the list of potential suspects—or Kanon, for that matter. I preferred to suspect people like the late Kelsey Glazer.

Sophie and I rode in silence for a while. I considered where the case was leading me. I was going to meet some of the people tonight who also had an association with Jerry, and I expected that I might find others I could add to the list of suspects.

I noticed how Sophie kept glancing at me. She seemed to have something on her mind. She finally spoke. "Dallas," she said softly, "you don't have to help tonight. When Kanon realizes you're hurt, he won't insist. Anyway, you're only doing it out of friendship."

Of course, she had no idea how little friendship had to do with it and how much my obligation to Mrs. Grady was what was driving me on. "I'll do as much as I can," I said. "I promised Kanon, and I believe in keeping my promises."

"I'll do more to help if it's needed," she said. "Really, you've got to take it easy."

I didn't argue anymore. I had to do what I had to do, and that was all there was to it. She frowned, brushed the hair out of her eyes, and looked straight ahead. My mind went back to the case. I wanted to know how it was going with Hank, Milt, and Pete Richards and his partner, the local detectives who were helping them. But I wouldn't know how the search turned out until later. I also wanted to know who owned the white Chevy Cavalier that had been following me. Hank knew I would be with possible suspects, so he was not going to call unless it was an absolute emergency. If I got a chance, I'd call him, but I had to be very careful.

Sophie directed me to the area Kanon and Razorback had staked out. They were both making last-minute adjustments to their blue-and-white Chrysler when we pulled up. Kanon looked up and grinned. Jerry's murder was giving Kanon an opportunity that might never have been his had the crime not been committed. That was a sobering thought. Although he'd seemed unsure about driving when he'd suggested I take the wheel as we'd worked on the Chrysler in his garage, things were not always as they seemed. I couldn't shake the thought as I hoisted myself gingerly from my truck. However, once my feet were under me, I steeled myself and strode quickly toward the other guys, hiding my pain from them as effectively as I could.

"Good to see you guys," Kanon said with a wide grin as he wiped his greasy hands on a rag before shoving it back in his pocket.

"How's it running?" I asked.

"Great," Kanon said. "This is a good car."

"It does have a good engine," Razorback agreed. "If Kanon can keep from getting hit too hard, he'll have a good chance of making some money tonight."

"I'm glad. What do we need to do now?" I asked as Sophie caught my eye and shook her head just the slightest bit.

"Nothing at the moment," Kanon said. "I think we're ready to roll."

"That's good," Sophie said, turning a relieved smile on me. "Maybe Dallas and I can kind of stroll around and get a look at some of the other cars, then, if you guys don't mind."

"Go ahead," Kanon said, grinning widely at the two of us. I think he might have been hoping for a romance. I was just hoping that Sophie was innocent of any part in the murder.

She took my hand and steered me away from the others. "That was lucky," she said after we were out of earshot. "Maybe you can get feeling a little better if we just walk around."

"That will help," I agreed. "A little walking will probably take some of the stiffness away."

"By the way," she said, flipping her long hair from her eyes and looking up at me, "Do the cops know about the burglary at Mrs. Grady's house and the assault on you?"

"Yes," I said, stretching the truth. Detective Wakefield knew. Of course, he had no local jurisdiction, but at least it allowed me to answer as I did without too much guilt.

There were derby cars all over the area, each in a designated spot, and each with crews seemingly busy at work. "I guess Jerry knew all these people," I said, trying not to make it sound too obvious that I was interested in his death. I added, "And I suppose Kanon does as well."

"A lot of them," she said. "There are some people—Jerry was one of them—who race all over the state at all of the derbies, even out of state sometimes. I guess they think of themselves as professionals of a sort. Others just show up at certain races."

She still had hold of my hand. I felt self-conscious, but I wasn't about to jerk loose. "Who are some of the more professional ones?" I asked. "You know, ones who might drive in places like Duchesne that are sort of out of the way."

"Right over there," she said, pointing at a large, bright red car. "That belongs to Jake Frankland. He and Jerry have been at almost every derby together." She chuckled for a moment and then added, "Jerry almost always beat him. But I don't know if Kanon can. Probably not, since he has no experience."

We veered in that direction. A fellow of forty or so was leaning against a pickup a few feet from the red car. He was a well-built man of maybe six feet or a little more. He had long black hair, long sideburns, and a large moustache. As we approached he was fiddling absently with the moustache while talking to a woman who had her back to us. She looked like she was only a couple inches shorter than the fellow. She turned as we approached, throwing her long blonde hair across her shoulder with one hand while she gave a little wave with the other. Her eyes were dark brown and quite piercing. She was a pretty woman with a full figure and darkly tanned skin.

"Hi, guys," Sophie called out in a friendly tone as she let go of my hand. "I'd like you to meet my friend Dallas Rowen. He's helping Kanon and Razorback with their car."

The man grunted, the woman smiled—a smile that did not go to her eyes. "This is Jake Frankland and his girlfriend, Lucia Root," she said to me. "Jake's one of the best drivers out there."

He acknowledged the compliment with a nod of his head but not a hint of a smile. "You driving or is Kanon?" he asked while looking directly at me.

"Oh, not me. Kanon will be driving," I said.

"Too bad," Jake said. "The kid has no experience. He'll get stomped."

"You're probably right," Sophie agreed. I glanced at her, and I could see irritation in her eyes, but she forced a smile. "After Jerry was killed, Kanon decided he'd keep driving at least for a while. Who knows, maybe he'll get good after a few times."

"Maybe, but I doubt it," Lucia put in rudely.

I didn't like this pair, and I had barely met them.

"Haven't seen you around before," Jake said to me. "You must have just moved into the area."

"I've been in the army," I said. "I'd had all I could take and decided to try my hand at being a mechanic. With Jerry Grady dead, I heard there was an opening at Jim's Garage. So I applied for it and got it. So far, it's not a bad job."

"I hear there's another opening," Lucia said. "Are you putting in for it, Sophie?"

Sophie forced a chuckle. "No, I'm happy with what I'm doing. It's too bad about Kelsey."

"He was a jerk," Lucia said. "No big loss."

I wondered if they considered Jerry a jerk too and assumed they probably did. I didn't bring up Jerry's name again, but Jake did. "That's two of Jim's mechanics that have been killed," he said. "Maybe it's not a very good place to work. You could be next, you know."

I shivered. I really didn't like this pair. Just then a fellow of about thirty joined them. He'd come walking in past some other cars to the west. Jake turned toward the newcomer. He was shorter than Lucia, but not much. He had thinning brown hair and was quite stocky. "Will you look at what the dog drug in," Jake said. "If it ain't Kade Squire himself."

I did a double take. That was the name of Alexandra's stepbrother. "Who are your friends?" he said, nodding toward me and Sophie.

"These guys are helping Kanon Storm. He thinks he can take Jerry Grady's place racing. I've got news for them," Lucia said. "What are you doing here?"

Sophie had clearly had enough, although I was in no hurry to leave. I wanted to get a little more of a feel for this Squire guy. But Sophie said, "We better get back and see if Kanon needs any help. He's got a good car, and I'm really pulling for him."

Her comment brought daggers from the eyes of Lucia, Jake, and Kade. She didn't seem to care. "Come on, Dallas," she said, taking me by the hand again. "See you guys around," she added to the other three. As we started away, my eyes met those of Kade. He stared at me with undisguised hatred. I quickly turned away, thinking we needed to learn a lot more about the stepbrother Jerry had not liked.

We walked past a couple of other cars where the pit crews were busy working. Sophie seemed intent on getting back to where her brother was. After a minute or two, she said, "Those guys are jerks. I've always tried to be friendly to them, and so has Kanon, but they think they're better than anyone else. I shouldn't have introduced you to them."

"No, that's okay," I said. "I just hope Kanon beats them."

"He might," she said. "Especially when I tell him what they said about him."

"That other guy, Kade—I take it you've never met him," I ventured, giving her a sidelong glance.

She stopped, removed her hand from mine, and with a shake of her fist, she said, "I don't know why he acted like a stranger. He doesn't live here on the Wasatch Front, but he comes up a lot. I'll have to ask Kanon and Razorback, but I wouldn't be surprised if he was in Duchesne. I think he helps Jake with his car once in a while, not usually at the races, just at his shop."

"Really?" I asked. "It didn't sound like they'd seen each other for a long time."

"That's probably not true," she said as she turned and started walking again. "I don't like Kade; neither did Jerry, even if he is family."

So she knew his relationship to Alex and Jerry. I didn't tell her that I also knew. So I said, "He and Jerry are related?"

"Yeah, Jerry didn't like to admit it, but he and Kade are stepbrothers," she said.

"So that makes him Alexandra's stepbrother too. I wonder if she knows he hangs around with Jake."

"I have no idea about that. Kade's dad married Jerry's mother after his father was killed," she said. "He's older than both of them, and for some reason, Jerry told us, Kade always resented them. He fits in much better with Lucia the witch and Jake the jerk," she said, her eyes filled with anger. Then she put a hand over her mouth. "I'm sorry, Dallas. I shouldn't talk that way. Forget I said that."

I couldn't help but agree with her, but my mind was so busy going over the facts I had just learned that I felt a need to get off by myself and give Hank a call. Why hadn't Alex mentioned that Kade knew Jake unless, like Sophie had just suggested, she didn't know?

"Dallas, are you okay?" Sophie asked, concern in her eyes.

"I'm hurting," I said in an attempt to avoid her learning what my real concerns were.

"You need to sit down," she said. "Come on, let's get you back to your truck." She took my arm and led me that way again. "You need some aspirin or something too. I'll try to find—"

"I've got something in the truck," I said quickly. "I'll take a couple of capsules and then I'll be fine, I'm sure."

But a little farther on, she spotted a man just ahead of us. She said, "There's another one of the guys who races a lot. His name is Lyle Wertz. But I won't take time to introduce you to him right now."

"No, that's okay. It'll only take a minute," I said as I steered us in that direction.

She introduced me to Lyle. "Dallas is helping my brother, Kanon. Kanon's going to be driving Jerry Grady's car tonight," she said.

"Boy, that'll be tough," Lyle said, brushing some dirty, stringy hair out of his face, a few strands that had escaped from his ponytail. He was a little guy in his early twenties. He was unkempt but he didn't seem antagonistic toward us. "Kanon really hasn't had any experience, has he?"

"No, but he's watched Jerry a lot."

"Yeah, and that's good for something. Too bad Jerry can't be here himself to drive. But since he's not, I wish Kanon a lot of luck."

We visited for a minute more. Lyle didn't say one bad thing about Jerry. He might be a suspect, but he didn't make it very high on my list. When we left, he said, "Tell Kanon I wish him well."

We walked back to my truck after that. "Lyle seems like an okay guy," I said.

"I think he is. Jerry didn't like him, but Jerry didn't like anyone. Kanon says Lyle never harassed them like Jake did. One thing's for sure—he's not like Jake," Sophie said.

At the truck, I took a couple of pain pills. Twenty minutes later I was feeling a little better, and Sophie and I helped Kanon get into his car. His heat was coming up next, and he needed to get in line now. The car started right up, and Razorback, who had been once again fiddling beneath the hood, said, "It's ready to go. I think this car will do great." He grinned and added, "Unless Kanon lets himself get hit too much."

"I'm doing the hitting, just like Jerry taught me," Kanon said with more confidence than showed on his face.

With the rest of the little pit crew, I watched Kanon get ready to race. We were leaning against the fence along with a bunch of others. Sophie, standing next to me, said in my ear, "I'll be surprised if he gets past this round. He talks about Jerry teaching him, but it's like I told Lyle, all he ever did was watch Jerry and listen to him brag. I just don't know if that's enough."

"Let's hope it is," I said as the flag came down and the crashing, banging, roaring of engines, and cheering began.

Sophie gripped my arm when Kanon took his first lick. A large blue Chevy pounded him from the rear, but the damage didn't look too extensive. He gunned his car and gave more than he'd taken to a yellow Ford. Kanon, to me, appeared quite skillful as he roared around the arena, occasionally taking some small bumps but managing to get some pretty good hits in on other cars. One by one, the cars became disabled, and the drivers pulled their flags and then sat still, waiting for the round to end so wreckers could tow them out.

Finally, there were just three cars still running. One of them was Kanon's Chrysler. One rear fender was rubbing against the tire, but Kanon was still able to keep the car moving. He and the other two attacked one another with a vengeance. Kanon managed to hit one of them from behind, jamming it into one of the disabled cars. Steam blew from the radiator, and it was down to two. Kanon got lucky as the other car blew a tire and he was able to ram it hard enough in the front end that another tire blew. Kanon was declared the winner of the round.

"I can't believe this. Kanon did better than I thought he would. But now our work begins," Sophie said as we turned away from the fence. "We've got to get Kanon's car tuned up the best we can before he goes into a semifinal round. He made it through this one, but it will get harder now. I just hope Jake Frankland's car isn't in that round. He will go after Kanon right from the start if he is."

I didn't disagree with her. Unlike most of the drivers, Kanon was able to drive his car from the arena on its own power. We went right to work on it. Razorback and Kanon began working on something in the engine. Despite my injuries and with Sophie's help, we were able to get the fender bent out so that it was no longer rubbing against the tire. We also straightened out a couple of other damaged areas, although there was nothing too serious.

When the four of us were satisfied that the car was ready for the next round, Sophie and I walked back to my truck, where I swallowed a couple more pain pills. "I still can't believe how well Kanon did," Sophie said. "I guess he watched Jerry more closely than I thought."

"Yeah, the kid did okay," I agreed as I put the cap back on my bottle of water.

"Do you want to rest in your truck for a few minutes?" she asked. "I'll go talk to the guys while we wait for the next round. When we're ready I'll come get you."

"That sounds good," I said, and I climbed into my truck. She stayed with me for a minute, and then she rejoined her brother.

Finally alone, I pulled my cell phone out and called Hank. "Are you in Ogden?" he asked me when he answered.

"I am," I said. "And I've learned some things. But I may only have a minute or two to talk, so tell me what happened when you guys searched Kelsey's car and house."

"Yeah, well, it was interesting," Hank began. "We found a letter in his car, the one he drives to work, a green Ford Explorer. It was from Kade Squire, the guy the white Cavalier is registered to, the guy I think has been following you."

That rocked me—Alexandra Grady's stepbrother had been following me! And he was even here at the derby. I didn't like where this was going. "What did the letter say?" I asked, trying to keep my voice calm.

"It was kind of strange, actually," Hank said. "Kade asked Kelsey in the letter if the job was still open at Jim's Garage—you know, the one you filled. He said he was planning to move back from St. George and that he expected Kelsey to help him get a job, that Kelsey owed him."

"Did he say why he owed him?" I asked.

"No, but I get the feeling this Squire guy is a hard character. We need to find out more about him," Hank said.

"I can tell you some," I revealed. "He's here in Ogden right now."

"How do you know that?" Hank asked.

"I just met a guy and his girlfriend who drove in the race in Duchesne, and who, by the way, don't seem to have cared too much for Jerry. We need to learn more about them. Anyway, this guy walks up and starts talking to them. He looks about thirty or so and has shoulder-length brown hair, thinning in the back."

"How tall is he?" Hank broke in.

"He's about five-ten. And I'd guess he weighs a little under two hundred pounds," I responded. "I didn't like the way he looked at me. The other people told him who I was, and they said his name was Kade Squire."

"The description is right," Hank said.

"Kanon's sister, Sophie, was with me."

"Who were the people he was talking to?" Hank asked before I could say more about Kade.

"Jake Frankland and Lucia Root," I answered as I looked out my window and saw Sophie turn away and start toward me.

"Those were also names you got from Alex Grady," Hank said.

"Yes. Listen, I've only got a moment before I am no longer alone here," I said as I continued to watch Sophie. "There's something you ought to know. Sophie told me something I already knew, something Alex told me that first night when we met at Arby's. Kade Squire is the stepbrother of Jerry and Alex Grady."

For a moment it was silent on the other end of the line. Finally, Hank said, "That throws a whole new twist on things, and I don't like it a bit."

"That's exactly what I've been thinking," I said. "Listen, I've got to go now."

I put the phone away before Sophie got to the truck. I rolled the window down for her. She smiled and said, "Are you doing any better?"

"A little," I said.

"Good. It'll only be a minute or two before we have to get Kanon and his car in line again. I thought it would be a little longer."

"That's okay, the pain pills are kicking in," I said.

She reached through the window and tenderly touched my face. "You really need to get some rest," she said. "I can make excuses for you to Kanon if you'd like to get on your way home. I can ride back with him and Razorback."

I shook my head. "No, I promised. I'll come now."

chapter TWELVE

As LUCK WOULD HAVE IT, Kanon was in the same semifinal heat as Jake Frankland. After we'd helped him into the car, he took the key out and kissed the lucky-charm key chain. "What's that about?" Sophie asked.

"Jerry always did that before each race. He used to tell me he didn't believe in God but that he believed in his lucky charms," he said with a grin. "It can't hurt, can it?"

"It's stupid," Sophie said with disgust. But Kanon ignored her and put on his helmet. A moment later, he drove toward the line that was forming at the gate to the arena.

Good to his word, Jake Frankland focused on destroying Kanon's car from the beginning of the heat. Sophie silently watched, her face in pain. She held my arm and even leaned into me for support as Kanon's car was bashed over and over again. Razorback wasn't so calm. In fact, he was very angry. He cursed and shook his fists each time Jake's car hit Kanon's. Sophie was the first to notice Alex's stepbrother standing a few feet away, right next to Lucia Root. Sophie poked me and pointed. I spotted Kade and Lucia without her having to say a word.

Kade had a gleeful look on his face, and once, when I looked over toward him, he looked my way. Our eyes met, and he simply nodded his head and held up two fingers in a V, the sign for victory. He smirked and turned away. Lucia Root never even looked at us, at least not that I saw.

Kanon tried his best to keep out of Jake's way, but the older, experienced driver was just too good for him. It wasn't long before Kanon's radiator began blowing steam, but the gritty young man didn't quit then. The next hit from Jake, though, bent his left back tire, axle and all, until it was almost sideways. A fender was crushed into the front right tire by another car only seconds later. Then, a moment later, flames spurted from under the hood. Men with fire extinguishers quickly put the fire out, but Kanon was finished. He pulled his flag, indicating that he was done so that other cars would no longer hit him, and he sat in the car as the race continued around him. His head was hanging, and I couldn't help but feel sorry for him.

Jake won the heat, and he drove his car out of the arena under its own power. Kanon's car had to be towed back to his area. As we all looked it over, he pumped his fist in anger as Razorback swore that Jake would wish he'd never done what he did. One thing was clear, but it was Sophie who voiced it, saying, "I'm sorry, Kanon, but I think this car is finished."

"There are more," he said without even turning his face toward her. "Jerry left us with a good supply. Let's get this piece of junk out of here. Next time we'll use the Cadillac. We'll crush Jake with it." I remembered the Cadillac key in the red toolbox and wondered where that car was. I decided that now wasn't the time to ask, but I would soon.

Using winches, we loaded the battered Chrysler onto Kanon's trailer, and then he and Razorback headed for Provo, both still voicing their anger at Jake Frankland as they pulled away.

Sophie and I stopped for dinner before we also started back toward Provo. I was less interested in food than I was in finding a place to spend the night. But I did eat some. I avoided coffee. It was hard for me, but I had made a decision that morning with Alex's help, not just for the sake of my landlady but for my sake as well. I had drunk my last cup. Sophie didn't eat a lot either. She was hurting for her brother; I could see it all over her face. She also turned down the coffee. I assumed it was simply because I hadn't accepted any. Then I recalled that she hadn't had any when we'd gone to dinner with Kanon and Razorback. They had both had a couple of cups each that night.

When she offered to drive after leaving the restaurant, I took her up on her offer. We talked about Kanon's defeat after we were on the interstate. I learned that she was more disappointed at the way Jake targeted and destroyed Kanon's car than the simple fact of Kanon having been defeated. "I hope he learned some things so he can do better next time," she said. "Maybe he can do better with the Cadillac."

"I hope so," I said as I reclined my seat in an effort to get comfortable. "Where is the Cadillac? It must be some car."

"I haven't seen it," she said. "In fact, tonight was the first time he has mentioned it. But, then, I know Jerry had some cars someplace else. I guess Kanon knows where they are, but I don't."

We rode in silence for a few minutes after that. I was starting to doze when Sophie suddenly said, "We've got to stop Kanon from driving again."

Startled, I asked, "Why? I think he'll get better. And like you mentioned, there is the Cadillac."

"Someone killed Jerry to keep him from driving. Kanon has taken his place," she reasoned. She looked over at me, her face scrunched with worry. "Whoever it was might also try to kill Kanon."

Sophie had opened the way for me to have the discussion with her that I had not known how to approach. I shrugged off the sleepiness and asked, "What makes you think Jerry was killed because of his involvement in demolition derbies?"

She looked my way again and fiercely gripped the steering wheel. "I can't think of any other reason. I just think it could have something to do with his driving. What if it does? He could have really gotten under somebody's skin."

"Like he did Kelsey?"

"How did you know that?" she asked.

I shrugged. "Kelsey told me. I worked with him, remember? Kanon can tell you. Kelsey couldn't say enough bad stuff about the guy I replaced," I explained. "Could there be others like him out there?"

Sophie slowed behind a semi, looked back, signaled, and then changed lanes. After she'd sped up again, she said, "I know he could be rude to people. But honestly, Dallas, it could have been another derby pro. He was probably rude with them like he was with everyone else. Or maybe one of them resented his beating them time after time. I wonder if the cops are looking at them."

"Maybe they don't know who they all are. You and Kanon could help with that, I suppose," I told her.

"Yeah, that's a good idea." She was thoughtful for a moment. "Maybe I'll get a list of names. But when I do, what do I do with it? I don't even know who to call."

"Give it to me. I'll call the sheriff in Duchesne, unless you want to do that yourself. That's who should be in charge of any murder investigation."

"Will you do it for me?" she asked.

"Sure," I agreed. "Get with Kanon and Razorback. See what the three of you can come up with. Then get it to me, and I'll call it in."

"Dallas, I really don't like Jake. He's scary."

"Then put him on your list," I said.

She nodded, her eyes on the road ahead. She was silent again for a few minutes. I felt like dozing off again. I was badly in need of rest. I leaned back, closed my eyes, and tried to ignore the results of the beating I had received just one day ago.

"Would Monday be okay?" Sophie asked.

It took me a minute, being half asleep, to process her question. Then I said, "Would what be okay?"

"The list we were talking about," she said. "I know you're going to want to spend tomorrow in bed, and I won't bother you until Monday with the list."

"Actually, I won't be spending the day in bed," I said. "I promised to—"

"You have to, Dallas," she interrupted. "You're hurt. Take care of yourself." She was pleading. I was touched.

"Sophie, I can't," I said. "I made a promise. I keep my promises."

"Promised to do what? You're not helping my brother with something again, are you?"

"No, it's my landlady. I promised to take her to church tomorrow."

"Dallas, I didn't know you went to church," she said, surprise on her face.

"I haven't been for years," I admitted, "but I told her I'd take her."

"Can't she go on her own? Surely she does that every Sunday, doesn't she?"

"She's in a hotel," I said. "Remember, I was attacked at her house. She's afraid to stay there."

"But you're going to?" Sophie asked.

"I don't think so, not for a day or two anyway," I said. "But I did promise to pick Mrs. Grady up at her hotel and take her to her ward."

"You're a good man," she said, again glancing at me. She smiled. "I have an idea."

"What's that?"

"I could go with the two of you," she said. "I can miss the meetings in my singles ward tomorrow," she said.

It was my turn to be surprised. "You're LDS?" I asked before I had time to think about it.

Sophie chuckled. "I'm not my mother, and I'm not my brother. How about it? Is it a date?"

How could I say no? "The meetings start at eleven. I'll pick you up at about ten thirty."

"I'll be ready," she said with a gentle smile.

Sophie dropped herself off at her home, but I did not go in since it was getting late. I did walk her to the door over protests of how much I must still hurt. I shook off her protests, and a moment later, I was glad I did. She kissed me lightly on the cheek and said, "I'll see you in the morning, Dallas." As a new friend, Sophie was great. The thought of her as a suspect was almost unimaginable. Sophie was a tremendous girl.

Sophie had not bothered to park behind the Storms' house like I usually did. Instead, she had pulled into the driveway. As I went to get back in my truck, I noticed a set of headlights as they were extinguished about a block up the street to the west. My stomach did an uncomfortable roll. I had not watched for anyone following us back from Ogden. Sophie had been driving, and I had been slumped back on my seat. That had been downright careless of me.

Maybe what I was about to do was foolish, but instead of going east, the way I normally would have done, I turned west as I left the driveway. No headlights came on as I gunned my truck that way. I was not surprised to see a white Chevy Cavalier parked there with someone slumped down in the seat. Had I felt better, I would have confronted my stalker right then, but I was in no condition to get into a fight. Instead, I simply drove on by, fully expecting the white car, driven, I suspected, by Alex Grady's stepbrother, to follow me.

My expectations proved to be accurate. Kade Squire was proving to be a real problem. I called Hank, who by then was at home, and told him what was happening. "Don't bother coming out," I told him. "I'm sure I can ditch him. I just thought you should know."

"It looks like we need to have a more formal discussion with Mr. Squire," Hank said. "I'm sure that Detective Wakefield will feel the same. Where are you going after you lose him?"

"First I'll drive by Ellen's house, but I won't go in. I just want to have a look. Then I will find a place to spend the night."

"If you have any trouble shaking Mr. Squire, give me a call back. I'll come give you a hand."

I didn't need to call my new boss again. Apparently Kade Squire wasn't very good at what he was trying to do. After five minutes of evasive driving, I couldn't see him anymore. I drove by Ellen Grady's house. It was dark and silent, like I expected it would be. However, I had no intention of looking inside tonight. I drove past and left the neighborhood. However, on an impulse, I drove back that way again. I parked two blocks away and got out of the truck. Sticking to the shadows as much as I could, I coaxed my pain-wracked body around the neighborhood. My impulse proved not to be misguided. The white car was parked on a side street near Ellen's house. I shook my head in frustration, and being careful not to let Kade see me, I returned to my truck and left the area once more.

I stayed in a different hotel than the one Ellen was in. I parked in the back and lugged my things to the third-floor room I'd been assigned, a room that looked out over the back of the hotel, as I had specifically requested. From my window, I had a clear view of my truck. Feeling some comfort in that, I prepared to make an effort at getting some much-needed rest. But before I had even made the attempt to insert my battered body between the clean white sheets, my cell phone went off.

"Dallas, are you okay?" Alexandra Grady, stepsister of Kade Squire, asked in a tender voice. "I thought you were going to call." I had never told her I would, and I wished she hadn't called me. I had a lot of concerns about her again.

"I'm doing a lot better," I answered her. That wasn't exactly the truth. The truth would be that I was feeling a little bit better.

"Where are you?" she asked.

I shivered, thinking about the man who might very well be her spy, as much as I hated to even think such a thing. "Where no one can find me and add to my bruises," I said.

"You can tell me," she coaxed.

No, I couldn't tell her, and I wasn't about to. She had been a great nurse during the worst of my discomfort following my beating, but I had every reason to be cautious. "I'm safe," I said elusively. "By the way, thanks for all your help. I don't know what I would have done without you."

"Dallas, you were hurt badly. Please, let me come make sure you're okay."

"Thanks, Alex, but someone tried to follow me again. I lost him, but for all I know he might try to follow you in an attempt to find me. I'm not taking that risk. You could get hurt." As much as it hurt to even think it, I couldn't avoid the possibility that Alex knew I was being followed and why. After all, Kade was her stepbrother.

"Not again!" she said. "Is it the white car, the one Hank said he'd take care of?" She honestly sounded like she was concerned and that she had no idea who was driving the white car. At some point, she and I were going to have a conversation about her stepbrother, but now was not the time.

Alex pressed me further, but when I skirted her desire to find out where I was staying, the other Alex returned. "You are a stubborn man, Dallas," she said hotly. "You make me so angry!" The call ended abruptly on that negative note. My heart heavy, I closed my phone, thinking about how volatile Alexandra could be. I wanted to trust her, to take her completely into my confidence. But there was no way that was going to happen anytime soon. There were just too many questions about her that troubled me.

I continued getting ready for bed, but I had barely finished brushing my teeth when I got another call. It was Sophie this time. "I shouldn't be bothering you," she said, "but I had to make sure you were okay."

"I'm fine," I assured her. "By morning, I'll be a new man."

"I've been working on the list. Kanon has been helping. I'm afraid it's not a very big list," she revealed.

"I'm sure the police will be grateful for whatever names you can give them," I said while thinking that I would be grateful as well.

"I hope I can help," she said.

"You can," I reassured her.

For a moment, it was silent. I wasn't entirely sure why she had called, although I couldn't help but be touched by her concern. When she spoke again, her voice was quite soft. "Dallas, who are you, really?" she asked.

Caught totally off guard, I stammered for a moment then said, "I'm Dallas Rowen. I'm a mechanic. I'm Kanon's friend. And . . . I hope I'm your friend."

"I know all that," she said, slightly louder now. "And yes, I am your friend. I like you, Dallas. I like you a lot. But I feel like I don't know the real you. I'm sorry, but there is more to you than I have seen."

"I would think so, considering what a short time we have known each other," I responded. "And I'm sure there is a lot about you that I don't know. I hope that I can get to know you better."

There was a light chuckle on the phone and then more silence. Finally, Sophie said, all mirth gone from her voice, "Somebody doesn't like you. I'm afraid for you. Please, tell me what you are doing, why you really got hurt at Jerry's grandmother's house."

Boy, did I ever want to tell her. This girl inspired confidence in me. She seemed to be genuinely interested in my well-being. Surely I could trust her, I thought. But I didn't dare. I wasn't at all sure about Kanon. He had profited by Jerry's death. I couldn't keep that thought away. I shouldn't. Sophie, though I could see no advantage to her from the death of Jerry, was Kanon's sister. And like I had just told her, I didn't know her that well. As with Alexandra, prudence called for caution.

"I think people don't like me," I finally said. "I seem to attract bad people. Did I tell you about getting robbed a few weeks ago?"

"No. What happened, Dallas?"

I told her, and she did not again express her doubts about my intentions. We ended our conversation on a good note. She didn't get angry the way Alex had. In fact, the last thing she'd said was, "I will pray for you tonight, Dallas." I found that I had a smile on my face when we disconnected.

I did something after Sophie's call, and partly because of her call, that I hadn't done for a very long time. I got on my knees. I folded my arms. I closed my eyes. I addressed a Heavenly Father I had long neglected. It felt awkward at first, but I soon found that it gave me a great deal of comfort. It wasn't so much the words that I spoke to God but the feelings that accompanied my expressions.

I must have been on my knees for ten minutes when I finally finished. I felt like a different man. My questions about who had killed Jerry were not miraculously answered. My doubts about two beautiful women were not erased, but I climbed into bed feeling confident that God cared about me. The most important thing in my life right now was restoring a relationship with my Heavenly Father, something that had been missing for too many years. I was determined to become a faithful member of the Church. Regardless of what happened with the investigation, my life would go in a much different direction now, and that brought peace to my soul. I was grateful to the Lord for leading me to Mrs. Ellen Grady. Her example had changed my life.

I climbed between the clean sheets of my hotel bed and was trying, with very little success, to find a comfortable position for my battered body when my cell phone again interrupted me. I grabbed it from the nightstand where I had placed it after my call from Sophie. "Hello," I said.

"Sorry to disturb you, Dallas. Did you find a place to stay tonight?" Hank asked.

"I'm in a hotel," I said, wondering what had happened that would cause Hank to do the very thing he said he was sorry about.

He wasted no time in coming to the point. "I found Kade Squire again," he said.

"I thought you were going to stay home." I swung my feet over the edge of the bed, thoroughly alert now. "Where did you find him?"

"Parked a short distance from our client's house," he said. Probably in the exact spot where I had last seen him, I was thinking.

"What did he have to say for himself?" I asked.

"Nothing," Hank responded. "I didn't get a chance to speak to him. I pulled in behind him after I spotted him, and got out of my car. I tapped on his window but backed off quickly when I saw that he was holding a gun. He pointed it back at me as I hustled behind my car. I thought he was going to shoot at me for a second or two, but he didn't. Instead, he started the car and peeled out. I followed him a ways but lost him. He was driving like a maniac."

I was shivering. This stepbrother of Alexandra's was not a nice man. "What do we do now?" I asked.

"Wait," he said. "I hadn't intended to confront him, but as I thought about him after your call, it made me mad. I suspected he might be watching Ellen's house, hoping you would come back. I was right, and I don't like it."

I didn't like it either. "This guy is probably behind his stepbrother's death," I said. "And he's feeling the heat."

"We can't be sure, but I'm thinking the same thing," Hank said. "I just got off the phone with Detective Wakefield. His boss, Sheriff Rutger, will be here tomorrow afternoon. We are going to try to find Kade. Hopefully, we can put an end to this thing."

"I'll go with you," I said.

"If you're up to it, that would be great," Hank said.

"What time should we meet and where?" I was thinking about my church date with Sophie and Mrs. Grady. I really didn't want to miss that.

"Sheriff Rutger will be here around three or so. He said he was going to church first. How about if I call you when he gets here? In the meantime, you can continue to mend," Hank said. "In the morning, I'll do a little poking around on my own, just to see if I can get an idea where Kade might be."

I had an idea, but I didn't mention it. I would save it for the next afternoon. "I'll check on our client in the morning," I said. "And I'll get her to church like you told her I would."

"Yes, you do that," Hank agreed. "Now get some rest. I have a feeling we are getting close."

I certainly hoped so. I also hoped that my cell phone would be quiet for the rest of the night. My body desperately needed a break from activity. I stepped over to the window and parted the drapes. My truck was sitting quietly, seemingly unconcerned about Kade Squire or anyone else. I stared at it for a minute, and then I turned back to the waiting bed.

chapter THIRTEEN

I T WAS AMAZING HOW MUCH healing a good night's rest could achieve. I rolled out of bed at about eight, feeling both refreshed and in much less pain. I didn't even feel the need for a pain pill. I showered, shaved, and watched the local news.

Alex called about nine thirty. "Are you feeling better this morning?" she asked pleasantly. There was no hint of the anger she had ended our conversation with the night before.

"As a matter of fact, I feel much better. I heal fast, Alex," I said.

"Good. I've been worrying about you." She sounded like she meant it, but I couldn't be sure.

"I'll be fine," I assured her.

"Do you remember that you were going to take Grandma to church today?" she asked.

"Yes, of course I do."

"I wish I could come too," she said. "But I'm at work. I don't get off until six this evening."

I was glad about that. Having her join us would be most uncomfortable, considering the fact that her grandmother and I would be accompanied by an attractive brunette. "I actually look forward to going to church," I told her honestly. "It's been a long time."

"Yeah, I know," she said. "Take good care of my grandmother. I've got to run now. I'll talk to you after I get off work."

Knowing what I had planned for that afternoon and evening, I wondered if she would really want to talk to me. I hoped we would have her stepbrother in custody. I wasn't at all sure how she'd like that. Of course, I said nothing about any of that. I simply wished her a nice day, and that was that.

Before getting in my truck, I inspected it carefully. I even peeked under-neath. I was sure Kade couldn't have found me here, but the aching reminder of my previous injuries caused me to be very cautious. I even felt just a shiver of nervousness when I put the key in the ignition and turned it. The only thing that happened was the familiar sound of my engine starting. There was no flash of light, no loud boom, nothing to cause my disintegration.

I stopped at the street and looked up and down it, alert for a white car. Upon seeing none, I began a roundabout route to Ellen's hotel. I was quite confident that I had not been followed. But just to be on the safe side, I drove on past and circled around, looking for Kade—or anyone else who might be after me. Finally, I pulled behind the hotel, parked, and got out. I greeted Ellen a couple of minutes later at the door to her room.

"I knew you wouldn't forget," she said. "But you are a bit early."

The fact that she said what she did made me wonder if she had ex-pected me to not appear as promised. "Of course I wouldn't forget," I said brightly. "And I'm glad you're ready early. We have to pick up someone else."

She smiled and invited me in. "Who's going to church with us?" she asked.

"A friend, the sister of one of Jerry's closest friends," I said, not mentioning that she was a very attractive friend. I explained that Sophie knew nothing about my involvement in the investigation of her grandson's death but that she had been very helpful, without knowing it, in getting me acquainted with some of Jerry's associates.

I helped Ellen with her coat, waited while she picked up her purse, and escorted her to the truck. I checked the street again before pulling onto it. Then I headed for the Storm home. Again, I drove a roundabout route, keeping a close eye for anyone who might be following.

I parked in front of Sophie's house and told Ellen I would be just a moment When Sophie and I came out a couple of minutes later, Ellen had moved to the backseat. I introduced her to Sophie. She smiled and said in an uncharacteristically icy voice, "It's nice to meet you, Miss Storm."

"Thank you, Sister Grady," Sophie said. "It's nice to meet you as well. Dallas has told me what a wonderful landlady you are."

Ellen blushed, and her stiffness toward Sophie seemed to vanish. "He's a very good renter," she said. "I'm very fond of Dallas."

I helped Sophie into the truck. She looked stunning in her dark red dress and white jacket. It was the first time I'd seen her dressed up like this, and I had to admit I really liked how she looked. As we drove toward the chapel where Ellen's ward met, we told her about the derby the night before. Ellen was seated in such a way that I was able to meet her eyes in the rearview mirror. When I said, "This Jake Frankland guy is a real jerk," she gave me an understanding nod. I got another when I added, "He seems to have disliked your grandson a lot. I'm sorry about that."

I was careful to avoid passing in front of the Grady house on the way to the church, although, because I knew that Sophie already wondered about me, I didn't make the same kind of evasive efforts I would have liked. I did keep a close eye out for the white Chevy. I did not make my observations obvious, I hoped. Nor did I mention anything about Kade Squire, although I did want to get Mrs. Grady's perspective on him after church, before I went with Hank and the officers to try to find him.

I parked behind the chapel in an effort to keep my truck from standing out too much. As we approached the entrance, I noticed that Ellen had warmed up to Sophie a lot. In fact, she chatted with her quite amiably. I held the door then followed them inside. Ellen was greeted warmly by several ward members, and she introduced us as her "renter and his sweet friend."

The bishop said, "So, you are a member of our ward," when he learned that I lived in Ellen's basement.

"It looks like it," I said. "And I'm glad to be here."

Ellen gave me a look of mild surprise, but she said nothing. The bishop asked, "Where did you move here from?"

"I've mostly been overseas," I told him vaguely. "I recently got out of the army."

He asked Sophie where she lived and what ward she was in. She explained about the singles ward. My landlady was looking more impressed all the time. Lots of heads turned as we entered the chapel. Sophie sat close to me, and I didn't make any effort to move away.

Childhood memories flooded over me as the meeting progressed. I found myself regretting my many years of inactivity, and I resolved that it would not happen again. I had truly come home.

After the meetings were over, I met Ellen and Sophie outside the Relief Society room. I was anxious to get to the truck and deliver my passengers to their homes. I wondered if Hank had tried to call, but I didn't dare turn my phone on and try to call him until I was alone, or at least after Sophie was home. When we reached the truck, my nervousness returned. I felt the urge to check the truck thoroughly before allowing Ellen and Sophie to get in.

I wanted to just ignore my nerves, but I couldn't risk the lives of my two lovely companions. So, much to Sophie's astonishment, I asked the ladies to walk back toward the church and wait while I checked my truck out. I walked all the way around it. I even knelt on the asphalt and peered beneath the undercarriage. My heart nearly stopped when I spotted a small, black metal object that didn't belong there, that had not been there the last time I'd looked. It was almost directly beneath the driver's seat. I took a deep breath and then stood up, my mind whirling.

Sophie and Mrs. Grady started toward me, but I signaled them to stay back. Ellen looked grave. Sophie was shaking her head in a puzzled sort of way. I waited while the nearest cars pulled away, leaving my truck by itself. Then I pulled out my cell phone and turned it on. I dialed Hank's cell number. He answered promptly. "Is everything okay, Dallas?" he asked.

"I'm afraid not," I said. "There's a black box fastened to the undercarriage of my truck. It wasn't there when I left my hotel. Unless I'm mistaken, it's probably a bomb." Sophie and Ellen stood silently as I spoke with Hank, their faces filled with worry, both watching me intently, probably wondering what I was saying and whom I was saying it to.

I looked out over the parking area. A familiar-looking white car approached on the street and then passed out of sight as it drove in front of the church. "Dallas, are you there?" Hank asked urgently when I was silent for a moment.

"Yeah, and I think Kade is too," I said. "I'm sure his car just passed on the street in front of the church."

"Give me your location. Are you at the church?" he asked.

"I'm parked out behind it," I said. "I can't believe he found me here. He must know this is where Ellen goes to church."

"Is Ellen with you right now?"

"She's standing over near the entrance to the church. She's with Sophie Storm, Kanon's sister. She came with us. I'll explain later why I brought her, but right now I need to figure out what to do. They don't know about the bomb yet, but they know something is going on. They saw me looking under the truck."

"Give me the address of the church," Hank said. "I'll need to have some cops go there."

"That's a must at this point," I agreed. "If this is a bomb, you and I can't handle it ourselves."

"Be alert. Walk over to the church. Take the ladies inside if you feel like you need to," he said. "Wait for me and the police to arrive. Are there other cars parked close to yours?"

"No. Most of the people from this ward are gone now."

"Okay, good. I'll call you right back."

I waited, watching a couple of nervous women. In less than two minutes, Hank called back. "The cops are on the way. There will be a bomb squad there before long as well. Do you see anything more of Kade's car?"

"No."

"Keep an eye out. Milt Wakefield is headed your way; so am I and the local cops. Can you trust Sophie?" he asked.

His question swirled about in my mind for a moment, and suddenly I felt a strong conviction that she was absolutely honest and trustworthy. "Yes, totally," I said with a feeling of relief.

"Good. Let her and Mrs. Grady know what's going on. Stay with them. Take them inside if you think you should. Don't let anyone else near your truck. Call me if you need to." Then he terminated the phone call.

The sudden decision to trust Sophie removed some of the stress from my mind. I eagerly walked toward her and my landlady. "There is a little problem," I said, trying to sound lighthearted. "But help is on the way."

"Dallas," Mrs. Grady said, her brow furrowed. "What is under your truck? Is there a bomb?"

"A bomb!" Sophie cried, grabbing my arm. "Why would there be a bomb under your truck?"

I spoke first to Ellen. "It is time to bring Sophie into our confidence," I said. "She is a good friend, someone I trust completely."

"Then you do that," Ellen said firmly. "You know that I trust you and that I know the Lord led me to you. I trust whoever you trust."

Sophie was looking up at me through puzzled eyes at that point, and she was clinging tightly to my arm. "Sophie, you asked me on the phone last night who I really am."

"Yes, I did. And I'm asking you again now," she said, her face serious.

"I work for a private investigator," I told her. "I am an investigator myself, and we are looking into the death of Jerry Grady. Mrs. Grady hired us to find the person who did it. We are working closely with the police, and they are on their way here now."

Sophie shook her head, followed by a shy smile. "I knew you were something other than a mechanic. I'm not saying you're not a good mechanic, but I just had this feeling," she said. She turned to Ellen. "If anyone can help you, Dallas can. You hired the right man."

"I know that," Ellen said. "And the fact that he has been threatened and even beaten is proof to me that he's getting very close to the truth. Somebody is afraid he's about to find out what they did."

I felt Sophie's grip tighten on my arm, and when my eyes met hers, there was something more than concern there—fear, perhaps. "It wasn't just a burglar in Mrs. Grady's house, was it?" she asked.

I shook my head. "Whoever it was must have known I was coming. He was waiting for me and caught me totally off guard. But I got lucky," I admitted. "I came out a lot better than I might have."

"Which wasn't very good," she said. "But I'm glad you're feeling better today. Okay, so what's with the bomb?"

I explained what I had seen and then added, "There will be a bomb squad here in a little while."

A pair of Provo City uniformed officers were the first to arrive. One of them looked beneath the truck, the same as I had, and got up, shaking his head. "I'm not touching that thing," he said. "There's a wire leading from it up into the engine block. It's lethal."

Hank was there just a few minutes later. Detective Wakefield was right behind him. Hank signaled for me to step aside with him for a private conversation. We walked a few feet away, and then he said, "I didn't see anything of our friend in the Cavalier as I was approaching the area. Sheriff Rutger will be here in a little while. We've got to find this guy. He sure seems to know where you are most of the time."

"I don't think he followed me here," I said, wondering if I had been too careless. "I was thinking that he might have known Ellen went to church here."

"Maybe, and maybe not. If he didn't know that, and if he didn't follow you, did someone tip him off?"

I felt like a rock had just hit me deep in the stomach. "Alexandra Grady," I said weakly.

"We are thinking alike. Do you know where Miss Grady is right now?" he asked.

"If she's where she claims to be, she's at the hospital where she works," I answered, wondering if she had lied to me about that on the phone earlier in the day.

"I'll get on the phone and find out if she is or isn't. In the meantime, we need to get that bomb taken care of without anyone getting hurt or doing any damage to the church—or your truck." He gave me a wan smile and signaled that it was time to rejoin our client.

The bomb squad did their thing flawlessly. By shortly after three, my truck was declared safe. The bomb, and it was in fact just that, was destroyed without doing any damage. Sheriff Rutger called Detective Wakefield, and they arranged to meet. I offered to take Ellen and Sophie both to their current places of residence before I joined them.

"Are you up to working the rest of the day?" Hank asked.

"I'm a lot better today," I told him, and I was being honest. Oh yes, there was a dull ache over much of my body, but it was nothing that would slow me down much now. I was ready and anxious to find and confront Mr. Kade Squire.

Hank whispered in my ear just before we separated. "See what you can learn from Ellen about Mr. Squire."

I did just that as we were riding back to Sophie's house. "I don't really know much about him," Ellen said in answer to my inquiry. "Most of my contact with my son's widow has been through Jerry and Alexandra. They never got along with their stepfather, and neither one has ever had much to say about Kade. He's older than both of them, and they were never around him very much as far as I know."

"Did they get along with him?" I asked.

"Jerry didn't like him. He was quite vocal about that. Alex has never said much. You'll have to ask her."

"That's what I'll do," I said. But it wasn't something I was looking forward to.

I walked Sophie to the door. "I'll call you later," I promised on her doorstep.

"Please do," she pleaded. "And please be careful." She punched me playfully on the shoulder. Then she gasped and said, "I'm sorry. That probably hurt."

"Not a bit," I said. Then, as I looked deeply into those dark brown eyes of hers, I added, "You be careful too. Ellen Grady has been threatened, and if Kade thinks you're helping me, he might cause you some problems as well."

I saw a flash of fear in her dark eyes. "I will, Dallas. I promise. Can I call you if I think I'm in danger?"

"I'll feel bad if you don't," I told her. She kissed me on the cheek, and a moment later I was back at my truck.

"She seems like a very sweet girl," Ellen said with a small smile. "I hope she doesn't get hurt, or her brother. It sounds to me like that other driver, Jake, is being very nasty. Do you think he might be the one we're looking for, or is it my step-grandson?"

"It could be either one. We are working on that," I said.

We talked more as I took a cautious route to her hotel. I watched closely to make sure I wasn't being followed. But as a precaution, I said, "Ellen, I'm going to walk you up to your room. I need you to promise me that you will not open the door to anyone but me or Hank. Use room service for your meals—you can open the door for them. I'm sorry you won't be able to join Hank and Shirley for dinner later. Call me if anyone suspicious tries to contact you."

Ellen did not argue with me at all. The seriousness of the killer's response to the investigation had really frightened her. As I left her at her room, she said she had one favor to ask of me. "Please, make sure that my precious granddaughter is safe. I'm afraid for Alexandra." Her eyes filled with moisture as she delivered her plea.

"I will do that," I said, wishing I didn't have to worry about Alex's possible involvement with Kade in his campaign of terror. I also took one more precaution to help keep my client safe. I talked to the head of hotel security. They promised to check on her room frequently, and I thanked them and left.

Ten minutes later, I was with Hank Pierce, Sheriff Rutger, and Detective Wakefield. We discussed where we were most likely to find Kade Squire. I had three ideas. "I think we should try finding out where Jake Frankland lives. He could be staying with him. I would also look around Ellen Grady's neighborhood. He might still think I'm returning there at some point, at least if he learns that I didn't get blown up."

I stopped. I didn't want to mention the third. The sheriff pressed me. "You said you had three ideas," he prodded.

"Yes, I did," I agreed reluctantly. "We might check and see if he's with his stepsister."

"With Alexandra," Hank said thoughtfully. "She is still at work at the hospital. I confirmed that earlier. She gets off at six."

"Then maybe we could check her apartment," I said, almost hating myself for saying it. She had been a kind and helpful nurse while I was hurting the worst two nights ago. But my suspicions lingered. I couldn't let my feelings interfere with the investigation.

"Okay, let's try those places first," Sheriff Rutger said with decisiveness. "We will need to split up. If any of us spot him, then we can just keep him under surveillance until we can all get to that location."

No one disagreed. The sheriff decided that he and Milt would try to find Jake while Hank and I checked out Ellen Grady's neighborhood and

Alexandra's apartment. Hank and I went together in his car, leaving my truck at the local police department. We didn't want to find more bombs attached to it, and they promised to keep a close eye on it in exchange for us keeping them apprised of our activities.

chapter FOURTEEN

HANK AND I HAD NO success the rest of the afternoon. The sheriff and his deputy told us at about six, when we all got together at Hank's home for dinner, that they had had an interesting visit with Jake Frankland. "He's not a very pleasant person," Detective Wakefield reported. "He did agree to talk to us. He claims that Kade Squire is no friend of his. He admitted that Kade helped him some but that he didn't particularly like the guy. He didn't hide his contempt for our murder victim, but he said that his dislike was not the kind of thing to be solved by killing him."

The sheriff spoke up. "His girlfriend came in while we were there. She had little to say. She didn't seem like a very nice person. She claims she wasn't in Duchesne the night of the derby. She told us she doesn't very often miss Jake's races, but she had to be out of state with her job that weekend."

"We'll check that out, of course," Milt added. "She's a regional sales manager for a women's clothing line."

Hank's wife interrupted to tell us that dinner was ready. The sheriff took up the narrative again after Shirley had us seated at her dining room table. "Jake said he had expected to beat Jerry that day in Duchesne. He even says he was angry when Jerry was killed because he'd never be able to prove now that he was the better driver. Kind of makes sense," he said with a shrug. "The last thing he told us when we left was that he wouldn't be surprised if Kade Squire had something to do with it, even though he admitted he hadn't seen him there that night."

"Did he indicate what Kade's motive might be?" I asked.

"Not a word," Milt said. "But he genuinely seems to dislike the guy. And yet he tolerates him. This still seems strange to me. If he dislikes him, why does he accept his help?"

"Free labor, maybe," Hank suggested. I nodded. That sounded reasonable to me.

Hank seemed particularly thoughtful. He finally said, "We've got to find Kade tonight. I'll work all night if I have to. I have to agree with Jake. Kade is the most likely suspect. I'd sure like to find out what the connection is between him and Kelsey Glazer, particularly to see if there was bad blood between the two of them."

The sheriff nodded in agreement. "I just remembered something else Jake said. There was a car he was going to buy, one he thought would make a great derby car. It disappeared back in July, shortly before he went to make the purchase. He told me the owner claimed it was stolen. He didn't know if that was true or not, but he's been watching to see if any of the other drivers come up with it. He's quite sure he'll recognize it if he sees it again."

"What make?" I asked.

"It was a big old Cadillac," Milt said. "Dark blue with a silver interior."

I thought about the collection of keys attached to good luck charms and of Kanon's statement about a Cadillac. The sheriff now had that collection of keys.

"I'd like to know if one of those keys in our victim's little red toolbox happens to fit the missing Cadillac," Sheriff Rutger said. "I'm quite sure one of them was a Cadillac key."

I stated the obvious. "To determine if it fits, we'll first have to find the car. I think I know how we can do that. Kanon Storm says he is going to use a Cadillac in the next race."

"Now that's something that could be very important," Hank said.

"I couldn't agree more, but it is not, I'm afraid, our highest priority right now," the sheriff said. "Finding Kade Squire is."

Somehow, I couldn't shake the idea that finding that Cadillac was very important. But I agreed that finding Kade was more so. After all, it looked like he was trying to kill me, and he had to be stopped. When that was accomplished, then we could pressure Kanon to show us the Cadillac. I was curious to find out what that car might be able to tell us.

It was about fifteen minutes before seven when the four of us, in two separate cars, pulled up in front of Alexandra's apartment. Her little lime green VW Beetle was parked in her slot. On the street in front of the complex there was a white Chevrolet Cavalier. "That's it," Hank said with a pump of his fist when he read the license number. "Dallas, you hit it on the nose. Good work."

If he thought I was happy that I had hit it on the nose, he couldn't have been more wrong. I wished the car would just vanish. I wished that Alex was what she had seemed when she had nursed me so tenderly. I didn't want her to be one of the bad guys. She should be one of the good ones. If she was bad, the hurt it would inflict on Ellen Grady, a woman I had truly come to admire, even love like a grandmother, would be devastating. I wanted to shout in protest.

Instead, I silently approached Alex's second-floor door and knocked. The other three men were close by but spread out in case Kade tried to make a run for it—we didn't want him getting away. Alex's eyes popped wide with surprise when she opened the door and found me standing there. "I need to talk to Kade," I said.

"Kade?" she asked, looking bewildered.

"Yes, Kade. I know he's here, Alex."

"Of course he's here. But why do you want to talk to him?" she asked as she brushed at a lock of bright red hair. "He came to ask for my help on a family matter."

I turned my head slightly and scratched my ear with my left hand, a prearranged signal. Hank moved into sight and hurried up the stairs to Alex's apartment. Sheriff Rutger and Detective Wakefield stayed out of sight, watching the back door, one that led onto a balcony with no stairs but one that a desperate person might jump from to escape from the apartment—if he so desired and if he was athletic enough.

Kade Squire was both. He jumped, landed quite gracefully, the sheriff later told me, and bounded away. The sheriff shouted, and Hank and I ran back down the stairway. But by the time we got around to the back, Detective Wakefield had caught and hauled Kade to the ground. He pulled a gun from inside Kade's jacket and handed it to the sheriff.

Alex came running after us. "What is going on?" she demanded as handcuffs were snapped onto Kade's wrists. We ignored her.

A siren sounded up the street, and a police car arrived a minute later. Kade was shouting obscenities. Alex was red-faced and demanding that someone, anyone, tell her why Kade was being treated as he was. She was also demanding that he explain to her why he'd jumped from the balcony when I appeared at the door. I wasn't sure whom she was most angry at, us or Kade.

None of us took the time to answer her questions right then. I simply said, "We'll explain shortly."

She didn't like that answer at all, turning away from us with a scowl. It was a relief that she had finally quit demanding answers from us. Kade, after he was dragged to his feet and forced to walk toward the patrol car, said, "Call me a lawyer, Alex. This is false arrest."

"I don't even know what you're being arrested for," she told him as an officer began to open a back door while the other prepared to push Kade in.

"Just call a lawyer," he shouted.

"What lawyer?"

"Any lawyer. These guys have got nothing on me."

"How about carrying a concealed weapon without a permit," Sheriff Rutger said as he displayed the handgun he'd pulled from Kade's waistband. "And there will be more to come."

Alex stood on the sidewalk, silent for now, and watched as the officers drove off with Kade after promising to make him available to the sheriff and his deputy if they would come to the station as soon as Kade's car was removed to the police impound yard by a tow truck. Sheriff Rutger told them he would see to it all, and then he turned to Hank and said, "This is the man who has been stalking your assistant?"

"It is," Hank said grimly.

"He can get his lawyer, but it won't do him a lot of good," the sheriff added. "At some point he's got a lot of questions to answer. We'll wait here with Kade's car while you and Dallas enlighten Miss Grady about why we are doing what we are doing."

Hank nodded. Alex looked at me. She suddenly looked very vulnerable. She was close to tears and shaking visibly. I took hold of her arm, expecting her to shake it free, but she didn't. "Let's go inside and talk," I said.

She nodded, and the three of us headed back to the stairs. Once we were in her small living room, Alex meekly invited us to sit. Hank said, "We'll answer your questions now, Miss Grady. Let me begin by saying that your stepbrother is a suspect in the murder of your brother."

Her hand flew to her mouth. "That can't be. He would never do that," she said unconvincingly.

"Maybe not, but things are definitely pointing in that direction," Hank said.

She shook her head, and her eyes met mine. "I know he and Jerry never got along well. I told you that before. But he came here asking for help from me."

"What kind of help?" I asked.

For a moment, she looked down, then, wringing her hands, she once again looked me in the eye. "He says that things have been strained lately between his father and him. He was hoping I could get my mother to help him in some way. He says he feels bad about it and doesn't want to be at odds with him."

"I see," I said, although I didn't. "Can you actually do anything to help?"

She slowly shook her head. "I don't think so."

"Did he say what caused the strain?"

"No, but I already knew," she said. "I had talked to my mother before Jerry was killed. She told me that Kade had called his dad and asked for money. He said he'd had a run of bad luck and if they could help him out that he would be able to repay it in a few months. But my stepfather told him no. Mom says that they've sent him money before, and he's never repaid a dime of it. His dad told him he was going to have to get himself out of the financial trouble he was in."

"So does that mean that he wants *you* to convince them to give him what he needs?" Hank asked.

She shook her head. "I'm not sure, but that could be it. We hadn't gotten that far when you guys came." She looked down again, and then she added, "That's when he took off. Why would he do that?"

"My guess is that he has a guilty conscience," I said.

She flinched. "I'm sure he didn't kill Jerry."

"How can you be so sure?" I pressed.

"I don't know. I guess I just feel it," she admitted.

"The same way you felt like I had just been released from prison?" I said coldly.

"You know I didn't mean that," she said hotly. "It was just the first thing that came to my mind when I found out you didn't work for Hank. I never thought you'd been in prison. But I'm not wrong about Kade. He's not the greatest guy in the world, but he's not a criminal."

"Do you know much about what he's done the past while?" I asked.

"He's been looking for work. Just like you were," she said with a bite to her voice. "You know how hard that is right now."

"Yes, I do," I agreed. "Can you explain why he has been following me?"

That question seemed to jolt her. "Are you saying I asked him to?" She was heating up again. "I admitted that I had someone watch you that one night, but it wasn't him. I just asked a friend from work to see what you were doing so I could be sure you weren't taking advantage of my grandma. Kade wasn't even in town then. He was still in St. George."

"Are you sure of that, Miss Grady?" Hank asked.

She hesitated. That was all the answer I needed. But she provided more. "He says he just came up here two or three days ago and has been looking for work ever since."

"It's true that I hadn't seen his car before that, but, Alex, he has been following me day and night since then. It was Kade sitting up the street when you and I went to leave your grandmother's house yesterday afternoon. He didn't provide Hank with any good reasons as to why he was doing that. He just denied it."

"Maybe he wanted to talk to me and just didn't dare come right out and do it," she suggested, but from the way she dropped her eyes, I was pretty sure she didn't believe that. After all, he'd come to her house this evening and knocked on her door.

"Why does he hang around with Jake Frankland?" I asked.

That question appeared to catch her by surprise. I waited. So did Hank. Finally, she said, "Does he?"

"You know I wouldn't have asked if he didn't," I said gently. "I met him in Ogden last night at the demolition derby. He was with Jake and his girlfriend, Lucia Root."

She slowly looked up at me again, and once more she was wringing her hands. "What was he doing there?" she asked.

"Keeping track of me, I'd say."

She didn't say anything, and Hank jumped in again. "Jake says that he and Kade aren't friends but that Kade occasionally helps with his cars—for free, it seems."

She shook her head and looked down at her hands. She stilled them. Then she again looked at me. Her eyes were watery. "How many times have you seen him watching you?" she asked.

"A whole bunch." I looked over at Hank and mouthed, "The bomb?" He nodded. I turned back to Alex. "He drove by the church today right after we came out. I checked my truck over before I would let the ladies get in. I discovered—"

She interrupted. "Ladies? Who was with you besides Grandma?"

"Sophie Kanon," I said.

She raised one hand and pointed it toward me. "Sophie, huh? That would be the first time she's ever been in church."

"How do you know that?" I asked. "I didn't think you really knew her."

That stopped her. She hung her head for a moment, and then she said, "She's Kanon's sister," as if that were all the explanation that was needed.

"And Jerry is your brother," I countered softly.

I think she got the point. "Sorry," she said.

"She is actually very active in the Church," I said by way of clarification. Then I went on. "There was a bomb attached to the frame under my truck."

Alex gasped and turned white. I could tell she'd made the connection I had intended her to make. She confirmed that a moment later as she said, "You think Kade put it there?"

"I'm almost positive. He's been following me. I'm making him nervous about something. You saw that for yourself when I came to your door," I said.

"And you think it's because he killed my brother," she said, her voice choking.

"I can't help but wonder," I said. "It was a real bomb. If I had tried to start the truck, it would have killed me as well as Sophie and your grandmother and who knows how many other innocent people from her ward."

Alex rose from the chair she'd been sitting in, her face pasty white. She began to pace. Hank and I sat and waited. She kept rubbing her eyes. When she finally stopped, she faced me. "You think I have something to do with Jerry's death, don't you?"

I didn't answer her question. I couldn't imagine her as a killer, and yet her association with Kade needed further explanation. I fervently prayed that she was truly one of the good guys. She glared at me for a moment and then resumed her pacing. She finally returned to her chair. "Should I get lawyers for us?" she asked, as much to herself as to Hank and me.

"That's up to you," I said. "But if you don't mind, maybe we could see if there's not another explanation for Kade's actions."

"So you don't necessarily think I'm involved?" she asked, her pretty eyes pleading.

I answered as honestly as I could by saying, "You certainly don't strike me as the kind of girl who would have anything to do with such a thing."

"I'm not," she said after again lowering her eyes. "I just have a hot temper, as you have learned. I've got to learn to control it. I know that."

I smiled in her direction as she again lifted her head. "Yeah, I have learned about your temper," I agreed. "But I've also learned that you are a compassionate and caring person. Now, let's talk about Kade." She nodded in agreement, so I went on. "Does he have a key to your grandma's house?"

She shuddered at that question. "No. Are you wondering if he had something to do with you being attacked the other night?"

"The thought has occurred to me, although I'm more inclined to think it was Kelsey—shortly before he was killed."

She nodded, and then she said, "Grandma has never had anything to do with Kade. Why would he be interested in her now?"

"When was the last time you saw him before today?" I asked, dodging her question.

"He was up here a few months ago. He came by the apartment one day," she said.

"What did he want?" I asked.

"I don't know. I can't remember. I guess he just wanted to visit, although I admit that I was quite surprised at the time. We'd never had much of a relationship."

"How many keys do you have to your grandma's house?" I asked.

"Just one," she said. "I keep it on the same key ring as my car keys and my apartment key."

"Did he ever have access to them?"

Alex gasped, and again the color drained from her face. "I let him borrow my car. I'd gone to work at the hospital at six. He showed up there and told me his car had broken down. He said he'd hitchhiked there."

"How long did he have it?" I asked.

"I don't remember for sure. Two or three hours, I guess. I know he had it back to me before midnight." She stared at me, glanced quickly at Hank, then back at me. "Do you think he might have had keys made?"

That's exactly what I thought. I was just glad she had come to that conclusion on her own. I did have another question for her, however. "Did he come to borrow your car before or after he asked your stepfather for money?"

"Oh, that was a quite a few weeks before I talked to Mom about him," she said. It was at least a couple of months before Jerry was killed. It might have been in June."

"What kind of car does he drive?" I asked.

That question startled her. "I . . . uh, I don't know. But it must be a white one."

"Yes, it's white," I confirmed.

Just then there was a knock on the door. It was Milt Wakefield. "Could I have a word with one of you before the sheriff and I leave?" he asked.

Hank and I looked at each other, and then Hank got to his feet. "Sure. I'll be right back, Dallas."

After they had closed the door, I said, "Didn't you ever see his car when he was at your apartment in the summer, or for that matter, today?"

She shook her head slowly. "The parking's kind of limited here at these apartments," she said. "Anyway, I never even thought about it."

"Did he say anything to you today about his money troubles?" I asked.

"Other than saying that he was out of work, I don't think he did," she answered.

"Did he say anything about Jerry today?"

"He hadn't been here very long when you guys came," she said. "But, no, he didn't."

"I'm assuming he wasn't at the funeral."

"No, he wasn't there. Of course, my mom and his dad were. It was after the funeral that his dad took Jerry's car. He drove it back to Arizona." The way she said it, I got the feeling that she didn't think that was right. I didn't pursue the matter. She spoke again. "Dallas, do you think Kade killed Jerry?"

"Honestly, I don't know, Alex," I said. "His behavior hasn't been that of an innocent man. Either he is involved or there is something else going on that we are missing. He surely came close to killing today. He had fully intended to."

She shuddered just as someone tapped on the door. Alex let Hank back in. "They are getting a search warrant for Kade's car. The sheriff would like us to join them in a few minutes to witness the search."

"What are they looking for?" Alex asked.

"Specifically, a rifle," Hank said. "But who knows what else might turn up."

chapter FIFTEEN

WE LEFT ALEX A FEW minutes later. As we drove to the police impound yard, Hank said, "Honestly, Dallas, I don't think that girl is involved in her brother's murder."

I was relieved to hear him say that. The girl had a way of getting up my ire, but I couldn't shake the tender, gentle manner in which she'd nursed my injuries. "I hope you're right," I said.

"We are also going to go to Jerry's place when we get through with the search of Kade's car. The landlord wants to get it rented out again. Do you think Alex would like to be there?" he asked.

"Probably, unless she has to sleep. She might be going back to work in the morning."

"Why don't you call her right now? Tell her it will be around eight thirty or nine."

I did that, and when I told her what I wanted, she said, "I do have to work in the morning, but I will go with you guys tonight anyway. What time and where should I meet you?"

"I'll pick you up about eight thirty," I said.

She was agreeable to that, and I ended the call. At the impound yard a few minutes later, a search of Kade's car produced no rifles. However, there were other items of extreme interest. In Kade's suitcase, which we found in the trunk of the Cavalier, there was a black pullover sweater and ski mask. We also found a paper that appeared to have been printed from a computer site. It contained specific instructions for making a car bomb. In addition, there were copies of one of Alex's checks and one of Ellen's. Both were blank and unsigned. There was also a piece of paper that contained information from a couple of credit cards. Both of them were Visa cards, and above the numbers of one, Alex's name was listed. Above the other, Ellen's name appeared. There was also a list of numbers there. It read: *Spin once to the right and stop at 1. Then spin twice to the left and stop at 16. Spin three times to the right and stop at 57.* It was the combination to a lock somewhere.

The list of incriminating items didn't end there. We found a ring of keys in Kade's jockey box. I compared one of them to the one Ellen Grady had given me. It was an exact match. Another was very similar. I said to Hank, "I wonder if this might be the missing key to Ellen's back door."

"She's missing one?" he asked in surprise.

"She is, and I can't help but wonder if this is it. He's been in her house, that's for sure. How else could he have gotten her check and credit card information?" I asked.

Hank shrugged. "He's been in Alexandra's house before today, too. He obviously didn't steal that information from her just before we showed up there."

I couldn't argue with that. "I've thought all along that it was Kelsey who accosted me, but now I suspect that Kade's footprints are all over my side and back," I said.

"If you're right, I wonder what he was doing," Hank began thoughtfully. "He could have been lying in wait for you. Or I suppose he could have been after something else and you just surprised him," Hank suggested. "He probably saw you go into your apartment, assumed you were going to stay there, and went back to Ellen's to do whatever he was going to do."

"Like steal the sweet old lady's identification," I said, feeling my anger building. "Kade might not be the one shot Jerry, but he's certainly capable of acts like that. I think I'll call Mrs. Grady, if that's okay with you."

"Do it," Hank agreed, and I dialed the number to her hotel. I watched the Provo detectives who were still searching the car. They were being thorough. I couldn't imagine what else they might find by pulling the doors apart, pulling up the seats, and so forth, but you never knew.

Ellen answered the phone in her hotel room after three or four rings. "Ellen, it's Dallas," I said. "How are you doing?"

"I'm still very upset and scared," she responded with a trembling voice. "Why would someone want to blow you up?"

And blow you up, I thought. "We are working on it," I assured her. "I have a question for you. When did you last remember seeing your back door key?"

She was silent for a moment, then she said, "It has been several months, I think. I kept it hanging on a ring in a kitchen cupboard. I went to get it one day a few weeks ago. It was gone. I used it in the spring, I'm sure. I must have left it somewhere. Why are you asking?"

"Just curious," I said. "Remember, don't let anyone in but one of us."

"Oh, believe me, Dallas, I won't. I'm a tough old woman, but I'm not ashamed to admit I am very frightened right now."

"I have hotel security keeping an eye on your room, so you'll be safe as long as you don't open the door. I'll call you or even swing by in the morning," I said. "By then I think Hank and I will have something to report."

"Thank you, Dallas. By the way, have you seen Alexandra? I am so afraid she's done something she shouldn't have."

"I've seen her, and she's okay," I said. "You keep saying she's a good girl," I said, thinking of Kade and what he had both done and probably been planning to do to her. My faith in Alex was restored. "You are right, and don't you forget that."

"Oh, Dallas, are you sure?" she asked. "It would be more than I could take if I were to learn that she had done something bad."

"She's a good girl," I said. "And I am sure of it."

"That is such a relief. How is your friend, Sophie?" she asked.

"I haven't talked to her since I took her home this afternoon."

"I hope she's okay. She's also a good girl, Dallas. You keep her safe."

Under the direction of Detective Pete Richards, the law enforcement officers were still finishing up the search of Kade's car when I told Hank that I'd head for Alex's place. "Okay," he said in a strained voice.

"Hank, what's the matter?" I asked.

"I'm not feeling very good all of a sudden," he said. "I better go home. You guys can finish without me tonight."

"I'll take you home," I said. "I don't think you better drive. You are pretty pale all of a sudden."

Sheriff Rutger noticed us, and he said urgently, "Dallas is right, Hank. You need to be in bed. I'll take you home while Dallas gets Miss Grady."

"No, I'll . . ." Hank began, then he clutched at his chest, his eyes suddenly wide with panic and pain. The next thing we knew, we were lowering him to the floor. "It's my ticker," he said weakly. "I don't think I'm . . . going . . . to make it." His voice trailed off.

I was almost in a panic, but Sheriff Rutger was already on his cell phone calling 911. The Provo officers were administering CPR. I was silently praying. As soon as the sheriff had completed the call, he said, "An ambulance is on the way." Then he turned to me and said softly, "I think this is a serious heart attack, Dallas. I hope they can save him. Did he ever say anything to you about having a heart condition?"

"All I knew was that he hadn't been feeling well lately. That's one of the reasons he hired me," I said.

An ambulance took him to the hospital. I called his wife, who said, "I knew this was going to happen. I hope you can carry on without him for a while, Dallas. I'll go meet him at the hospital."

I was numb with shock and didn't tell her how desperately ill Hank appeared to be. Hank, according to the paramedics, had in fact just suffered a major heart attack. Hank had been more ill than he had let on. I continued to pray that he would be okay. As soon as we finished with Jerry's place, I would head for the hospital. My worried thoughts were interrupted by a phone call. It was Sophie. She sounded as stressed as I felt. "What's the matter, Sophie?" I asked.

"Jake Frankland just called me. He was really mad," she said.

"About what?" I asked as my stomach began to churn even worse than it already was.

"He says that Kade Squire called him from the jail and asked him to bail him out," she revealed. "I asked him why he was calling me. He said he'd wanted to call Alex because Kade was her stepbrother, but he couldn't find a phone number for her. He said he called me because I was Kanon's sister and he assumed I knew Kade since Jerry and Kanon were friends. He said he knew I could get a message to Alex."

"What message?" I asked.

"He said that I better call you or Alex or somebody and tell them to let Kade know not to bother him again. He told me that if Kade did, Jake'd break the guy's neck. I think he meant it."

"I wouldn't be too sad if he did," I told her. "He's up to no good."

"If he's in jail, it must mean you found him," she said.

"Yes, and he tried to run, but Detective Wakefield from Duchesne caught him. He's a bad guy if I ever met one," I said, unable to mask my anger.

"There's more," Sophie said. "Jake knows you are working with the cops. He said that I should tell you and your cop friends to leave him alone. He said he had nothing to do with Jerry getting killed.

"I told him none of it was my business. I was just trying to get him to hang up. But that apparently really made him mad, and he said he'd break my neck if I didn't tell you guys to leave him alone."

"He threatened you?" I asked incredulously.

"Yes, and now I'm scared. Kanon's so mad he says he'll go make Jake wish he'd never been born."

"You tell Kanon to stay out of it. Does he know I'm an investigator?" I asked.

"I didn't tell him, but he overheard the call, so he might have figured it out," she said.

"Is he there?" I asked.

"He's in the living room. I'm in my bedroom."

"Take the phone to Kanon. Let me talk to him. Then I want to talk to you again."

"Hi, Dallas," Kanon said a moment later. "I guess you're more than you let on."

"I am, Kanon," I said, trying to be firm. "This is a dangerous situation we are in. But you've got to let me handle it, me and the cops. Tomorrow morning I'll let Jim know that I can't work there anymore. But I will need to have you help me with something important. If he can't let you off work, then I'll have to wait until your shift is over, but I need your help."

"Jake's got something to do with Jerry being killed, doesn't he?" he said angrily. "I hate that guy."

"I don't know who killed Jerry yet, but I'm working on it with the police. If it was Jake, he sure did something stupid when he threatened Sophie, but most killers aren't known to be the smartest guys in the world. They just think they are. You just say nothing to anybody about this, okay?"

"If you say so," the young man muttered.

"I say so," I said. "Have you said anything to Razorback about this?" I asked.

"No, should I?"

"Absolutely not! Don't say a thing to anyone about any of this. Please, do I have your word?"

"You've been good to me," Kanon said. "I know I can trust you. So, yes, you have my word."

"Good, I'll see you tomorrow, then. And Kanon, there is one more thing."

"What's that?"

"Don't you let anyone touch your sister."

"You can count on me for that," he said.

"Good, now let me talk to her again."

"I don't know what you said to Kanon, but it looks like you have his attention," Sophie said a moment later.

"I hope so," I told her. "Are you going to be okay, or would you like me to come pick you up? We can find a safe place for you tonight. I'll pay for it."

"What are you doing right now?" she asked, her voice trembling. "I'm really afraid of Jake."

"I'm going to pick Alex up as soon as we finish here at the impound yard. She's going with us to search Jerry's apartment. I'm closer to your place, so I'll come get you first if you'd like me to," I said, hoping I wasn't going to cause a lot of problems having both girls together.

"Are you sure it's okay with her?" she asked.

"It doesn't matter if it is or not," I said. "I'll be there in a few minutes."

"Thanks, Dallas. I'll be waiting," she said.

I had no sooner concluded the call than Milt Wakefield shouted, "Hey, Dallas, look what Detective Richards just found."

Pete was holding several bundles of green cash. "These are hundred-dollar bills," the Provo detective said. "There is five thousand dollars here. They were inside the door panel on the back passenger door."

"Maybe he's a drug runner too," Sheriff Rutger said.

I had my own suspicions, but I said nothing to them about that. I did say, "My truck is over at the police department. I'll need a ride so I can go get Alex and Sophie."

When the sheriff volunteered to take me, I took the opportunity to fill him in on the threat Sophie had received from Jake.

"That makes things even more interesting and dangerous, Dallas," he said. "We've got to make sure the two young ladies stay safe," he added. I was determined to do just that.

One of the Provo officers said they'd secure Hank's car in the yard and that I could get it in the morning. When the sheriff dropped me off at my truck, I told him that I'd see him at Jerry's apartment after awhile. A few minutes later, Sophie was seated next to me, and Alex was by the passenger door of the front seat of my truck. "Alex," I said as soon as we'd pulled away from her apartment, "we found some interesting stuff in Kade's car." Without mentioning the other things we'd found, I told her about the two blank checks and the credit card information.

"Kade stole our identities," Alex said through gritted teeth.

"It looks that way," I agreed. "We also found a small ring of keys. When we finish at Jerry's, the officers and I are going to go to your grandmother's house and see if the keys we found in Kade's car fit her doors. I suspect they do, but we have to know for sure."

"What else did you find—not that that isn't too much already?" Alex said, sounding very dejected.

"He had some clothes in a suitcase, all normal stuff but a couple of the things. There was a black hoodie and ski mask and a paper on how to make car bombs."

Sophie gasped and grabbed my arm tightly. "It was Kade that hurt you, wasn't it?" She concluded. "You did say that whoever was in there was wearing a black hood thing, didn't you?"

"That's right. So was whoever broke into my apartment the first time I got bumped around. But I think that might have been Kelsey, not Kade. It was a black car that first time, not a white one. I'll have to sort it out later. There is something else puzzling. There was the combination to a lock of some kind written on the same paper as the Visa information."

It was Alex that gasped this time. "Do you remember the combination?"

"I wrote it down," I said. "It's in my notebook there on the dash."

"Do you mind if I look?" she asked.

"Not at all. It's on the last page I've written on," I said.

She turned on the dome light, opened the notebook, and studied it. "I'm almost positive this is the combination to Grandma's safe," she said.

"She has a safe?"

"It's in the basement. It's built into the wall down there. She keeps a lot of cash in it," she said. "I always tried to tell her to use her bank savings accounts. She has a lot of money in several different banks, but she said she just felt more secure knowing that she had a little money in the house. She kept hundred dollar bills in it."

"Oh boy," I exclaimed, thinking about the stash of cash that had been recovered from Kade's car. "How much did she have in there?" I asked.

"Not as much as she did before she hired you," Alex said with just a trace of snip to her voice. Sophie gripped my arm again. I looked over at her, and she gave me a quick grin. Alex wasn't through. "There should have been several thousand."

"That just might wipe out the drug trafficking theory," I said.

"What are you talking about?" Alex asked.

"Kade had five thousand dollars in hundred dollar bills hidden in one of the door panels of his car," I said.

Alex threw my notebook back on the dash and angrily pounded her fists. "He robbed my grandma," she said. "What a creep. And I thought I could trust him."

"Maybe he did, and maybe he is trafficking drugs. We'll find out later tonight."

We rode in silence for a while. "Is Hank going to meet us at Jerry's house?" Alex asked a few minutes later.

"I'm afraid not. He had a serious heart attack just before I picked you guys up. He's in the hospital," I told them.

"Oh, Dallas, no!" Alex said.

"How serious?" Sophie asked.

"I'll find out after I go to the hospital later tonight. They took him to the Utah Valley hospital, or whatever it's called," I told them.

"It's called the Utah Valley Regional Medical Center. Now what will you do?" Alex asked, sounding very concerned. She still didn't appear to have much confidence in me.

"I guess I'll just have to carry on," I said.

"Can I go see him when you do?" she asked.

"You both can," I said. "If they'll let us see him, anyway."

We again rode in silence. The sobering news about Hank had all three of us thinking, I guess. Life could be full of unexpected twists. Silently, I prayed that Hank would be okay, both because he had become a very good friend and also because I needed his help. We were making progress, but we still didn't know who had killed Jerry Grady.

chapter SIXTEEN

THE PREVIOUS SEARCH OF JERRY'S apartment had been quite thorough, but the officers that had conducted it then didn't know exactly what to look for. They had mostly looked for clues as to why someone would have murdered Jerry, the sheriff explained. They really hadn't expected to find anything else. But there was one specific item I was interested in searching for. Most of Jerry's things were still there. The apartment had been paid up several weeks in advance, and Alex said they still had until the end of the month to get everything out of it. "The landlord has been harassing me about getting his stuff packed up, but I just haven't been able to face it. We don't have to for a few more days anyway."

"We can help," Sophie volunteered.

"Would you?" Alex said, her face lighting up. "It hurts me too much to even look at his stuff."

"Yes," she said as she looked at me, a question in her eyes.

I couldn't turn her down. "I'll help when I get a few minutes," I said.

We finally found what I was looking for. It was in a shoe box under Jerry's bed. The box had various receipts and other papers in it, but beneath the papers was an envelope. It had the name of a local bank on the front and inside was a key. We had found the key to Jerry's safety deposit box. I had more to do the next day than I could manage.

Our next stop was Ellen Grady's house. The sheriff, Detective Wakefield, and the two Provo detectives met us there. As I suspected, two of the three keys fit her doors. The other one, when Alex compared it to her own, was a duplicate that would open her apartment. She shuddered as she reached that conclusion.

We trekked into the basement where we discovered that the combination found in Kade's papers opened the safe. It was empty. We confirmed via a phone call to Ellen that she had left money in the safe. She thought she'd had five thousand dollars there. Kade had stolen it all. It was all too much for Alex, and she broke down in tears. I was afraid I was guilty of having sorely misjudged the girl. I had not misjudged Sophie—she showed me what a kind, sweet woman she was. She put her arms around Alex and simply held her until the tears dried up.

I spent a few minutes conferring with the four officers while we planned the next morning's work. After agreeing to meet again at eight at the police department, I told my passengers that I was going to the hospital to see Hank. "I'll take you guys if you want, but you don't have to go."

"I'm going," Alex said.

"So am I," Sophie concurred. "Then I've got to figure out someplace safe to spend the night."

"We'll find a room at the hotel where I'm staying, if there is one available," I suggested.

"That won't be necessary," Alex said. "She can stay with me."

"Oh, I hate to put you out," Sophie said.

"I'd be glad for the company," Alex said. "Please, say you will."

Sophie looked at me. I didn't say a thing. This was her decision. She looked back at Alex. "Thank you, I'd like that," she said. It looked like these two could become good friends. I had certainly not expected that. Alex slid into the truck next to me this time, and Sophie sat by the door.

We talked of the case as we rode toward the hospital. None of us could be sure about who had killed Jerry. However, none of us, especially Alex, felt like Kade should be removed from the list. "I think he's greedy, and that's why he's stealing from us, but at this point I wouldn't put anything past him," she said.

"Alex, remember that first night when you and I met at Arby's and you filled me in on what you knew about Jerry's friends?" I asked.

"That seems like a long time ago," she said. "This has been a long week."

"It sure has," I agreed. "Anyway, I couldn't figure out how anyone knew we had been there."

Alex looked over at me and nodded. "Kade was following me then," she said soberly.

"That's what I think," I said. "None of us saw his car, but we weren't expecting anything like that at the time. So we might not have noticed."

"I need to call my mother. She has some money and some stocks and bonds worth quite a bit," she said thoughtfully. "I wonder if Kade is busy cleaning her and his dad out too."

"That's very likely," I agreed. "Is it too late tonight?"

"Probably, but I think I should do it anyway. Who knows, if Kade is already bothering people about getting him out of jail, he might have called them," she said as she pulled her cell phone from her purse. "His dad might have already made arrangements to get him out." She shivered, and Sophie moaned. It was not a pleasant thought.

I listened as Alex talked to her mother a minute later. Alex said, "Has Kade called you guys tonight?" She listened, and then she asked, "What did he say he wanted?" It was hard to see her face in the dim light of the inside of my truck, but I could see her well enough to know what her mother had said. "Dad didn't do it yet, did he?" she asked with panic in her voice.

Her free hand pinched my arm as she listened to her mother's voice. "Stop him!" she cried a moment later. "Kade robbed Grandma Grady and tried to kill her and some friends of mine. He stole from me, and he's been doing some other awful things, Mom. He might kill me if he gets out." There was real panic in her voice. Her mother must have been able to hear that panic on her end of the phone call, because Alex finally said, "Thanks, Mom. Make sure he doesn't get Kade out. And Mom, you might want to make sure he hasn't stolen your identity and his dad's. He's into that."

She talked a moment longer and then closed her phone. "Kade's dad was on the phone with a bondsman here in Provo. I called just in time," she said. "Mom stopped him." She gave a big sigh. "That was close."

Sophie was apparently having the same thought I was at that point. She quietly said, "Maybe he'll find someone who will get him out."

That made Alex shiver, and she again grabbed my arm. "We can't stay at my place," she said. "I don't dare now, and I won't put you in that danger either, Sophie."

"We'll get you rooms at my hotel," I said. I handed my phone to Alex. "The number is in there. Call them and make a reservation for a couple of rooms right now."

"One room would be okay with me," Alex said as she opened my phone. "I'd like to have company. Do you mind, Sophie?"

Sophie didn't mind at all. A room was reserved. I put the phone back in my pocket. "We'll stop by your place and get your car and some things when we finish at the hospital," I told Alex.

We arrived at the hospital, and I parked at the nearest spot I could find, which wasn't very close. We got out of the truck and headed for the main entrance. I was surprised when Hank's wife, Shirley, met us as we came into the hospital. Her eyes were red, and she had been taking a walk outside in an attempt to relieve some of her tension. "How is Hank?" I asked, afraid of what the answer might be.

"He's in surgery right now. The doctor thinks they can save him, but . . ." Her eyes filled with tears, and I put an arm around her shoulders.

"He'll pull through," I said. "The three of us are praying for him."

Sophie and Alex agreed with that. "Thank you, kids," Shirley said.

"Do you need someone to sit with you?" Sophie asked. "I would be glad to."

"That's not necessary," Shirley said. "Our children, all three of them, are on their way. Our oldest daughter lives in Logan. She will be here shortly. I think I'll just hang around the front here and wait for her."

"Shirley, what can I do?" I asked.

She smiled wanly. "Just keep this investigation going," she said. "Hank has a great deal of confidence in you, and so do I."

I wished I had the same confidence, but I refrained from saying so. Instead, I said, "I'll do my best. I'll come back tomorrow and check on Hank. If you think of anything more I can do, would you let me know?"

She nodded. I hugged her and said, "Then we'll be going." Sophie and Alex each gave her a hug too, and we headed back to my truck, Sophie with her arm through my left one, Alex with hers through my right. I'd never had so much feminine attention.

Nor had I ever had so much attention paid to my truck. Someone with a long ponytail was kneeling beside my right back tire, his back to us, as we approached. Both women tensed. I shook free of their arms and whispered, "You guys wait here."

I moved forward as quickly and silently as I could. The damage Kade had done to my body was bothering me. I needed rest again soon. Had it not been for that and whoever it was kneeling beside my truck, apparently expecting me to have a longer visit in the hospital, I might have gotten hurt again. But the guy didn't even look around until I was almost to him. When he became aware of my presence, he sprang to his feet as quickly and lithely as a cat, turning toward me, a knife in his hand. I didn't wait to see what he planned to do with the knife; my fist hit his face so hard that it half turned him and slammed him against the truck with a sickening thud. The knife clattered to the pavement, and he slowly slid to the ground, falling on his side. I hoped I hadn't killed him.

Alex and Sophie ran over as I quickly knelt to check the guy's vital signs. He was unconscious, but his heartbeat was strong and he was breathing fine.

The tire he had been kneeling beside was flat. "Did he slash your tire?" Alex asked angrily.

"I'm afraid so, and they are brand new," I said as I rolled the guy onto his back.

The guy looked familiar. I knew I'd seen him before. My companions both recognized him. Alex said, "It's one of the guys that raced against Jerry."

"It's Lyle Wertz," Sophie said, dropping beside me on her knees. "What's he doing here?"

His identification caught me by surprise. I remembered meeting him at the derby in Ogden and concluding that he was a pretty nice guy. He'd been talkative and acted friendly at the time. Of course, he had no idea at that time who I was and what I was up to. However, as I looked gloomily at my tire, I guessed he must have known or someone had told him later.

Alex was still standing over us, and she said, "Is he okay? You throw a pretty mean punch. Not that I blame you. That's a nasty-looking knife." She bent and picked it up as she spoke.

"He just needs a minute, and I think he'll come around," I said hopefully. The last thing I wanted was to seriously hurt someone. I'd done far too much of that in the wars I'd fought in.

The three of us waited for a minute. Alex knelt beside him, laid the knife beside her, and began to check his vital signs. After he still hadn't stirred, Sophie said, "Should I call the cops or the hospital or something?"

"No, let's give him a minute more first. I'd like to be able to talk to him before the cops advise him that he can keep his mouth shut," I said. Even as I spoke, he began to come around.

Lyle was a little guy, and despite my aching body, I easily lifted him up. "Let's put him in the backseat of my truck," I said. "Would one of you open the door?"

Alex moved quickly, picking up the knife and then opening the door with one hand while she held the knife with the other. I put Lyle in, shoved him over, and climbed in beside him. He slowly came to as I searched him for more weapons, but there were none. Finally, he shook his head, reached a hand up, and grabbed his chin where my knuckles had struck him. "What did you do that for?" he asked as his eyes focused on me under my interior light.

"You had a knife," I said. "What would you have done?"

"I wasn't going to try to use it on you," he said as he continued to nurse his chin.

"It didn't look that way to me, Lyle," I said. "Now, from here on out, I'll ask the questions and you'll provide answers, if you know what's good for you."

Just then, the far door opened, and Sophie leaned in. "Dallas, is the jack behind the seat? I'll put your spare tire on while you talk to Lyle."

"It is, but you don't have to do that, Sophie. I can do it in a few minutes."

"It's okay. I don't mind, and I'll even bet that I've changed more tires in my life than you have."

She was probably right. "Lean forward, Lyle, while Sophie gets the jack from behind the seat."

She worked quickly, and in a moment, she had the jack and tire wrench loose. "Lyle," she said, hesitating, "you need to tell Dallas whatever he needs to know. I'm really disappointed in you." Then she stepped back, turned, and shut the door with her hip.

"What can I do to help?" I heard Alex say to Sophie before I turned my attention to my captive.

"Okay, Mr. Wertz," I said, not attempting to disguise my anger at him. "Let's start at the beginning. How did you know where I was?"

He looked at me, stubbornness showing in his eyes.

"Next time I'll bust your chin so badly you'll be on a liquid diet for six months," I threatened. I'd never do it, but I apparently convinced him that I would.

"Jake told me to follow you, that you were causing him trouble and that you were going to cause me trouble too," he said.

"Do you mean Jake Frankland?" I asked.

"Yeah. He said you were going to mess both of us up so we couldn't win no more derbies. He said someone told him that. He didn't say who it was. But he said he believed the person."

I chuckled mirthlessly. "I didn't know you'd ever won any," I said, knowing nothing about his derby career.

I had apparently hit pretty close to the truth, for he said, "I will soon. I'm still learning a lot."

"Interesting," I said. "I can see why Jake wouldn't want me messing with his driving, but why would he care if I messed up yours? I thought he wanted to be top of the pack and that anyone who tried too hard to beat him would get thrashed—or worse."

"We ain't exactly friends," he admitted. "But Jake, he didn't never bother me none."

"That's because you weren't a threat to him," I guessed. "Anyway, how much did he pay you to follow me and disable my truck?"

He got that stubborn look in his eyes again, and I doubled my fist and pulled it back. My threat, even though I'd never carry it out, loosened his tongue. "Two hundred bucks," he said.

"That's not much money for risking your life," I said. "Do you know who I am or anything about me?"

"I know you're a friend of Jerry's sister and that you're helping Kanon with his cars."

"Of course you know that," I said with disgust. "Sophie and I talked to you last night. What I want to know is if you know who I *really* am."

Fear suddenly showed in those small hazel eyes of his, and he shook his head. "I guess I don't," he said, his voice trembling.

"I am your worst nightmare, and that sliced tire isn't going to make your dreams any sweeter," I said darkly.

He squirmed and tried to move toward the far door, but I had one hand on his left arm, and I gripped it tightly. I guess he could tell at that point that trying to get away from me would be a wasted, even dangerous effort on his part, so he sat still again. "Who are you?" he asked.

"I am someone who is going to find out who killed Jerry Grady and take care of that person when I find him. If you are the *him* I'm looking for, you could save yourself a lot of pain and suffering by just telling me now. I don't want to have to beat a confession out of you."

I was aware of the back left quarter of the truck slowly rising. Sophie was getting right after the tire changing business. The door opened behind me, and Alex asked, "Did he say why he cut your tire?"

I glanced back at her. Her face was worried, and she was teasing a strand of bright red hair. I smiled and winked. "He's about to," I said. "Give us a couple more minutes here, and then maybe I can tell you why."

She nodded as she looked at me, worry still clouding her eyes. I winked again, hoping she would see that I was all bark and no bite. I didn't want her thinking that I would hurt Lyle again. She smiled a weak smile and shut the door. "She wants to know who killed Jerry," I said. "I'm not going to disappoint her. So you are going to tell me why you killed Jerry."

"I didn't have nothing to do with that!" he protested, the color draining from his face.

"Listen, you little worm. You had something to do with it. Two hundred bucks isn't enough motivation for an innocent person to mess with someone who's killed as many people as I have," I said, hating the fact that I let myself go so low. I had killed in the wars I was in, but it was nothing that I felt good about. In fact, I got sick just thinking about it, but I was getting desperate. I didn't know how I was going to find out who the real killer was unless I forced someone like Lyle to buckle. I convinced myself that the means justified the end. And I wanted this case to end soon.

He looked at me with slowly widening eyes. "Who are you?" he stammered for the second time.

"I told you," I said fiercely, grabbing him by his shirtfront until my face was just inches from his. "Now tell me why you really followed me, and I want the truth. Then I want details. And in case you don't know, you are not the first one who's been following me. The last one, as of this afternoon, won't be following me again." I hoped.

"Who . . . was . . . that?" he asked as if he didn't really want to know.

"Another of Jake's so-called pals," I said. "Do you know a guy by the name of Kade Squire? He was in Ogden last night."

Lyle nodded, tears filling his eyes now. He tried to speak, but apparently fear was shutting off his vocal cords. "Unless you want to go where he went," I said, my voice low and threatening, "you will tell me everything you know about Jake and whoever else is involved with him."

"Okay," he finally managed to say, although I had a hard time understanding him. "But you gotta promise me you won't let Jake hurt me."

"Jake is the least of your worries, Lyle. Now start talking."

He did have more to say, and by the time he'd finished I had learned some more things of interest, very important things. "Now, Lyle, I expect that you have been telling me the truth. If I find out you haven't, I'll come looking for you."

"I've been honest with you," he said.

"I hope so, for your sake," I said.

"What about Jake?" he asked, his hands trembling visibly as the back of the truck began to descend.

"What about him?" I asked in return.

"How you going to keep him from hurting me?"

"I don't remember saying I'd do that. Don't know that I could if I'd promised," I said. "I guess you're on your own there."

"But Kelsey—he's dead," he said.

"Yes, he is, and I would guess that you will do what you have to do to avoid that same fate. There are other states you can live in, you know."

He gave me a blank look. Finally, he said, "You're serious."

"Murder is serious. Death is serious. And yes, I am serious, Lyle. Now, before I let you go, I'll need that two hundred Jake gave you."

"But I need—"

I cut him off. "Lyle, you ruined a brand-new tire. The two hundred will help pay for it."

"But, Jake, he gave it to me—"

I cut him off once more. "You are a slow learner. If you feel like you've been cheated, go take that up with Jake."

"But I can't do that."

I held out my hand. "The money, Lyle."

He pulled out his wallet and extracted the two bills and handed them over. "Thank you," I said. "Oh, there is one more thing. How long have you been following me?"

He hesitated. I gave him a threatening look. "Since you were at Jerry's place," he said.

"Thanks. Now you can go," I said, feeling like a dupe for allowing myself to be followed again. I had to be more careful. I wasn't sure how many times I would get lucky.

I opened the door behind me, scooted backward, and stepped out. He followed me, but after he was standing on the pavement, he didn't move. "Go. Before I change my mind," I said, waving my hand.

"I need my knife," he said.

I actually laughed at that. "You think I'd give you back the knife after what you did? No way; now go," I said fiercely. He finally went. I called after him. "Remember our deal. I don't want to see you again."

"Why did you let him go?" Alex asked, looking puzzled.

"He's no threat," I said as I noticed Sophie starting to pick up the ruined tire. "Hey, the least I can do is lift that into the truck."

I did that and then put the tailgate up. I leaned back against it and took a deep breath. I wasn't feeling well again. I watched Lyle get in an old rusty pickup and drive off. I pushed myself away from my truck, suddenly aware that my two nonsuspects were watching me with worried faces. "I'm fine," I said. "Just a little stiff still is all. Should we go? I think we could all use some rest."

chapter SEVENTEEN

After we'd left the hospital parking lot and pulled onto the street, Alex asked, "So did Lyle tell you why he slit your tire?"

I reached in my pocket and pulled out the pair of hundred dollar bills. "For these," I said. "But he decided that I could have them to pay for the tire he sliced. So I guess he did it for nothing."

Sophie, who was seated next to me this time, poked me playfully in the ribs, causing me to gasp involuntarily. "Oh, Dallas, I'm sorry. I forgot. Did I hurt you bad?"

"Just surprised me was all," I lied valiantly.

"Sorry," she said again. "Who paid Lyle to do that?"

"Jake Frankland."

"Jake!" she exclaimed. "I didn't know they were friends."

"I don't know that they are. After tonight, they definitely aren't. Poor guy's scared to death of Jake. I have a feeling that he's going to be moving."

"To get away from Jake?" Alex asked.

"That's what he says," I answered. "And after what he told me, I think it might be a good idea if he wants to stay healthy."

"Dallas," Alex began again. "Did Jake kill Jerry?"

"I'm not sure," I said honestly. "Well, let me put it this way, if he didn't, I'm pretty sure he knows who did. But I could be wrong."

"Why did you really let Lyle go?" Sophie asked. "You could have gotten him put in jail for what he did."

"That's true, but it wouldn't have gotten us any closer to the full truth. Thanks to him, I know where to look next. That's the best I could expect from a guy like Lyle," I said. "I'm really tired. Are you, girls?"

Both looked over at me. I looked back and smiled. I knew they wanted me to tell them more, but I was still digesting what Lyle had revealed. I wanted to figure some things out before I told them more. I sure wished

Hank was okay. I'd love to spend a few minutes discussing what Lyle had told me with Hank. Maybe he'd feel better in the morning and I could do it then.

I was much more cautious this time and took a roundabout route to Alex's apartment to try to shake anybody who might be tailing us. "Who could be following us now?" Sophie asked anxiously.

"It could be anybody, or preferably nobody, but I'm not taking any chances. I've had quite enough trouble for one day," I said as I pushed my luck at a light that was already yellow and which turned red as we entered the intersection. Looking in my rearview mirror, all other traffic—only three vehicles—stopped at the light. I made a quick right at the next intersection, then ducked down an alley and circled around and took another couple of seemingly foolish maneuvers. I was feeling quite rash, but neither of my passengers complained.

When we finally arrived at Alex's apartment, tail free, I hoped, the three of us went together to her door. I went in first, and when I was sure we were alone, the women followed. Alex quickly gathered some things, including a nursing uniform, and then we went back to the truck. "I should take my car. I'll need it to go to work in the morning," Alex said. "But I don't know if I can do all that fancy driving."

"Look, there's no need to take your car," I said. "Let's leave it here, and I'll bring you back to it in the morning."

"It will be early, and you need rest. I know that you are far from healed from the beating you got from Kade," she protested.

"This is not the time to worry about little inconveniences," I said. "I insist."

She didn't argue further. In fact, she was visibly relieved. I parked as near as I could below the window to my room. When we checked in, I made sure Alex and Sophie's room was close to mine like I'd requested. We got lucky, and they were given a room just two doors down. "We should be able to see your truck too," Sophie said. "I'll check on it every so often."

"It should be okay tonight," I said, even though I was not convinced that I was right. There was only so much a person could do. I had barely entered my room when I had a disturbing thought. I didn't hesitate to go back out into the hallway and down to their room again. I knocked on the door. Sophie answered almost immediately.

"Is something wrong already?" she asked, looking concerned as Alex joined her.

"No, but I think that we need to move Alex's car," I said. "I would feel better if it were here."

They needed no explanation as to why I might feel that way. "Then let's go get it," Alex said.

"No, you two go to bed. If I can just take your key, Alex, I'll call a cab. I can have it back here in a few minutes."

"You need your rest," Alex said, but I raised a finger.

"I promised your grandmother that I would try to keep you safe," I said. "So let me do this myself. Please, no arguments."

"Okay, but don't be long," she said.

"I'm coming too," Sophie said.

"That's not necessary," I argued.

"Let her go," Alex urged. "It's okay."

I was too tired to argue, so I called a cab, and we waited in the lobby. I helped Sophie into the cab and then had another thought. "Just a minute," I said to the cabbie. "I need something from my truck. I'll be right back." Sophie gave me an inquiring look, but I just smiled at her and hurried around the hotel.

I grabbed what I was after from the jockey box of my truck and then hurried back to join Sophie. We relaxed in the backseat while the cab driver did the work. I nodded off and was embarrassed when Sophie said, "We're there, Dallas."

I had fallen asleep, my head cushioned against her shoulder. "I'm sorry," I said.

"Don't be," she replied with a tired smile. "I don't mind at all."

I paid the cabbie as Sophie started toward Alex's car. "Not yet," I said. "There is something else we need to do first."

Sophie was getting to know me, I guess. She didn't ask what, just quietly followed me as I went up the stairs and walked to Alex's room. I took the tape from my pocket and applied a piece to the crack at the top of the door. "What's that for?" she asked.

"The next time Alex comes here, I want her to be able to tell if anyone has been in her apartment," I explained.

"You really are cut out for this line of work," she said as we started back toward Alex's car. "How did you know to do that?"

I grinned at her. "Detective novels."

She touched me lightly on the arm and chuckled. "Let's get back. I don't want you falling asleep at the wheel."

I groaned when we reached Alex's car. There was a note under the windshield wiper. I pulled it out, opened it, and stepped into the glow of a street light. "What does it say?" Sophie asked.

I read it out loud. Someone had written in very neat, and by now, familiar handwriting: *This is not a game. Back off, Alex, and tell your hired lackey, whatever his name is, to do the same. If you don't both do as I say, things will get ugly.* That was it.

Sophie fell against me, and I put a hand around her shoulder. "When will it end?" she asked.

"When we catch the guy," I said as I thought about what Lyle had told me in the backseat of my truck while trembling out of fear. I just wished that he'd have known more. "Stand over there," I said, pointing. "I want to check this car out before we leave. I don't want you getting hurt in case I mess up."

"Oh, Dallas, please be careful," she pleaded as she followed my instructions.

Everything seemed okay, and we returned to the hotel without incident. I walked Sophie to her room. Standing outside her door, I said, "Let's not mention the note to Alex until tomorrow. There's no need for her to worry about it tonight. For the sake of her patients she needs her sleep."

"I'll leave that to you," Sophie said. She kissed me lightly on the cheek and said, "You are a rock, Dallas. Thanks." Then she put her key in the door.

As tired as I was, I spent a few minutes with my notebook after entering my room. I recorded the events of the day. Then I wrote down, as closely as I could remember, the information I had obtained from Lyle Wertz. Finally, I put pen and notebook down and got ready for bed. After a fervent prayer, I crawled between the sheets, thinking with a smile that I'd probably fall asleep as quickly as I had on the cab ride with Sophie.

It was not to be. I lay there, my body aching and my mind working in a fragmented fashion. I thought of beatings, burglaries, slashed tires, stolen money, stalking drivers, bombs fastened to vehicle undercarriages, and . . . out of nowhere, I thought of high-powered rifles.

I sat up with a start. Jerry had been killed with a hunting rifle. Someone out there had the ability to kill from a distance. This past week, Kelsey had died by a handgun. I had nearly been killed by a bomb and could have died from a beating. But no one had been shot with a rifle. That might not mean anything, but again, it could be important. I needed to learn who was good with a rifle.

I began to sweat. Not all of the threats and danger had come from the killer I was pursuing. Kade Squire might have been nothing more than a dangerous diversion, one of his own making, I was quite sure. If he was not the killer, he had caused the cops and me to waste valuable time, time we should have spent looking for the killer—a killer who could shoot with amazing accuracy from a long distance. Whoever used that rifle to commit murder was getting more nervous by the day. I might be wrong, but I couldn't help but think that the killer was one of the people I'd crossed paths with this last week. Alex and Sophie were in the clear with me. The same was not true of several others, including Kanon and Razorback, as much as I hated to think that.

My mind churned on for several more minutes. I made a mental list of what needed to be accomplished the next day. Then I cleared my mind and tried to go to sleep. I must have succeeded, because the next thing I knew my alarm was going off. I had set it for five. I knew that Alex was due to leave for work at five thirty, and I wasn't about to let her go there alone.

I took a fast shower after checking my truck and Alex's car through the window. Then I shaved, dressed, and was standing outside Alex's door when she opened it and came out—followed by Sophie. "What, don't either of you guys think I can go to work by myself?" Alex asked. "I'm a big girl, you know." She smiled though. That was a good sign. When she was not happy, it showed, as I had learned on several occasions this past week.

"I guess I'm kind of thinking we make a good team. So if you don't mind, we'll make sure you get to work without any harassment," I said with a smile.

"Thanks, guys," she said seriously. "Are you going to be able to get this thing wrapped up today, Dallas?"

I had been wondering the same thing. "I wish I had Hank to help me, but maybe with the sheriff and Detective Wakefield, we can at least make some good progress."

"Do you want to ride with me or with Dallas?" Alex asked Sophie as we waited for the elevator.

"We will all go together," I said. "And we'll go in my truck. I'll pick you up at whatever time you say. I'm not taking any chances."

"And I'm not letting you work alone today, Dallas," Sophie said. "I'll call in to my job and take the day off and cut classes as well."

The elevator arrived. We got on, and as it descended, I said, "Sophie, you don't need to do that."

"I insist," she said.

"And I concur," Alex said. "By the way, I forgot my name tag. I need it. Can we stop by my apartment really quick, and I'll run in and grab it?"

Sophie and I exchanged glances. "Sure," I said, "but we'll go together."

We got out of the elevator and headed for the back door of the hotel. Suddenly, Alex stopped. "Is there something you two haven't told me?"

"Yes," I said, "but it can wait until we're in the truck."

I checked the truck before getting in. Everything seemed okay. As soon as we were underway, Alex, who was seated next to me, said, "Okay, give. What haven't you told me?"

I fished the note out of my pocket and handed it to her. "This was on the windshield of your car when we went to pick it up last night."

As she read it, her face went so pale her freckles stood out like moles. "Oh my! This is scary," she said as tears filled her eyes. "What are we going to do?"

Sophie put an arm around Alex. Her eyes were also shining with tears. I felt determination fill me from head to foot; I would catch whoever was doing this and do so as quickly as possible.

By the time we arrived at Alex's apartment, Alex's emotions had changed dramatically. She was as angry as I had seen her. She expressed her anger with every word she could think of without using profanity. She was pumping her fists as she raged. When I parked the truck and we got out, she bounded toward the stairway. "Alex, wait!" I shouted. "Don't go in there until I say."

She turned her anger on me. "I'm the one who lives here. I can go in my apartment anytime I want to. Don't you tell me what to do," she raged.

I ran after her, aware of Sophie right behind me. "Don't, Alex. Please. There could be a trap set for you."

She beat me to her door and was inserting the key when I got there. I grabbed her and pulled her back. She angrily thrashed at me with her fists. I just held her. Sophie stood close, her eyes wide. Gradually, Alex calmed down, and then suddenly, she spun around and threw herself against me, wrapped her arms around me, and sobbed uncontrollably. My eyes met Sophie's as I held Alex. Her eyes again filled with tears of sympathy.

Finally, Alex gained control and pulled back from me. "I'm sorry, Dallas. I just feel so helpless."

"It's okay, Alex. I don't blame you. You have been through a lot. But I promise I will do everything I can to get us through this," I said.

"Thank you," she said. "I'm sorry I ever doubted you." Her eyes turned to Sophie. "Help keep him safe, will you?"

Sophie nodded soberly. "I'll do what I can," she said, shaking her head in dismay. "But I don't know what I can do."

"Just stand by Dallas. You're good for him. I can see that." She looked at her door. "Can we go in now?"

"No, not yet!" Sophie said urgently. "The tape's been broken."

I looked up and saw that she was right. The tape had been torn in two. This door had been opened since she and I were there the night before. "What tape?" Alex asked.

Sophie reached up and pointed to it. Alex looked puzzled. "How did that get there?" She asked.

I explained, and she again grew white. "So the door has been opened since you guys were here last night?" she asked.

"That's what it means," I said.

Sophie groaned, and I looked at her face. It was nearly as white as Alex's. "Dallas," she said in a weak voice. "Whoever it was might have been watching us last night."

I felt an uncomfortable weight stir in the pit of my stomach. "Possibly," I acknowledged. "You ladies stand back while I check the door."

They moved several steps away. A neighbor came out of the room next door and asked Alex if she was okay. "I'm fine," she said. "But someone has been in my apartment. I wasn't home last night."

The woman, someone I judged to be in her late forties or early fifties, told us that she'd heard a noise during the night. But she had just assumed it was Alex. "It wasn't me," Alex said. "Stand back here with us while my friend opens the door."

The key was still in place. Alex had let go of it when I'd jerked her away from the door. I slowly turned it, keeping my face turned away. Then I tried the knob, hesitated, and shoved the door open. When nothing happened, like getting myself blown to tiny little pieces, I let out my breath, not even aware that I'd been holding it.

The girls moved toward me. I lifted one hand and said, "Let me give it a quick check first." I moved through the door, my eyes darting quickly around the small living room. I had expected to see it trashed the way mine had been, but that was not the case. Then my eyes settled on the sofa. Leaning against it was what looked like a picture frame of some type. It was about two feet square and partially covered with a bath towel.

I was certain it had not been there when Sophie and I had waited in this very room for Alex to pack her bags the night before. I turned back to the door. Alex was standing there with Sophie watching over her shoulder. The neighbor seemed to have left. "What is that?" Alex asked.

I signaled for them to join me. "That's one of my bath towels," she said. "I didn't put it there—or what it's covering. Will you pull it off, Dallas?"

I moved next to the sofa and reached down and grasped the towel. I lifted it, and both girls gasped. Alex stared for a moment then began to slump. Sophie moved quickly and caught her, lowering her gently to the floor. I stared in shock at what the towel had been covering. It was a picture of Alex from the shoulders up, enlarged from some snapshot someone had taken. A target had been drawn over her face in crude circles of red ink. The center of the target was right between her eyes. To the side of her face, written in the same red ink and in handwriting that was beginning to haunt me, were the words: *Enough meddling. Back off or you die.*

I dropped the towel back over the picture and turned my attention to the girls. Sophie was on her knees beside Alex. She was gently brushing at Alex's short red hair with one hand while holding one of her hands with the other. She looked up at me, her beautiful face stricken. "She's fainted," she said softly.

"Let me get a wet cloth," I said. When I returned from the bathroom with a washcloth, Alex was beginning to stir. "Take this," I said to Sophie. She reached up and took the cloth from my hand and applied it to Alex's forehead.

Alex's eyes opened, and one hand fluttered. "Just lie still for a minute," Sophie said tenderly. As I watched them, I couldn't imagine what luck had brought two such incredible women into my life. I had developed a deep respect for both, and I found myself feeling fiercely protective of them.

I dragged my eyes from them and pulled out my cell phone. I dialed Sheriff Rutger's number. When he answered, I told him where I was and what I'd found. For a moment he was silent, and then he said, "I'm in Heber, heading for Duchesne. We've had a kidnapping there, a custodial thing. I'm on my way to deal with that. But I'll call Detective Wakefield. I'll have him contact Detective Richards and see if the two of them can meet you there. Don't go anywhere, any of you."

"Alex is supposed to be at the hospital in twenty minutes," I said as I glanced at my watch.

"Call in for her. And keep her in sight, Dallas. She's in danger. Where is the other girl, Sophie?"

"She's here with us," I said.

"Good. Keep an eye on them. When Milt gets there, he can tell you what else to do. But you have got to keep them safe, both of them," he said urgently. "I hope I can get back soon. But until I do, Milt is very good, and so is Detective Richards. You and Sophie, with their help, have got to get this thing solved if you can."

I walked over and shut the door and locked it. Then I crossed back over to where Sophie was now helping Alex sit up. "What is the number to your work?" I asked her.

"Why?" she asked suspiciously.

"I've just been on the phone with Sheriff Rutger. He told me to take care of you, both of you, actually. I can't do that if either of you goes to work," I explained. "He suggested we call in and get you excused from work. I'll do it for you if you'd like me to."

"Would you?" she asked, and she gave me the number.

chapter EIGHTEEN

DETECTIVE RICHARDS FROM THE PROVO Police Department showed up and took the lead on the investigation. He took the picture and note I'd found on Alex's car, a look of deep concern on his face. I was more than concerned, and so was Milt Wakefield. We were both ready for action—but where to begin? I conferred with him for a few minutes while Detective Richards and his men were processing the scene and Sophie and Alex sat huddled on the sofa. I again shared my concerns over someone using a high-powered rifle and who among our suspects, if any, were expert shots with such a weapon.

We talked about the safety deposit box. "We can't access that until nine o'clock," he told me. "And you need to check on your boss."

"We also need to check out what Lyle told me," I said. Then I gave him a quick version of the events at the hospital and what Lyle had divulged.

"I'll get on that with the help of these fellows," Milt said, pointing in the general direction of the Provo detectives. "You work on the matter of the bank and then try to find the Cadillac. After that we'll get together again and decide what to do next. This thing here and the problem in my county have upended the plans we made last night."

"I've got to quit my job at Jim's Garage. I'll do that at nine, and then I'll visit the bank. After that, I'll get Kanon from work and we'll go see this Cadillac, wherever it is," I said.

"What if he balks about showing it to you?" Milt asked.

I just shook my head. "Leave that to me. He'll cooperate," I said darkly.

"Okay, and what about Alex and Sophie?" he asked.

"I'll try to get them to stay at the hotel. I'll talk to security there and have them provide protection, even if it costs us."

"And if they won't stay?"

"Then they'll just have to go with me," I said in a tone he chose not to argue with.

"Let's go see your grandmother," I said to Alex as she and Sophie and I left the apartment a few minutes later.

"She'll be terribly worried," Alex said faintly.

"She's a strong woman and has great faith. We could use her prayers today."

"Yes, we could. But what if someone tries to follow us again?" she asked.

"Just hang on, you two. Me and this old truck are getting good at this stuff."

That brought a weak grin from both of them. After we were on our way, Sophie asked, "So what do we do after we visit Mrs. Grady?"

"I guess I should take you two back to the hotel. Then I want to go see how Hank is doing, and I'll go from there," I said, glancing over at her.

Both girls gave me a hard stare. "I take it you don't want to stay there. I can have security provide protection for you like they've been doing for Mrs. Grady. Or is there someplace else you would like to go?"

"With you," they said in perfect unison.

"That's what I thought, but you've got to promise me one thing, both of you," I said soberly.

I mostly ran a red light and then said, "Will you do whatever I ask if things get sticky?"

"I trust you, Dallas," Alex said. "I'll do whatever you ask, within reason. And if I get mad, just give me minute to get over it. You know how I am."

I sure did. "And you, Sophie?"

"You have my word," she said.

Being on good terms with Alex seemed to mitigate the bad news we'd been given that morning.

Ellen hugged Alex for a full minute or more. I also got a hug, as did Sophie, who appeared to feel a bit awkward. Not that I blamed her.

"I'm sorry about keeping you holed up here like this," I said. "I know it isn't easy."

"I'm just lonely," she said with a sad shake of her head. "I've got books, the TV, even my knitting, but I should be cleaning and cooking. They do all that for me here."

Alex got a strained look on her face and began to wring her hands. "Alex, what are you doing today?" her grandmother asked.

"Well, they don't want me to go to work, so I was planning on going with Dallas and Sophie but . . ."

She trailed off and looked at me. "Dallas, would you mind terribly if I stay here with Grandma? I think she needs me more than you guys do."

Ellen's face brightened noticeably. "That would be fine," I said. Ellen simply glowed after that. But I looked Alex right in the eye and said, "Promise me you will stay right here. It is dangerous for you—"

She cut me off. "I know, and I promise. Remember, it was my face behind that target," she said with a shudder.

Ellen gasped. "What happened?"

We explained the morning's events to the sweet elderly woman, and I then asked a favor of her, which she readily granted. Alex looked at me with worried eyes but nodded her approval. She understood the danger and why I had made the request. I also promised to have security keep an even closer eye on them.

So it turned out that it was just Sophie and I who stopped at the hospital a few minutes later. We were told at the main desk that Hank was in a private room with his wife, but considering who I was, they said that a short visit would be all right. We found the elevators and rode up to Hank's floor. A minute later, we tapped on his door, which was hanging partly open. Shirley looked up from her chair at the side of Hank's bed, quickly rose to her feet, and met us at the door.

"How is he?" I asked in a whisper.

"He is going to make it," she said, wiping at her eyes. "I've prayed all night. Oh, Dallas, I've been so frightened. I love that man."

I hoped that someday someone would love me like she loved Hank. I counted him a lucky man. "Is he sleeping?"

"Not really. I think you should come in and say hi," she suggested.

Sophie followed me, and we approached Hank's bed. There were tubes everywhere, and his face was puffy. He opened his eyes and tried to focus for a moment. Then he recognized me. "Dallas," he said weakly.

"Good to see you, Hank."

"You too," he said. "Sorry."

"You just get well. I'll take care of things the best I can."

"Call Shirley if you need to," he said slowly. "She knows a lot."

"I'll do that," I said.

He closed his eyes. I could tell he didn't have enough energy to say more. I stood and watched him for a moment. It was only when I turned to leave that I realized Sophie was holding my hand. I wasn't sure when she'd taken hold of it, but I was glad she had. We moved together to the doorway. Shirley followed us. "Call me if you have questions," she said. "And, Dallas, Hank did say earlier that you needed a pistol. There's one in the office, in the safe. There are bullets there too. Go get it before you do anything else."

"Thanks," I said, my eyes meeting Sophie's. We were both thinking of my earlier request of Ellen Grady.

My next stop was at the office, and I got the pistol. I didn't intend to carry it anywhere but in the truck unless I felt that my life or someone else's was in danger. I put it in the jockey box of the truck as soon as we got back in it. I looked at my watch. It was after eight o'clock now, but seeing we still had extra time, I said, "Let's go to Mrs. Grady's house now. We have a lot to do this morning."

"Yeah, let's," she agreed.

I had placed tape on her doors after we and the cops had left the night before. The tape was intact. "I didn't see you do this last night," Sophie said.

"You and Alex were talking," I said. "I did the back door right after we found out the money was missing. She was upset and . . ."

Sophie knew. She'd been the one comforting her. I had slipped out and done it and come back in before they'd even missed me. "I did the front door as we left," I said as I removed the tape and we went in.

A fine sheen of dust covered the tables and chairs. That would disturb Ellen. She kept the place spotless. I could almost see her bustling about the house, getting rid of the slightest traces of dust. I only had one purpose in this visit. I headed into the basement. I got Ellen's husband's rifle from the gun cabinet there, took a box of bullets, and said to Sophie, "I wouldn't have asked Ellen to borrow this if I'd known Hank had a pistol for me. But I still want it just in case."

"I agree," she said.

"I suppose you know how to shoot guns," I said.

"I do, but I'm not real good. I could get by if I had to."

I left tape on the door again. Then we drove to Jim's Garage.

Jim Ralsen was there when we arrived. I came right to the point. "I haven't been entirely honest with you," I began. "I'm going to have to quit. I have another job as a private investigator."

Jim rubbed his belly for a moment, and then his face split into a grin. "Well, I'll be snookered," he said. "'Course, I didn't think you'd stay anyway. You struck me as a man with a lot of ambition. Who's the young lady?" he asked. Before I could answer, he said, "Wait, you're Kanon's sister, aren't you?"

"Yes," she said.

Jim turned to me. "Let me guess. You are investigating Jerry's murder."

"That's right."

"Was Kelsey involved?" he asked. "He really seemed to dislike Jerry far more than seemed reasonable."

"What do you mean by that?" I asked as Alice Berryman walked in.

"Good morning, Alice," Jim called out. "I was talking to *Detective* Dallas Rowen and Sophie Storm about Jerry's murder. Our detective is done being a mechanic."

The heavy woman's eyes popped. Then she said, "I thought there was more to you than met the eye, Dallas. Have you got it solved yet? Jim and I think Kelsey had something to do with it."

"We were just talking about that, but as I was about to say to Jim, I don't know yet."

"If it wasn't Kelsey, I hope you catch the scum, whoever he is," Jim said. "In answer to your question, Dallas, Kelsey was just plain mean to Jerry. Granted, Jerry could be a real jerk, but so could Kelsey. I can see Kelsey sitting on a hill with a rifle, pumping a round into Jerry. I'm glad he's gone."

"But how are you going to get the work done here?" Alice asked. "Now we're down to just Randy and Kanon. First thing you know you and I will have to grab a wrench and get greasy."

"I can if I have to," Jim said. "But you—now that's a different matter." They both laughed and then Jim turned to me. "Is there something I can do to help?"

"As a matter of fact, there is, but you are not going to like it," I said.

Jim frowned. "Okay, so what is it?"

"I will need to borrow Kanon in a little while."

Jim looked from me to Sophie and back again. "You aren't telling me that he's somehow involved, are you?"

"I hope not," I said for Sophie's benefit, although he was still on my list of potential suspects. "There is a car I need to take a look at. He knows where it is. I hope it won't take too long."

"Okay, we'll make do. I should have some potential workers coming in for interviews today. I hope to be up to a full crew soon."

"I hope so, and I appreciate you being so understanding about me," I said. "Sophie and I need to go now, but I would appreciate it if you don't tell Kanon that I'm going to be back to talk to him. It's okay if he knows I quit, but don't tell him why. Let me break that to him."

Jim looked at Alice. She nodded, and he said, "No problem."

"Great, then we'll be on our way."

Kanon had not yet arrived for work when Sophie and I left. I looked at my watch. He was five minutes late already. I didn't mention it to Sophie. I didn't want her worrying. Anyway, for all I knew, he was often late. After all, I'd only worked at Jim's for four days.

The closer we got to the bank, where I hoped to find Jerry's safety deposit box, the more I worried. I hoped that Kanon hadn't let his temper get the best of him and tried to get even with Jake. Sophie seemed nervous too. Finally, she said, "I saw you look at your watch when we left Jim's Garage. Was Kanon late?"

"Just a little," I said. "He probably is from time to time."

She clutched at my arm. "He's never late," she said. "My dad taught both of us to never impose on other people's time. He shouldn't have been late."

"Maybe he blew a tire or something," I said, trying to ease her worry.

"Maybe," she said, but I could see that I had not eased her mind in the least. She didn't say any more about it.

We arrived at the bank and went in. I presented the official ID Hank had issued to me and explained my business. It took fifteen minutes, several phone calls—including one to Alex, as next of kin—and the Provo police before they let me use the key we had found in Jerry's shoe box and open the safety deposit box.

There were two fat envelopes and a small cardboard box. That was all. I opened the larger of the two envelopes first. The address to a private storage place in Salt Lake was written on a paper, along with a list of cars. There were also pictures of each one, a total of seven in all. One was a dark blue Cadillac. I suspected I could find the Cadillac now without Kanon's help if I had to.

"I wonder where Jerry got all those cars," Sophie said. "I wish Kanon would get out of this business. I'm afraid he's headed for trouble if he doesn't."

I agreed but didn't say so.

I opened the little box next. It was filled with lucky-charm key rings. "He really is into lucky charms," Sophie said. "Why don't people just put their trust in Heavenly Father instead of false gods like these things?"

I looked over at her where she sat next to me at the little table in the room that housed the safety deposit boxes. "From what Kanon said, Jerry was apparently into what could only be described as worship of these things. There's nothing wrong with them otherwise. I think these used to be Alex's."

"Really? She collected them?" Sophie said. "I wonder why she gave them to Jerry."

"She didn't," I revealed. "He stole them from her."

"That's awful, Dallas." I didn't disagree. The more I learned about Jerry Grady, the less I liked him, and that was pretty sad since he was dead.

I put the key chains back in the little box and put the lid on it. I picked up the last envelope and opened it. I pulled out two pieces of paper. They were each folded over. One was folded three times, and on it was written in large letters, *Alexandra*. "I probably have no business looking at this one," I said. "Maybe I should just take it to her."

"That's your decision, Dallas. You could call her and ask her though," she suggested.

I looked over at her and grinned. "Thanks. You are a lot of help."

She smiled back and touched one of my hands with hers for a moment. I pulled out my phone and dialed Alex's cell phone number. She answered quickly. "How are things going?" she asked.

"Okay, I guess. We are at the bank right now," I said.

"And you want to tell me what you found in Jerry's box," she said. "Before you do, tell me how Hank's doing."

I gave her a quick rundown, and she expressed relief. "Now, back to what we've got here. First, I think I found the rest of your lucky charms," I said.

"Jerry had them at the bank!" she exclaimed. "Whatever for? They aren't worth that much."

"Maybe to him they were. Kanon told us at the derby the other night that Jerry once told him that he trusted in the charms a whole lot more than he did in God."

"That's blasphemy," she said angrily. "I can't figure out what was wrong with that guy." She hesitated, and then she added. "But he was my brother, and I still love him."

"Of course you do," I said. "There's more here." I then told her about the list of cars and pictures and where the cars were most likely located.

"Are you going to go look at them?" she asked.

"What do you think?" I asked.

"I think you should. I wish I could be with you guys, but I can't leave Grandma today. She's having a bath right now, so I can talk a little more freely," she said with a little chuckle. "I love her to pieces, but honestly, Dallas, I'm bored to death. Is there anything else?"

"Yes, there's a note that's folded over with your name on the front. I haven't unfolded it. That's why I'm calling. Would you like me to bring it to you?" I asked.

"No, open it and read it to me," she replied. "I can't imagine that it can be very important."

"Okay, hang on while I open it," I said. There was a piece of tape on it. I sat my phone on the table while I slit the tape and unfolded what turned out to be several pages, all handwritten. I flattened them out on the table and then picked up my phone again. "Are you ready?" I asked. "This is several pages long. It will take a few minutes."

"Why don't you read it first, and if it's important, call me back and read it to me then," she said. "Or you can just bring it to me later."

"Are you sure?" I asked, hoping she was since I was very curious.

"Yes," she said. "I'll talk to you later, then. Just let me know what you decide—you know, whether to read it on the phone or bring it to me later."

After closing my phone, I said, "For some reason, Alex doesn't seem too anxious to hear what her brother has to say to her."

"Is it okay if I read it?" she asked.

"I can't see what it could hurt,"

So together, we bent over the paper and each of us began to read silently. The note read:

Alex, if you are reading this it's because I'm dead and you found my safety deposit box. I don't expect to die, but you never know when you might get in a car wreck or something. It's been a long time since I wrote one of these confessionals to you. I don't know why I am now. I guess just for old time's sake. Anyway, my first confession is that I've been a crappy brother. I'm sorry about that. I just never wanted to tell you that face-to-face. And I'm also sort of sorry for stealing your lucky charms. I know you thought I did it, and you were right. But I needed them worse than you did. You know that I never had much use for God. I don't really even believe there is such a creature. I know you will scoff at this, but the lucky charms I've used on key rings (I use them on my derby cars) have brought me lots of luck. You've got to admit that I'm the best driver in the state. And I give the charms credit. Anyway, I'm sorry that I hurt you.

The first page ended there. I glanced at Sophie to make sure she'd finished reading then pulled the other one to the top.

"This is so sad," Sophie said. I glanced at her again. Her eyes were filled with tears. "Poor Alex. Jerry wasn't a very nice guy. I'm surprised he wrote this." I looked at her, silently questioning whether she wanted to read on. She said, "Let's read the rest."

The second page read: *I guess that since I must be dead and you must not be, I can tell you some other stuff. You know me. I like to brag, but some things I've done I can't brag about except this way. I guess this is the real reason I'm writing this. I wanted someone to know that I was a pretty good car thief. Yeah, that's what I said. I'm probably the best car thief in the state. But don't think too badly of me. I never steal anything but old cars—big old cars that I can use for racing. The guys, Kanon and Razorback, think I bought them, and I did buy some of them. I bought this really neat old Cadillac. I was trying to figure out a way to steal it when I found out that Jake Frankland and his girlfriend were going to buy it. I hate that guy, and I hate his girlfriend, or whatever she is. I think you've met her. Her name is Lucia Root. She was the one that was going to buy it. The guy that had it said she was getting it for Jake as a birthday present. So I bought it. He said he wouldn't sell it to me until I offered him more money than Lucia had. I still laugh when I think about it. I heard them talking about it at the next derby. Of course, they don't know it was me that bought it. The guy promised he wouldn't tell them. I gave him an extra hundred bucks to keep his mouth shut when they came back for it. I won't use it for a while. I've got to find a way to disguise it. I think they'd kill me if they knew.* That brought another page to an end.

I straightened up when I could see that Sophie wasn't quite finished. A few seconds later she also looked up. "Maybe Jake found out," she said soberly.

"Yeah, this could be an important piece of information." We both looked down again as I pulled the next page to the top. The letter went on: *I had to wait a couple of days before I could pick it up. Kanon helped me get it. The guy I got it from said that Lucia and Jake threw a fit. It was on his birthday that they went after it. Ha, ha! I guess I showed him. The guy I bought it from got a lot more for the car than it was worth. But I got even with him. I stole a big Ford from him about a month later. He doesn't have a clue it was me. Why would he? I paid him big money. He thought I was a great customer. Ha, ha! I got one over on Jim Ralsen too. I asked him for a raise. He wouldn't give me one. He said he couldn't afford it. He had a big Chrysler out in the backyard behind his house. I waited about a month, then I slipped in one night when he and his wife were on a trip and hauled it off. He should have treated me better. I wouldn't have taken it, but I figure he owed me. That's only two of several that I stole. I'm pretty good at it. Tell Kade when you see him. He thinks I can't do anything right. He's a thief, you know. Actually, you probably don't know. But I am a better one than he is. I guess that's about all. I'll put this in one of those bank lock boxes or safety deposit boxes, whatever they call them, with the lucky charms I haven't used. If there are any left when you find this, you can have them back. Ha, ha! Sorry, but I think it's funny. That's all.*

I felt exhausted after finishing the letter. Jerry was not only dishonest, but he had the gall to brag about it to his own sister. It was amazing, simply amazing. No wonder somebody had killed him. The question now was which somebody. This letter added another name to my list of suspects, an unlikely one, I would have thought, but maybe not so, after all. Jim Ralsen, if he suspected what Jerry had done, also had a motive.

I looked at Sophie. She looked at me. We both sighed. She said, "Poor, poor Alex. And poor, poor Mrs. Grady." Sophie cared about others. It made me think highly of her.

Together, we looked at the rest of the papers. There were three of them. Each was a handwritten bill of sale for the cars, including the Cadillac. "That's good," I said when I showed it to Sophie.

"Why is that good?" she asked.

"Because now I know who he bought the Cadillac from. I can ask the guy if he actually kept his mouth shut. And I also know that Jake was lying about it being stolen, if this is the car he was referring to, and I'll bet it was."

chapter NINETEEN

TAKING THE CONTENTS OF THE safety deposit box with us, we left the bank. "I don't know whether to call Alex or not," I said to Sophie after we were back in the truck and headed for Jim's Garage again to talk to Kanon.

She shook her head and placed a hand on my arm. "I would hate to get something like this from Kanon. Alex is going to feel awful."

"How about if we just wait and give it to her later?" I asked.

"I guess. I feel so sorry for her." After about five minutes, she spoke again. "I just hope my brother isn't involved in any of the stealing."

So did I. "Kanon seems like a good guy, Sophie. Jerry didn't even pretend to be. Plus, Jerry's letter says Kanon didn't know."

I didn't know if that relieved her worry. I suspected it didn't because she was quiet the rest of the drive to Jim's Garage. I was quiet too. I was thinking about how and when to talk to Jim about the Chrysler Jerry had stolen from him. He struck me as a smart man. He might well have suspected what Jerry had done. I decided that I would put this decision off until I had a chance to brief Detective Wakefield. He was experienced and would know when and how to proceed.

When we arrived at Jim's Garage, Sophie looked and acted nervous. She was playing with a strand of her long black hair. "Kanon's probably here now," I said.

He wasn't there.

"Did he call in?" Sophie asked Jim.

"I heard from him a few minutes ago," Jim said. "He said he was sick. But he didn't sound sick. I really needed him today. It's not like him to just not come in. I did get lucky though; I hired a new guy a little bit ago, but he can't start until tomorrow. Frankly, I'm getting desperate." He paused and then looked expectantly at Sophie. "You should know if he's really sick. Did he seem okay when you left this morning?"

"I wasn't at home last night," she said. "That's why I'm asking."

"Oh yeah, sorry," Jim said.

Sophie was not her usual calm self as we drove as fast as I dared back to her home. "Something's happened to him," she said, wringing her hands. "He's in some kind of trouble."

I put my hand on her arm, "We'll find him, Sophie," I said, trying to act confident while worrying myself. "He'll be just fine."

When we got to her home, Kanon wasn't there. Sophie's mother was already drinking, and she said that she thought he'd gone to work. We checked the shop out back. His truck and the trailer he used to haul cars were gone. "He's after a car somewhere," Sophie said thoughtfully.

"Do you have a phone number for Razorback?" I asked. "We might try calling him."

"I don't," she said. "I don't even know where he lives. What are we going to do?"

"We are going to go to Salt Lake and check on the cars Jerry has stored there. Maybe Kanon's after one of them." That thought had come to me the moment I saw that the trailer was missing.

"Okay," she said, trying to act hopeful, but she was clearly worried about her brother.

The closer we got to our destination in Salt Lake, the more worried she became. We found the storage yard and hurried to the office. It was open, so I walked right in. Sophie stayed in the truck. I talked to the man who was sitting behind a small desk cluttered with papers. I told him who I was, showed my ID, and then asked if anyone had inquired that morning concerning the cars he was storing for Jerry Grady.

He looked at me in surprise and told me that Kanon Storm had called, claiming he was taking over Jerry's business. But he hadn't seen him yet. I told him that I wanted to look at the cars. He shrugged and led the way back outside. He unlocked the gate and pointed toward the far southwest corner of the lot.

I got back in the truck with Sophie and said, "Kanon called the guy. He's expecting him today."

"We didn't pass him, did we?" she said.

"I didn't see him, but maybe he stopped somewhere. I'm guessing that he'll be along soon. Let's go have a look at the cars."

We found the neatly parked row of cars behind an equally neat row of large boats. I recognized the Cadillac from the photograph Jerry had left in the safety deposit box. "Well, here we are," I said.

Sophie seemed more herself after hearing that Kanon had called. She let me open the door for her and then got out and walked toward the Cadillac. Before looking closely at the Cadillac, however, I compared the other pictures we'd found in the safety deposit box to the other cars. They were all there, including the one stolen from Jim Ralsen. I put the pictures back in the truck and then joined Sophie. The doors were locked, but I had a key—a copy of the Cadillac key taken from the red toolbox. It fit, and I opened the door.

There was a musty smell inside and dust on the dashboard. I slipped behind the wheel and tried the key in the ignition. Nothing happened, indicating that the battery was dead. I pulled it out, put it back in my jacket pocket, and began to look around the interior of the car. I wasn't sure what I expected to find. Sophie slipped into the car on the passenger side. She opened the jockey box, where she found a single sheet of paper. She pulled it out, looked at it for a moment, and then said, "Dallas, you've got to read this."

I took the note from her hand. The neat, precise handwriting was familiar. In fact, I was pretty sure the same handwriting had been on each of the notes I'd found. The difference between those notes and this one was that this note had a signature. The note read: *To whoever bought this car: You think you are so smart. Whoever you are, you know there was already a buyer. I will figure it out, and when I do, I'll make you pay.*

In the same handwriting, there was a signature. It was signed *Jake*.

My eyes met Sophie's. "Jake killed Jerry," she said.

"Or had someone else do it," I amended. "One thing's for sure; it's time to focus on him." I had been so anxious to find this car, wondering what it would tell me. Now I knew. The hunt was narrowing. "There is one thing that puzzles me. This note had to have been put in after Jerry paid for the car but before he picked it up, and yet he either didn't read it or ignored it if he did because in his letter to Alex he said no one knew about what he'd done. We also know that Jerry knew who had planned to buy this car. This note should have put him on alert."

"Maybe he thought he was untouchable," Sophie said. That was probably an accurate assessment.

We didn't find anything else of interest in the car, but as we closed the doors and locked the Cadillac, Kanon came barreling around the line of boats, the trailer bouncing behind his truck, and slid to a stop beside us.

He jumped out, a big grin on his face. "Pretty nice car, isn't it?" he said.

"And you want to beat it up in a demolition derby?" Sophie asked with a frown. "Why don't you restore it instead? You'd have the nicest ride in the neighborhood."

"That's not what Jerry bought it for," he said, his excitement gone.

"Jerry's not here anymore," Sophie reminded him. "If these cars are really yours, then why don't you do something productive with them instead of demolishing them?"

"You know I've always wanted to drive in the derbies," he said.

I stood back and let the two of them work this out. When Sophie finished, I'd have some questions for Kanon, but I could wait a minute or two.

"That was before your run-in with Jake. You can do better things with your time," Sophie said. "Just think what you could do in restoring cars if you wanted to. Dad sure left you a good shop to do it in."

"I don't know—maybe," he said.

"Think about it, Kanon. And if I were you, I'd pay more attention to your job. Jim's not very happy with you today."

"How do you know?" he asked, turning his back on her and stepping over to the Cadillac.

"Dallas and I were there. We were looking for you," she said as she joined him beside the long blue classic car. "He said you called in sick. That's not like you. You aren't a liar."

"I know it's not like me. But I've been dreaming about this car ever since the last derby, and when Jake called and threatened you, I knew I had to beat him at the next derby. I have to get it home so I can work on it."

"What about these other cars?" she said. "Are you going to give them back?"

The look of surprise that crossed his face told me what I had suspected. Apparently it did the same to Sophie, because when Kanon turned away from her she stepped around in front of him. "You could go to prison."

"For what?" he said, his face red but his voice full of anger. "These were Jerry's cars. We were partners, so they are mine now."

I decided it was time for me to step in. "I suppose you have that in writing someplace," I said. "Because if you don't, then these cars are Alex's, not yours—those that were legally Jerry's anyway."

His face paled.

"Kanon," Sophie said, "Dallas doesn't really work for Jim. Remember, he's a private investigator."

The slump in Kanon's shoulders told me a lot. He slowly faced me. "What am I supposed to do?" he asked meekly. "I want to keep driving, and I can't without cars."

"Forget that. Think about prison," I said harshly. "Believe me, if Jim knew that you had his big Chrysler here, he'd have you arrested, and of course, he'd fire you."

"What Chrysler?" he asked, visibly shaken.

"Probably that one over there," I said. "Let's see if I have a key that fits it." I walked over to my truck and brought out the duplicates Shirley Pierce had had made from the ones taken from Jerry's red toolbox. "Here's one that might." I showed a Chrysler key to Kanon. "How about if we try it out. Would you like to?" I held it out to him.

He hesitated. "Where did you get that key?" he asked. I took a moment to explain that it was a duplicate from Jerry's small red toolbox. "I thought you gave that to Alex," he said. "Did she give it back?"

"No, I actually never gave it to her. I gave it to the police," I admitted. "I have duplicates, but they have the originals."

"Oh," he said. "I guess that makes sense. So now what happens to the cars?"

"The cops are going to want to take most of them. Here, try this key." I walked over to the Chrysler and patted the hood with my hand and once again held it out to him.

"Go ahead," he said, shaking his head.

"It's not hot," I said. "Well, the car might be, but the key is fine."

When Kanon again shook his head, I walked to the driver's door. It was unlocked, so I slid beneath the wheel, inserted the key, and turned it. Amazingly, the battery was still charged; the engine turned over several times then fired up. I let it idle for a minute then shut it off and got out of the car. "So, I guess this is Jim Ralsen's Chrysler, the one he kept in his yard at home—the one Jerry stole from there and brought here. And you want to claim it now." I shook my head sadly. "That doesn't seem like a very good idea to me. That's admitting that you are in possession of a stolen car."

"Kanon," Sophie said. "Did you know Jerry stole this car from your boss?"

He worked the muscle in his jaw for a minute then said, "I wondered where he'd gotten it, but I didn't know it was Jim's."

Sophie's eyes filled with tears, and she turned away. Seeing how hurt she was angered me. But I kept that anger in check, stared at Kanon, then said, "Listen to me, Kanon. Most of these cars are stolen. I only know where the Cadillac and Chrysler came from, and technically, the Cadillac isn't stolen, but there is a way to get these other vehicles returned without you going to jail."

"How?" he said, looking at me hopefully.

"Sophie and I were going to have you show us where these cars were being stored," I explained. "But we learned from . . ." I hesitated and looked at Sophie, who was watching me now, her eyes red. I swear she was holding her breath as if she were praying for a miracle. I hoped I could pull this off for her sake as well as her brother's. I went on. "We learned about their location from a different source," I said, deciding not to tell him about the safety deposit box. "So if you will simply drive away from here and go home, I'll let my law enforcement friends know about what we have here. And then we'll let them take it from there. Your name doesn't need to come up."

Sophie let out her breath. Kanon slumped back against Jim Ralsen's Chrysler. He looked like the wind had been knocked out of him. "You'd do that for me?" he asked, almost in disbelief.

"Of course." I stopped and stared hard at him for a moment, and then I added, "There are some conditions that you will have to agree to though."

"Anything," he said. "I'll do whatever you ask if you'll keep me out of trouble."

I glanced again at Sophie. Her eyes were gleaming, and she nodded in agreement. "Here are the terms, Kanon. First, you've got to agree to quit driving in the derbies."

"I have to anyway. I don't have any cars now," he said.

"You could get something pretty cheap, and you know it, but frankly, Kanon, you'd be better off doing other things," I said. I hoped he truly saw the wisdom in it. "My second term is that you answer every question I have about Jerry or anything I think might help me and the police in our investigation."

"So I have to talk to the cops?" he asked.

"Not if we can avoid it, but if it comes to that and I decide you need to, then yes, you'll have to."

"What else?"

"You won't like this one, but if Alex is okay with it, I'd like to have her offer to sell the Cadillac to Jake Frankland. I will help with it."

"Why should we do that?" he asked.

"So he won't kill you," I said bluntly. "Sophie found a note in the jockey box of the Cadillac that I think you should read, if Sophie agrees."

Sophie had remained silent throughout the entire exchange between the two of us. She spoke now. "I agree with you, Dallas."

I pulled it from a pocket where I had put it for safekeeping until I could turn it over to Detective Wakefield. I unfolded it and said, "Here, read it."

He read. His face went pale again. His hands shook as he gave it back to me. His voice sounded like it had gravel in it when he said, "Jake wrote this."

"That's right; it was from Jake. Didn't Jerry tell you that he bought it knowing it was about to go to Jake?"

"He didn't tell me that, but he did show me a bill of sale."

I smiled. "Like he *didn't* on these other cars?"

"Yeah, that's right," he admitted. He was thoughtful for a moment, and then he said, "Jake killed Jerry, didn't he?"

"Could be," I agreed. "We don't know that for sure yet. But I don't think you want to turn up with that car, because, for all we know, he might carry out his threat against you, since Jerry is dead already."

I had made my point. "Sophie," I said, "are there other conditions that you would like to impose as part of this deal?"

"There sure are," she said sternly. "I expect you to treat Mom with respect. Maybe if the two of us try hard enough, we can get her to quit drinking."

"I'll help with that too," I said, renewing my previous promise to Sophie.

She acknowledged me with a smile. But she wasn't through with her conditions. She said, "Come to church with me for at least a month. Then, if you can't handle it, I won't make you. But I do insist that you don't drink."

"How did you know I drink?" he asked, his face now red.

She grinned at her brother with affection. "I didn't," she said. "I suspected it, but now I know it. Those are my terms."

"Okay, I'll do it," he said, uncertainty in his voice.

"Kanon, as your friend, I'm going to hold you to this," I said.

"I guessed you would. So what questions do you have for me?"

"Not now," I said. "We'll talk later. Right now I'm going to call my cop friends. You take that truck and trailer of yours home. I don't want you anywhere near here when they arrive."

Sophie gave her brother a hug. "I love you, Kanon," she said tearfully.

"Love you too, Sophie," he said, and a minute later, as I was calling Milt, he was driving away.

"Thank you, Dallas. You are a great friend," Sophie said ten minutes later, after I had concluded a long conversation with Detective Wakefield.

"He's on his way with another officer," I said. "He says they have learned some interesting things as well. When they get here, we'll compare notes. In the meantime, I'm going to ask the manager here to lock this place down while you and I go grab a quick bite to eat."

"Dallas, thank you for what you're doing for my brother." She stepped toward me, threw her arms around me, and gave me a hug. I was looking beyond her as we hugged. Behind the storage yard there was a large, empty lot filled with weeds. Beyond it was a road. There was a vehicle parked on the road, and someone was leaning over the vehicle. It was several hundred yards away, and I couldn't make out any details, but I did catch a glint of light that alarmed me. "Get down!" I shouted as I shoved Sophie to the ground.

We both dropped together as a rifle was fired. The bullet hit one of the boats behind us. "Don't move," I told Sophie urgently as I scrambled on my knees toward my truck. I retrieved the rifle and fired at the distant car even as another bullet whistled by. I got a second shot off before the car squealed away.

"Did you hit him?" Sophie asked.

"I might have hit the car." I said.

Sophie got to her feet, trembling. "That was close," she said. "How can you be so calm?"

"It's not the first time I've been shot at. I was a soldier," I said.

She laughed nervously. "Well, it's not natural to me. I'm scared to death. And I'm worried about Kanon." She was trembling.

Her mention of Kanon sent me into action. I grabbed my cell phone and began to dial. Even as a 911 operator answered, the yard manager came running around the line of boats. Before he could ask, I held up a hand and said, "Yes, we were just shot at." Then I told the operator what was going on, and she promised to get someone there quickly.

So much for a nice lunch with Sophie. The next hour was busy with cops looking at bullet holes, collecting bullets from a boat, questioning the two of us and the manager (who had absolutely nothing to add), and just generally doing what police do in this kind of circumstance. Sophie called Kanon several times. I was relieved when she stepped close to me and said, "Kanon is home."

"Did you tell him to stay there?" I asked.

"Yes, and I think he will. He's scared too."

"Sophie," I said, thinking now of her safety, "I thought keeping you with me was a good idea, but it almost got you killed. We need to take you back to the hotel and—"

"I'd rather be with you," she said, her eyes moist. "Please, don't make me leave now. I want to help."

That girl had a way of getting to me. I didn't know what to do. I said, "We'll see."

I was glad for the presence of Detective Wakefield. I felt like the local officers were treating me like a suspect until he showed up with Detective Richards and convinced them that I was legitimate. I was quite sure that I knew who was behind the rifle that shot at us, but I didn't mention any names to the local officers. I simply said that I felt like it had to be connected to my investigation. "If I find out," I promised them, "I'll let you know."

The focus of the investigation turned to the cars that Jerry had stored there. There was a lot of interest when I told the police that most of the cars we were looking at were stolen, the Cadillac being an exception. The officers gave the manager of the property an order to keep the cars secure while they investigated the thefts. The Provo officer volunteered to contact Jim Ralsen about his Chrysler, but Milt and I convinced him to let us do that, as he was technically a suspect in the murder of Jerry Grady. He might have somehow learned that Jerry had stolen his car and chosen to take revenge.

I didn't mention the note I'd found in the Cadillac until after the local officers had left. Even Detective Richards had to get back to Provo. I finally pulled out the note when Sophie, Milt, and I were sitting in a restaurant, finally getting some lunch. He read it with interest. And then, when I handed Milt the note from Jerry's safety deposit box, he read in awe.

"Wow, this is dynamite," Milt said. "Jerry stirred people up, didn't he?"

"It seems that way," I agreed. "So let's narrow things down and decide where to focus our next efforts."

"First, let me tell you what I've learned—the reason why the Provo guys are concentrating on the murder of Kelsey Glazer," he said, "as well they should."

"Does that mean the information Lyle Wertz gave me checked out?" I asked.

He nodded his head. "Indeed it did. He was right about Kelsey and the cars. Besides the green Explorer, which people say Kelsey always drives and his wife thinks is his only vehicle, he owns both a black van and a black sports car, a Mazda RX-8, which he has registered under an assumed name."

"So where are they? I wish Lyle could have told me the name they are registered under," I said. "That would have helped find them. Lyle could only tell me that nobody even knows Kelsey owns the other cars, let alone that he has another complete identity."

"That's right. He doesn't keep either one of the cars at his house. He never even drives them to it. Apparently, he keeps them at a place he either owns or leases up in Magna. The Provo officers, after a lot of good police work, found both of them but not in Magna. The black van is in a shop in West Valley City getting new glass. The sports car turned up abandoned on a dirt road out by Utah Lake. There were traces of blood both in the car and around it. We think that was where he was shot. DNA will confirm that."

"And then he was dumped at the hospital, where he died," I mused. "Well, at least now I know for sure that it was him that broke into my apartment and tried to kidnap Ellen, although I've believed that ever since Lyle gave me that information. And since that is true, I'd bet Lyle was also right about Jerry knowing Kelsey had cars and a residence in a different name. And who knows, he might have been using that in some way against him. That could explain why Kelsey disliked Jerry so much. The other thing he told me, is that true as well?"

"It sure is, and it could also be very important. Kelsey Glazer and Lucia Root, Jake's girlfriend, are first cousins, just like Lyle told you."

Sophie gasped.

Milt continued. "Kelsey's widow confirmed that to us. But she says she didn't know what Kelsey was up to." He glanced at Sophie. "She says their marriage was a sham."

Sophie grunted. "You think?"

Milt glanced at her. He didn't know her dark history with the creep. She didn't expand for his benefit, so I moved the conversation forward. "Did Kelsey's wife say whether Kelsey and Lucia had been in contact with each other lately?"

"They had. Jake and Lucia had come around several times the past few weeks," Milt reported. "That was unusual. One time, Lucia called when Kelsey wasn't home. She seemed quite upset that he wasn't there, according to Mrs. Glazer."

"What kind of relationship did Kelsey have with Jake and Lucia?" I asked.

"It was generally okay, I guess, until the past few days."

"Did something happen to change things?" I asked.

Milt scratched his chin. "Apparently it had, but Kelsey's wife doesn't have a clue what it might have been over. In my estimation, she didn't have much of a clue about anything." He chuckled and then went on. "Lucia and Jake didn't like her, and they didn't ever say much to her, or so she claims," he reported.

We ate silently for a moment. I was thinking things over carefully. Lyle had been right about Lucia and Kelsey being cousins, about the black vehicles, and about Kelsey's other identity. And he was clearly afraid of Jake. At this point, I couldn't help but wonder if Jake might have killed both Jerry and Kelsey. There was just one thing that bothered me—motive. Why would Jake kill Kelsey? The motive for him killing Jerry was, in my mind, well established.

"You're thinking awfully deeply," Milt said.

"Yeah, there are several things I think we need to do this afternoon," I said. Sophie was watching me intently.

"Besides find Jake and see if you put a bullet in his car?" Milt asked.

"Yes, besides that. I'd love to nail him for shooting at Sophie," I said.

"Hey, he was shooting at you," she said with a hint of a smile.

I smiled at her. "We also need to get a search warrant for his house or apartment, for all of his vehicles, and for the place he works, if we can find out where that is," I said.

"I'll work on that," Milt said. "You are right. What else are you thinking we need to do?"

"Well, there is still Jim Ralsen. Jerry stole his car. I'd like to know if Jim knew that. We can't rule him out."

Milt nodded in agreement. "Other than asking him what anyone might have had against Jerry, I haven't grilled him much."

"Same here," I said thoughtfully. "There's still more we need to do about Jake. It has to do with the Cadillac Jerry bought out from under his girlfriend."

"What exactly are you driving at?" Milt asked, scratching his chin again.

"I think I know," Sophie said.

She was sitting next to me. I turned toward her. She was pulling at a long strand of her glossy black hair. I looked at her expectantly. It may or may not have been what I was thinking, but I wanted to hear what she had to say. "You want to know if the guy who sold the Cadillac to Jerry broke his promise," she suggested.

"Yeah, that's it exactly," I said. "Jake might have gone to him recently and, with Jerry dead, the guy might have figured it wouldn't matter if he broke his promise. After all, he might simply think that nothing could be done to a dead man."

Detective Wakefield said, "I think we are heading in the right direction here. Is there anything else we need to check on right away?"

I slowly nodded my head. I was an expert marksman with any kind of rifle. Whoever shot Jerry was also an expert. I voiced my thoughts. "I think we need to know who among those we know about are expert marksmen. I would include Kelsey, even though he is dead and obviously couldn't have shot at Sophie and me. I would also include Kade Squire. Besides things like theft and identity theft, he showed us that he was not above killing people, Sophie and me included. I don't think we should rule him out."

"So who all do we need to check on?" Milt asked.

"Kade, as I just said, Jake, Lucia, Jim Ralsen, the late Kelsey Glazer, maybe even Lyle Wertz," I responded. "Of course, even if we don't find that any of them have training or experience with rifles, it doesn't mean that they couldn't have hired someone to kill Jerry—someone who isn't even on our radar."

Milt made some notations. We split up the assignments, with Milt's first one being to work with the authorities in Utah County, and mine to contact Jim Ralsen and the man who had sold the Cadillac to Jerry. I was also going to make a visit to Mrs. Grady's hotel and talk to Alex, get her reaction to Jerry's safety deposit box letter, and finally, try to persuade Sophie to stay there with them.

chapter TWENTY

ON THE RIDE BACK TO Utah County, I spoke seriously about the danger of what I was going to be involved in later that afternoon. "Please," I said, "don't argue with me about this, but I insist that you stay at a hotel, either with Alex and Ellen or back at our hotel."

I braced myself for an angry outburst. But this was Sophie, not Alex. There was no display of anger, just gently falling tears. "I'd rather stay with you," she said. "I'm worried that you might get hurt."

"Having you along will just make it harder and more dangerous for me," I told her bluntly. "I need to concentrate on keeping myself safe while I work. If you are with me, I'll have you to worry about too, and that could be risky. It would divide my attention, and I can't let my attention be divided. Please, you've got to understand."

She wiped the tears away, laid her head against my shoulder, and said softly, "I don't want to do anything that might get you hurt. You are the best guy I've ever known."

I knew that couldn't be true, but I was touched. "Thank you, Sophie. Where would you like to go?"

"To our hotel, if that's okay."

"Of course it is," I said. I didn't tell Sophie what was worrying me the most. We were being followed again. It wasn't the car the shots had been fired from. That one had been blue, if I wasn't mistaken—either blue or green. The one I kept noticing now was silver. I had noticed it first when we'd pulled out of the restaurant parking lot. It had eased away from the curb nearly a block away. I'd seen it back there from time to time all the way to the freeway. I hoped that it wouldn't get on the interstate when I did, but my hopes were dashed. Finally, it exited when I did in Orem.

"Just in case someone sees us, I suppose I better do some evasive maneuvering again," I said. "I'm getting tired of driving like a maniac, but I'm not taking any chances on leading anyone to Ellen and Alex."

Sophie snuggled a little closer and said, "You aren't fooling me, Dallas Rowen. I've seen how closely you've been watching your mirrors. Someone is already back there. Who do you think it is? If it's the guy that shot at us in Salt Lake, why don't you call Detective Wakefield and have him help you stop them?"

I glanced at her, and she smiled at me. I said, "I couldn't tell much about whoever that was, but I'm sure the car was either green or blue. This one is silver. Right now my first priority is to make sure you're safe. I'm going to lose him now," I said firmly.

"When you do, can we go by my house so I can get some of my books? If I am going to sit in a hotel room, I might at least make good use of my time and do some studying."

"I have a better idea," I said. "Let's make whoever is back there think that I left you at your house."

"How?" she asked.

I explained. She agreed and made a phone call while I changed the direction I was driving. We pulled in behind her house a few minutes later, out of sight of the street and whoever was driving the silver car. I was relieved to see Kanon's truck parked there. The trailer had been unhooked in the backyard. The doors to the shop were all closed. So was the garage door where Mrs. Storm kept her car. Sophie, at my instruction, went into the house alone. I kept my eyes peeled until she came back with her arms full of books—and with what she had told me earlier was her father's pistol. "Kanon and Mom are gone, like you suggested," she said. "So was Kanon's pistol. At least he's doing what you want him to. I'm sure he's scared. Mom probably is too. I just hope he keeps the booze from her like I told him to when I called."

Sophie had been climbing into the backseat as she was talking. As soon as I knew she was safely hidden, I said, "Okay, hang on now. Hopefully, they'll think you're at home and come after me, thinking I'm alone now," I said. "I'll tell you when it's safe to sit up."

I didn't see the silver car until I was three blocks away from Sophie's house. Whoever was driving it was a skilled driver—much better than Kade and whoever else had followed me the past few days. I feared it was Jake. Sophie made a comment to that effect when I did crazier driving than I had before. I eventually lost the silver car. When I was sure we were safe, I pulled to the side of the road while Sophie scrambled up front with me.

We parked at the back of the hotel when we got there, and I accompanied her inside. Once she was safely in her room, I said, "Don't let anyone in but me—not even room service."

"I wish I could go with you," she said after giving me a kiss on the cheek and a quick hug. "But I know this is best."

"Yes, it is. Now, like I did for Alex and Ellen, I'll have security keep a close watch on your room. And you keep that gun handy." I felt very alone when I drove away from the hotel after talking to the chief of security.

My next stop, after giving my truck another workout, was Ellen's hotel. Alex hugged me when I entered the room. "Where's Sophie?" she asked. "You didn't leave her alone in the truck, did you?"

"No, she's at the other hotel."

"I'll bet she likes that," Alex said facetiously. "I think she likes you. She's not the only one, if she does."

Wow, was this the same girl who had once said she hated me? I let her comment pass. "She's scared. We had a close call. When I told her that I wasn't taking any more chances with her safety, she didn't argue."

"Are you okay, Dallas?" Ellen asked in a worried voice.

"Don't I look okay?" I said lightly. "Yes, I'm fine, but I did waste a couple of rounds of your rifle ammunition."

Alex went white. "What happened, Dallas?"

I explained, and she sank down on the bed. "Oh, Dallas, this is getting worse all the time."

Ellen also had to sit down, but she chose a chair. I gave them a fairly detailed account of what had happened. However, I left Kanon's involvement out of my story. The only mention I made of him was that, at my request, he'd picked his mother up at their house and had taken her someplace out of the way until the cops and I could get to the bottom of this.

"Do you have the note you found in the safety deposit box?" Alex asked when I had finished.

I pulled it from my pocket and showed it to her. "It's several pages long," I said. She took it from my hand and patted the bed, inviting me to sit beside her. She unfolded it and began silently reading. She looked up after barely getting started. "I told you how we used to write to each other like this and then hide what we'd written where the other was sure to find it."

"Yes, you did."

"You never told me," Ellen said.

Alex gave her a brief account of their confessionals, as she called them. Then she went back to reading. She had to stop and wipe her eyes several times. At one point, she stopped reading again and looked at me. "I was right about him stealing the lucky charms. It just took him a long time to confess to me," she said. Then she again lowered her eyes to the paper. I knew when she'd reached the part about the cars and how he had stolen so many of them, because she gasped, let go of the papers with one hand, and grabbed my arm. "He stole cars," she said, her voice quavering.

"Yes, he did."

"He even stole from Jim Ralsen. I can't believe he'd do that. Does Jim know yet?"

"That'll be my next stop, Alex."

She finished reading the letter, slowly folded it, and handed it back to me.

"May I see it?" Ellen asked.

"It's very sad, Grandma," Alex said. "It'll make you cry. Jerry was a lot worse than either of us thought. It's little wonder he got killed."

I couldn't argue with that. I handed the papers to my client. As she read, sobbed, wiped her eyes, and read some more, Alex held my hand tightly, her head bowed and eyes closed much of the time. Occasionally, she would wipe a few tears away. We were silent until Ellen had finished and handed the papers back. I folded them and put them back in my pocket.

"Is there more you'd like to report?" Ellen asked in a weak voice.

I told her about Kelsey's relation to Lucia and Jake, as well as the story about the black vehicles.

"I wonder if Jerry knew about Kelsey's other life," Alex said thoughtfully.

"I would guess he did," I answered. Then I pulled out the note I'd found in the Cadillac and read it to them.

"That looks like the same handwriting on the note you found on my car," Alex observed. "And it's signed by Jake."

"That's right," I said. "Now I better get going. I have a lot to do."

"You be careful, Dallas Rowen," Alex said as she followed me to the door.

"I will. You ladies stay put."

She suddenly flung herself at me, threw her arms around me, and sobbed as she hugged me tightly. "Dallas, I'm so sorry I doubted you. You are the best guy I've ever known." It was no truer when she said it than it was when Sophie had said the same thing, but it sounded nice—really nice.

Jim Ralsen was glad to hear that I had found Kanon. "He's in rough shape," I said, not telling him that *rough* referred to his emotional rather than physical state. "Hopefully, he'll be able to get back to work pretty soon," I said. "But it may be a day or two."

"I'm sorry to hear that," he said. "Are you sure you can't spend a few hours working here this afternoon?"

"I really can't," I said. "I've got more to do than I can possibly handle."

"Welcome to the club," he said harshly.

"Jim, there is one thing I need to talk to you about. That's why I came by," I said. "Can we go in your office for a minute?"

"Alice, would you hold my calls?" he said, and then he led me in and we both sat down after he closed the door.

"What's on your mind?" he asked. "You look pretty serious."

I got right to the point, watching Jim carefully for his reaction. "Did you used to have an old Chrysler in the yard behind your house?"

His eyes narrowed, and he leaned as far forward as his ponderous stomach and desk would allow. "How did you know about that?" he asked.

"I'll take that as a yes," I said. "Do you have any idea where it is now?"

I thought he couldn't lean farther forward. He proved me wrong—he did it with such force that his desk slid several inches across the floor toward me. "I gather that you already know it was stolen," he said, his face going red. "That car was in mint condition and had low mileage. It was my dad's car. He took good care of it. There was sentimental value to that car." He finally sat up again. "You know something about it?"

"What would you do if I told you that I know who stole it?" I asked.

I flinched when he again shoved the desk with the weight of his body and said with a fierceness I hadn't guessed he was even capable of, "I'd kill the dirty bugger that took it."

I gave him time to think before I said, "Somebody already did."

He jerked and rose to his feet in one motion, hitting his desk so hard that much of the disorganized stuff on it fell to the floor. He seemed not to notice. His eyes, narrowed and angry, focused on my face. "Surely you don't think I'd really do that?" He shoved his chair back and came around the desk.

I jumped to my feet, not sure what he had in mind. He stopped right in front of me. "I didn't kill anybody, if that's what you think," he growled.

"I didn't accuse you of anything, Jim," I said calmly, although my stomach was churning. I had just seen a side of Jim I hadn't known existed.

"That was just figure of speech, what I said," he told me as he pulled a handkerchief from his pocket and began wiping his brow. "I would never kill anybody."

"Why don't you sit down again?" I pointed to the chair behind his desk.

He glared at me for a moment and then slowly shuffled back. Once he was seated again, I sat down as well. "Who do you think stole your car?" I asked. "You must have some idea."

"I do now," he said as he folded his arms across the top of his stomach and looked at me suspiciously. "It was either Jerry or Kelsey. They're the only ones I know of who have been killed."

"Do you still hunt?" I asked as my eyes settled for a moment on a framed picture of Jim on the wall behind his desk. I had not been in his office before. He'd hired me right out by Alice's desk, and she'd done the paperwork there. The picture was of Jim, younger and slimmer, squatting beside a huge bull elk. He had one hand gripping the large rack. The other held a rifle with a scope.

"Not much," he said. "I let myself get too big. It's hard to get around in the mountains like I used to."

"That's a beautiful bull," I said. "How did you get close enough to bring him down?"

"I didn't need to be close," he said. "I shot him at a good five hundred yards or more. I'm a good shot," he said.

"What's the caliber of your rifle?" I asked.

"It's a—" He stopped and squinted at me. "Now you know I'm a good shot. You sneaky bugger, you. You are about to tell me that it was Jerry Grady that stole my car, and you're thinking that I shot him with my rifle because it's the same caliber he was killed with."

I didn't say anything for a moment, just kept my eyes steady on his face, studying the movement of his eyes, the color in his cheeks, and the way he was gulping breaths of air. Finally, I said, "Where's the rifle now?"

"It's at home," he responded. "It's in my gun cabinet with my other guns."

"It's not out in your car?" I asked, remembering that he drove a Ford sedan to work, a *dark green* one.

His face grew darker. He looked like he was about to have a heart attack. I stood and opened his door. "You fixing to look?" he asked. "You think I'm lying."

"Alice," I said after I got up and opened door. "What time did Jim get back to the garage this afternoon?" It was a shot in the dark, but I figured that if I asked him and he was lying about where his rifle was, he'd say he hadn't left the office. I needed to get Alice's response before he had a chance to tell her what to say.

"About an hour ago," she said. "Why?"

"Just needed to know," I said, smiling at her and closing the door again.

"What was that all about?" he asked with a scowl. He mopped at his brow again. "You're being mighty sneaky, Dallas."

"Where did you go? I only worked here for a few days, but it was long enough to know that you hardly ever leave the garage during the day," I said.

"I'm shorthanded, thanks in part to you," he growled. "I had to make a run for some parts."

"How long were you gone?" I asked.

"Maybe an hour. Maybe two."

"It doesn't take that long to get parts, Jim. What else did you do?"

"I don't have to answer your questions," he said angrily, starting to get to his feet again.

"No, you don't. But I think it would be a good idea if you did. Where is your rifle?"

"It's at home," he said.

"Should we go have a look in your car, Jim?"

"Who stole my old Chrysler?" he countered.

"You already know that," I said.

"It was Jerry?"

"It was."

"And he was going to use it in one of those demolition derbies. Did he already use it? Is it a piece of junk now?"

"It's as good as the day he stole it," I said.

"Where is it?"

"The Provo Police Department picked it up," I said. "They have it in their impound yard."

He seemed to relax a bit. He sat back in his chair and took a couple of deep breaths. "Jerry was a good worker," he said. "But he was also a trouble-maker. He always had someone mad at him."

"Including you?" I asked evenly.

"Actually, it's like I told you before, I got along fine with him. I didn't have any idea he'd stolen my car," he said as he heaved himself to his feet again. "Let's go look in my car. There's no rifle in it."

I followed him outside, leaving Alice with questions in her eyes. I kept mine on Jim. If he was the killer, I needed to make sure I protected myself. He unlocked his car and opened the trunk. "Go ahead, have a look," he said.

Warily, I looked inside, checked under the seats, where there was no room for a rifle, and finally looked in the trunk. The rifle wasn't in the car. I also looked the exterior over while Jim stood with his hands folded on his belly. If it had been his car on the road south of the storage lot in Salt Lake, my shots had missed it. There were no bullet holes.

"Satisfied?" he asked.

"Getting closer," I said. "Where did you go that took you an hour or two?" I asked. "You could make this easier for both of us if you'd just tell me."

"I went to the employment office," he said.

That would be easy to check, and I certainly would do so. "Why didn't you just say so?" I asked.

"Dallas," he said, unfolding his arms and scratching his ear. "What you said shook me up. I'm no killer, but it sure seems like you came here to accuse me."

"I came here to tell you that Jerry had stolen your car and that I had found it for you," I said. "You assumed a lot. Should we go look at your rifle? I'd like to borrow it for a while, have some ballistics run on it."

"Why should I let you do that?" he asked.

"To prove that you are telling me the truth," I said. "I have a hard time thinking of you as a killer. But unless you let me take that rifle, I'll have a hard time proving that you're not. And while we're at it, I'll need to know where you were the evening Jerry was killed."

"You don't give up, do you?" he said.

"I've been hired to do a job, and I intend to do it," I said.

"I hired you to do a job too. You don't seem too anxious to do what I hired you to."

"Sorry, Jim, but this job comes first. Where were you that night?"

"What night was it?" he asked.

I told him, and he said, "I was home all day and night, I'm sure."

"What were you doing?"

"Probably watching football," he answered. "My wife can tell you."

"Let's go talk to her and have a look at your rifle."

"Just wondering," he said. "But what happens if I say no?"

"Then I'll call my cop friends, they'll get a warrant, and we'll get it anyway," I said, trying to stay patient.

"That's what I thought you'd say," he said. "Okay, let's go, then. I don't know why I'm being such a jerk. I didn't kill anybody, so I'll let you prove it."

"Thanks, Jim," I said. "I'll follow you to your place."

I got on the phone and called Detective Wakefield, told him what I had learned, and agreed to meet him at the Provo Police Department as soon as I had the rifle. I wasn't sure what to think about Jim. I honestly hoped his alibi checked out and that his rifle wouldn't prove to match the bullet taken from Jerry's head or the ones taken from the boats that had been meant for me that afternoon.

I was wary of him as we went into his house. He let me get the gun from the gun cabinet. I noticed that he also had a pistol. I would have liked to have taken it too, but I didn't know what caliber weapon Kelsey had been shot with, and Jim was being cooperative, so I didn't push my luck.

His wife was in the kitchen. He called to her. She came out, and he introduced us. Then he mentioned the day of Jerry's murder and asked her to tell me that he was at home watching ball games on TV. She agreed that that was what he did a lot of Friday nights, but I thought he was going to faint when she reminded him that she'd spent that entire week at their daughter's home in Logan.

chapter TWENTY-ONE

A SEARCH WARRANT FOR JAKE'S house and cars had been obtained. "There is a catch," Milt said. "The issuing magistrate is a stubborn old judge. He restricted us from searching unless Jake's with us. And we can't find him. The neighbors say they haven't seen him all day. There's an officer watching the place. When he shows up, we'll hit the place as quick as we can get there."

"Have you learned anything about what kind of marksmen some of the persons of interest are?" I asked.

"Not yet. I mean, we've tried, but we haven't learned anything yet," he said. "You seem to have been the only one to have gotten anywhere. Maybe if we can find Jake, we can duplicate what you accomplished with Ralsen."

"Do you know if Kade Squire is still in jail?" I asked.

"He is," Milt replied. "His father is refusing to bail him out, and he doesn't appear to have anyone else to turn to. Anyway, the judge raised the bail. It's at a million dollars now."

"That's good. It should be! Do you think his father would cooperate with us if we called him? He should know if Kade is good with weapons or not," I suggested.

"That's a good idea," he said. "Do you want to call him or should I?"

"I'll do it, if you'd like," I said.

"Then I'll head for the state crime lab," he offered. "They have the bullet taken from Jerry's body. And I'll call the cops up there who responded to this afternoon's events. We can also run the bullets fired at you against this rifle," he said, waving the one I had just handed over to him.

So Milt headed back to Salt Lake, and I, after prioritizing my tasks, headed for the address of the man who'd sold the Cadillac to Jerry. I also wanted to verify with Workforce Services that Jim had been there earlier. But depending on the results of the ballistics tests, that might not even be necessary. So that could wait.

The day had been wearing on. I checked my rearview mirror several times, but there was no sign of anyone following me, so I headed for the address I had for the man who had sold the car to Jerry. On the way, I checked in with both Alex and Sophie by phone. They were both okay but bored. Ellen was worrying about cleaning her house, Alex told me. Kanon and his mother had driven to Brigham City where a sister of Mrs. Storm lived and were reasonably safe for now was the report from Sophie.

I still didn't think anyone had been following me when I arrived at the home of Cyrus Turner. It was a nice brick home in Payson with a well-kept yard. Large poplar trees offered shade along both sides of the yard. A late-model silver Cadillac was parked in the driveway. I pulled in behind it and approached the door. But before I had knocked, a slender, gray-haired man in his sixties came around the house and called out, "My wife isn't at home. Is there something I can help you with?"

"If you're Cyrus Turner, you can," I said.

He wiped grease off his hands with a rag as he approached. "I'd offer to shake hands, but I've been working on a car—my hobby since I retired. As you can see, I'm a bit greasy. So what can I do for you?"

"My name is Dallas Rowen," I said. "I'm a private investigator. I just needed to talk to you about a car you sold two or three months ago, a Cadillac."

He smiled. "I sort of favor Cadillacs," he said. "Sometimes I restore them and sometimes I just make them drivable and resell them. If you can describe the car in question, I might be able to help you."

"It is a dark blue Cadillac, quite old," I said, "but in pretty good condition."

"Yes. I remember that car. A lady wanted it. She was probably not quite thirty. She was nice looking, with a full figure. But she wouldn't give me money to hold it. When she came by later to get it, I'd already sold it to a young fellow who said it had really caught his eye. He was later murdered, as I recall. It's too bad. He was so young. What is your interest in that car?"

"I'm working with the police and with his family. I'm trying to figure out who killed him and why," I said. "I just wanted to clear up a few things. First, you say you sold it, not that it was stolen?"

"That's right," he said. "Did someone say it had been stolen from me?"

"Yes, but I was pretty sure he was lying," I responded as I thought about what Jake had said about the stolen blue Cadillac. "Did the young man that bought it take it the day he gave you the money?"

"No, he paid me on a weekday, I don't remember which one, but he said he'd come back for it on the weekend. And that's what he did."

"Was the car drivable?" I asked.

"Other than a weak battery, it was running like a charm." Cyrus stopped and grinned. "Funny thing that, me using that word."

"What word?"

"Charm," he said. "When the kid bought the car, he put the key on a lucky-charm key ring and handed it back to me. I remember it because he said he always had lucky charms on the key rings of his cars. He said it made him a winner. I don't know what he meant by that, but he seemed quite serious."

"Did he drive the car away from here then?"

"Oh no, it wasn't registered or insured. And he said he wouldn't bother with that, that he was going to be doing some more work on it before he used it. He and some real skinny guy came with a trailer and hauled it off," he said.

"You say the woman that had come earlier came back again?"

"You bet she did, she and the boyfriend both. They accused me of selling it out from under her, but I didn't do any such thing. I had asked her for a deposit, and she had refused to give it," he said with a scowl. "I remember it well because she said she'd be back, but then this kid comes along and buys it outright. And after the way those two acted, I was glad he had it and not them."

"How did the guy that bought it act?" I asked.

"He was a perfect gentleman," Cyrus said. That was a first. No one I had spoken to about Jerry Grady had called him a gentleman.

"Was the car still here when the woman came back?" I asked.

"Yes, it was the day before the kid picked it up," Cyrus said. "After I told her it was sold, she walked over and looked at it. I remember her saying to her boyfriend, after she'd had a few choice words for me, that she wanted him to see it. It was in back, and I followed them around there. They spent a minute or two looking at it. The woman pulled some money from her purse, a wad of cash, and she told me her boyfriend really wanted it, and that she'd pay me more than what whoever had bought it had paid."

"You didn't agree with that, I take it?"

"That's right. I told her that I didn't work that way. They both said some not very nice words, and then the guy asked me who bought it."

"Did you tell him?" I asked.

"No, I'd promised the kid I wouldn't. That made them really mad, and they both swore at me again and then looked at the car once more. They even looked inside it. Then they left. I remember the guy saying something about how I shouldn't do business this way. I didn't like either of them."

"Do you remember their names?"

"They never gave me their names," he said.

"You've been a big help," I said. "I appreciate it."

As I started to walk back to my truck, I thought of something else. I turned back, and he was still standing there. "By any chance, was the key in the Cadillac when those two looked inside it?"

Cyrus was thoughtful for a minute, rubbing his chin and closing his eyes. Finally, he said, "Might have been. I don't recall for sure, but it seemed like I had moved it from where I'd had it parked so I could get another car in that spot. I might have left it in the ignition, but I know that if I did, I removed it later, because I remember I went in the house to get it for Mr. Grady when he came to get it."

"Thanks," I said.

I had learned all I needed to know. Jake most likely had known who had bought the car months ago. As I left Cyrus standing in his backyard, I wondered if Jake had asked Lucia to keep track of me. I shivered at the thought and went back to my truck.

I watched for the silver car when I left, but I couldn't see it. I drove around a bit and then stopped at a shopping mall, where I parked inconspicuously among thousands of vehicles. I spent a few minutes making notes, thinking about the case as I did so. Right now, it seemed to me that Jake Frankland and Jim Ralsen were in a toss-up for top suspect. I had a feeling that whoever killed Jerry had also shot Kelsey Glazer. They both had motive for killing Jerry, but I didn't have a clue yet as to why either of those two would have killed Kelsey. Also still on my active list was Kade Squire. It was about him that I made my next move.

I called the home of Alex's mother and stepfather. Her mother answered, but after explaining who I was, I asked to talk to George Squire. When he came on the line, I again introduced myself and stated my business.

"Are you the guy that got my boy thrown into jail?" he asked gruffly.

"No, he actually managed that all by himself," I said. "It seems he's been stealing from his stepsister and her grandmother, and he planted a bomb in my truck."

"But you're the one that caught him," he said. "He didn't turn himself in."

"Yes, I guess you could say that I caught him."

"Alex says he caught you by surprise and kicked you around quite violently," he said, his voice not quite so gruff now.

"Yeah, that's right," I admitted as I again felt the residual ache from those unrestrained boots of his. "I guess I caught him in the act of stealing from Ellen. But that's not what I'm calling about."

"I'm very sorry about what he did," George told me. "I thought I raised him better than that."

"I'm sure you did, but somewhere along the line he probably fell in with bad company," I said in an effort to save him the trouble of making excuses for Kade's criminal tendencies.

"I'm afraid so," he agreed. "But I would never have believed that he would steal from my wife and me."

"He did that?" I asked. I wasn't surprised, but it was news to me. "What did he take?"

"We don't even know for sure what he got away with," George said. "He's been using my identity and my wife's. He cleaned out one savings account. At least we're pretty sure it was him. We've been checking on that all day."

"Did he get a lot?" I asked.

"I'd say," George said, sounding like he was feeling a mixture of anger and grief.

"I'm sorry. Maybe it's not too late to recover some of that," I suggested.

"I hope it's not. And I hope he hasn't done us too much more damage." He paused for a second, and I waited. He finally went on, asking, "So what did you want to know?"

"I'm interested in what Kade knows about guns. How much he shoots, what kinds he likes, that sort of thing," I said.

"So he's stealing guns too," George said, making an assumption that I didn't feel the need to correct. "That doesn't surprise me now, not after what I've learned that he's been doing. Kade has always liked guns. And he's a whale of a good shot. He can outshoot me any day of the week."

"Pistols or rifles?" I asked.

"Both. I have always loved shooting for sport, and I taught him, but he was a natural. He could shoot the eye out of deer at two hundred yards."

"Did he ever shoot in competitions?" I asked.

"Oh yes, and he did right well. In fact, he got acquainted with some people up in the Utah County area in some of his matches," Mr. Squire revealed.

He had just elevated his son to one of the top three on my suspect list. "Does he own a 30-06 rifle?" I asked. George confirmed that he did. Then I asked, "Who here in Utah did he shoot with—you know, the ones you just mentioned?"

I don't suppose I was surprised when he said, "Some guy named Jake and a girlfriend of his."

"Lucia Root," I said.

"Yeah, I think that might have been the woman's name. He told me he gave them some pointers that helped them improve their accuracy."

I wondered if that was why he thought Jake owed him. I asked a few more questions, and after listening to a heartbroken father talk about his wayward son, I finally got off the phone with Mr. Squire. I got right back on it again, this time with Detective Milt Wakefield.

"It will be a little while before they can get back with us on the results of the ballistics testing," he said after I had filled him in on what I had learned. "They promised to put a rush on things when I explained where we were in the investigation and about someone shooting at you and Sophie. When we get those results, it will either bring our list to two or one."

I knew it would simplify things if it turned out to be Jim Ralsen, but my gut didn't feel good about that. Kade was in jail. If we could somehow get a confession out of him, it would narrow the suspects to him. And yet I was bothered. He couldn't have been the one shooting at me at the storage yard.

"I guess we will just need to move ahead while we're waiting," I said. "Are you staying up there while they do the testing, or are you coming back down?"

"I'm on the road right now," he said. "They promised to call me with the results."

"What should we do next?" I asked as I looked at my watch. It was almost seven in the evening now.

"What do you think?" Milt asked me.

I thought for a moment. It seemed strange that he, the experienced detective, would be asking me, but since he had, I shared my thoughts with him. "Milt, if I were to rate our three main suspects in this case, I would put Jake above the other two. In addition to that, we know where Kade is, and I don't think Jim Ralsen is going anywhere," I said. "At least I hope he's not."

Milt chuckled. "That's the advantage we cops have over you private eyes. We have a lot more resources. Detective Richards has him under surveillance."

"That's a relief," I confessed. "So the only one we don't know the location of is Jake. I think we need to find him. Anyway, that girlfriend of his is probably the one that's been tailing me this time. Let's try to find him again, and her, for that matter. If I see that car again, I'll let her keep me in sight until someone can stop her. She can lead us to Jake."

"If we don't get a call that he's returned to his home first," Milt agreed.

"We need to put all the resources we can muster into finding him," I said. "I'd like to wrap this thing up tonight."

"Sounds good to me, Dallas," Milt said. "I'll call Pete Richards and see if he can meet us at the police department. He can probably help get more officers to assist us."

Pete was waiting there when I arrived. I brought him up to date with our progress on the investigation. "I've already got people looking for the silver car," Pete told me. "Have you seen it lately?"

I told him that I hadn't but that I suspected Lucia hadn't given up on me, that Jake wouldn't let her. He agreed with me. While I called and checked on Alex, Ellen, and Sophie, he made some phone calls in an attempt to see if he could learn where else Jake might be hanging out.

My three lady friends were all okay but bored and restless and worrying needlessly about me. At least that's what I told them—I was being careful and didn't want them to worry. Sophie had just talked to Kanon, who was also bored and restless. I envied the four of them. It would be nice to be bored right now. I was very restless and far from bored.

chapter TWENTY-TWO

MILT WAKEFIELD HAD BARELY WALKED into the police department when Pete got a call from the officer at Jake's house. "Let's roll," Pete said urgently as he slammed the phone down. "Jake just got home."

"Why don't you ride with me," Milt suggested as we rushed outside.

"Thanks, that would be great, but let me get my pistol from the truck," I said.

Ten minutes later, Milt and I, along with Detective Richards and a couple of other Provo officers arrived at Jake's home. Milt and Pete walked to the door. I sat in Pete's patrol car, feeling like the odd man out, while the other officers watched the back of the house. I watched while Jake answered the door. The officers spoke to him for a moment and then signaled for me to join them.

"What's this nonsense about?" he asked angrily as we followed him into the house.

"We have a few questions," Pete Richards said. He introduced Detective Wakefield and then me.

"You're the guy that was helping Kanon up in Ogden Saturday night," he said. "So you're a rent-a-cop, huh?"

I didn't respond to the slur. I simply said, "Let's talk about a blue Cadillac that Lucia was going to give you for your birthday a few months ago."

"What about it?" he asked with an angry scowl. "Jerry Grady bought it out from under her. End of story."

"Not quite the end, Jake," Milt said. "In fact, it's sort of the beginning, I think."

"What are you talking about, man?" Jake asked with a sneer. "I ain't seen that car since. It was a beauty. I thought it was too bad that Grady was going to use it as a derby car. It was a classic, not the kind you beat up. But he got it, and that's all there is to it."

"Where were you today around noon?" I asked.

"Am I under arrest for something?" he asked, looking at Pete.

"Nope," Pete said.

Jake shrugged. "I was in Price. I have a friend down there that needed help with an engine. I've been there since this morning. I just got home fifteen minutes or so ago."

"Was Lucia with you?" I asked

"No, but my pals down there can verify it for me if you need that done for some reason," he said.

I asked Pete to verify it for me, and then Jake continued. "Why are you asking? Did something happen today that you think I know about?"

"It did," Milt said. "Do you have a large green car?"

"Nope," he said.

"How about a blue one?" I asked.

"Yep," he said. "It's a Pontiac. I let Lucia take it today. She likes to drive it. It's a really comfortable car."

My eyes met Milt's, and I felt a sudden twisting of my gut. I turned back to Jake. "Where is she today?" I asked.

"At work. That's why she didn't go to Price with me."

"Where does she live?" I asked as my brain was kicking into overdrive.

"Sometimes here, sometimes in her apartment in Orem," he said. "Why?"

"Just wondered," I said lamely. "Does she have a silver sports car?"

Jake shook his head in annoyance and moved toward the door. None of us had sat down, and it looked like he was about to invite us to leave. "Well, does she?" Richards pressed.

"Yeah, what of it? It's a Camaro, one I restored for her."

"Does she drive it much?" I asked as Jake opened the door.

"Not much. She prefers to drive my Pontiac," he said. "Now, if there's nothing more, you guys can go."

"Actually, there is more," I said. "Why did you hire Lyle Wertz to follow me and cut up my tires?"

Shock crossed his face, but it was fleeting. "I don't know what you're talking about," he lied.

"Sure you do. He says you'd been told I was trying to destroy your career as a derby driver and you wanted to discourage me."

"He lied," he said flatly.

"I don't think so. He gave me the two hundred dollars you gave him. Who told you I was out to destroy your career, such as it is?"

He looked at me for a moment, anger shooting from his eyes. But then he said, "Okay, so I asked Lyle to follow you. That's not a crime. But I didn't tell the little weasel to slash any tires. That was his own dimwitted idea if he did that."

"He did that," I said. "And I caught him in the act. He was quick to point fingers at you. But he said you wouldn't tell him who said I was out to ruin your career, which, by the way, isn't true."

"Ah, what the heck. It don't matter anyway. Lucia told me. And she got it from a good source. One you were working with."

"And who would that be?" I pressed.

"Kelsey Glazer," he said.

"Her cousin," I said. "So tell me, were she and Kelsey on good terms?"

Jake glanced at me, and a puzzled look replaced some of the anger in his eyes. "Funny you should ask that. I thought they were, but when he got murdered the other day and I told her about it, she didn't seem to care like I thought she would."

I took a deep breath. Jake was standing by the door. Nobody was moving. "Did you ask her why she didn't care?" I asked.

"She said that he'd been acting like a real jerk lately. She even said she told him not to come around anymore," Jake answered. "She didn't say exactly what he'd done, but I didn't care. I never liked Kelsey. But when she told him to get lost, that was when she says he told her what you were up to. Sort of made sense to me."

I shook my head. "What would be the chance of looking at your blue Pontiac?" I asked.

"I told you Lucia has it," he said. "But why would you want to look at it?"

"I would like to know if there's a bullet hole in the passenger side," I said.

"Of course there's not," he said. "That's stupid."

"You mean there wasn't one when you let her take it," I said.

His eyes narrowed. "What are you saying?" he asked.

"Why don't we go in and sit down. Then I'll tell you," I said.

"I guess it won't hurt," he growled. "But there better not be nothing wrong with my Pontiac."

We had scarcely sat down before Milt pulled out his cell phone. "It's the crime lab," he said and took the call.

"What's the crime lab got to do with me?" Jake asked. "Are you guys trying to set me up for something? If you are, you'll be hearing from my attorney. I ain't done nothing wrong."

"That call is not about you," I said as Milt stepped over to the door and spoke softly into his phone. "Now, let me tell you about something that happened today. Someone took a shot at me at a storage yard in Salt Lake. Whoever it was missed because I saw a glint of sunlight on the barrel of the rifle and ducked. I returned fire. I'm almost positive that I hit the car. I might have hit it twice."

"This is all very interesting," he said, cocking his head to one side. "But I don't see what it's got to do with me or Lucia."

Just then Milt closed his phone and rejoined us. "It's not a match," he said.

I nodded my head. I knew who had killed Jerry and Kelsey. It wasn't Jim. I'd known it before the call from the crime lab. I spoke to Jake again. "I was looking at a dark blue Cadillac," I said. "This key fits it." I reached in my pocket and pulled out the lucky-charm key ring and dangled it in front of him."

His face went pale. "You recognize this, don't you?" I asked.

"Of course I do. It was in the Cadillac the day Lucia and I went to pick it up from the guy that sold it to Grady. We were both mad. I'm still mad. That's not the kind of car you waste on a demolition derby," he said. "And that's exactly what Jerry was going to do with it. I know he was. I was just watching for the day it appeared again."

"So you and Lucia knew it was Jerry that bought it?" I asked.

"We were pretty sure, but there was nothing we could do about it."

"You have nice handwriting, don't you?" I asked, almost positive at this point that he didn't.

"Are you kidding me?" he said with a gruff laugh. "Lucia always told me I should let her teach me penmanship."

"She does have good handwriting doesn't she?"

"Very good," he agreed. "I still don't see where you are going with all of this," Jake said.

"Are you sure?" I asked. "Someone with pretty handwriting wrote some threatening notes. One was even signed with your name." I pulled out my notebook and a pen. "Here, sign your name for me." He balked, but he finally did it. He was right. His handwriting was atrocious. He hadn't written those notes. I knew who had. "So who do you think wrote the notes?"

He slammed one fist against the other. "I've no idea. Are you saying you put a bullet in my Pontiac?" he asked as if what I'd said earlier had just now hit him full force.

"If Lucia took a shot at me, I did. Like you and Lucia, I'm a good shot. And don't tell me that the two of you aren't crack shots. Even Kade Squire knows that," I said.

A whole range of emotions passed across Jake's face. I could see that he was struggling within himself. Finally, he said, "Lucia is a much better shot than me."

"Does she have a 30-06 rifle?" Milt asked. I'd been wondering when he was going to help me ask questions. But this was a key one.

Jake nodded and worked his mouth for a moment, but nothing came out. I think he had just reached the same conclusion I had. I looked at Detective Wakefield. From his face, I knew he was right there with me. I nodded at him to go ahead. I was pretty sure I knew what he was going to ask.

He didn't disappoint me. "Where was Lucia the night Jerry was killed in Duchesne?"

Again Jake worked his mouth. But this time he finally managed to speak again. "I don't know. She didn't come to the race that night. She said she had other things she needed to do."

I was afraid he was right. I stood up. The officers followed suit. "Should we go find your Pontiac?" I asked.

"I'd rather not," he said. But he finally agreed. Lucia wasn't at home when we got to her apartment. By then we had been joined by a pair of officers from the Orem Police Department. There was a blue Pontiac there, however, and my aim had been pretty good considering that I'd never fired Ellen's rifle before. The only thing that had saved the shooter was that one of my bullets had struck the passenger door just below the window, directly across from where Lucia had been shooting. And yes, I knew for sure it was Lucia who had tried to kill me.

Jake put a finger on the hole in his car, and then he called Lucia a few words that I won't use here. But he concluded with, "She must have killed Jerry Grady. I hated the guy, and I wanted to beat him, and I wanted the Cadillac, but you don't kill people over stuff like that. I can't believe she'd do that."

"Do you really believe Kelsey told her I was out to ruin you?" I asked.

I could see his mind working, and finally, he said, "I suppose he could have."

"But do you really think he did?"

He seemed to think it over again, and then he said, "He must have done. Why else would she tell me that?"

"So you would try to warn me off. She probably thought that I was getting too close to the truth about who killed Jerry Grady. When that didn't work, she decided to do to me what she'd done to him. Only I ducked in time, and she missed."

Jake's face was pale. "I don't believe it," he said, but there was no conviction in his voice.

Milt spoke up then. "Your car is implicated. We'll seize it as evidence, get the bullet out of it, have it tested, and prove that it came from the gun Dallas was shooting. Then we'll charge you as an accessory."

"You can't do that," he said angrily, shaking his fist at Milt.

"We can, and we will. In fact, we've got enough to take you in right now."

Jake threw both hands in the air, his face red with anger. He cursed, but then he said, "Okay, okay, I'll help you if that's what you want. If Lucia did what you say she did, then she doesn't care about me anymore."

"Okay, here's what we need you to do: call her and ask her to meet you either here or at the house," Milt said.

"I can do that, I guess, but what do I say?" he asked after a moment's hesitation.

"Don't let on that you know what she's done. She's your girlfriend; you'll think of something," Milt said.

"Ex-girlfriend," he said as he, in a sudden burst of anger, put a dent in his Pontiac with his fist. "She's a—"

I cut him off. "We already know," I said. "And I would say that we should have her come to your place. That way she won't know that you know about the bullet hole in your car until we get a chance to tell her."

The fierce Jake Frankland that had hammered Kanon's car in the derby in Ogden wasn't so fierce now. He was between a rock and a hard spot, and he knew it. And he knew who had put him there. We drove back to his house, and then he called Lucia's cell phone. He spoke for minute before he said, "Can you come over tonight? I'm lonely." It sounded natural. He'd obviously used that phrase before.

He listened for a minute, and then he closed the phone. "She's on her way," he said. His anger had given way to intense sadness. "I'd rather not be here when she comes," he said. "Would you guys mind if I leave for a little while?"

"You'll need to be with an officer," Detective Richards said. "But you can go with him down to the station, where I will get a full statement from you later."

He shrugged his shoulders. "Do I have a choice?" he asked. "I just wanted to go get a cup of coffee," he said. My mouth watered. That sounded good, but I had consumed my last cup. "I'm not going to run off," he whined.

"That's right, because we'll see to it that you don't." A minute later, a uniformed officer escorted him from his house.

The two detectives waited in Jake's house for Lucia. They had left the kitchen light on, but the front room light was off. The porch light was shining. Jake had told us she would not knock, that she would just walk in. A couple of other officers waited, hidden in the shadows by the front corners of the house. I was also in the house, but they asked me to wait in one of Jake's bedrooms, one that faced the street. It was my job to let them know when she arrived.

When Lucia Root came into the driveway, I alerted my detective friends. She approached the door, her purse swinging in her hand. They were standing, one on each side of the door when she opened it and stepped in. "Jake, I'm here," she called out.

She screamed and struggled when Milt and Pete grabbed her, but she didn't stand a chance. After Pete and his fellow Provo officers had taken Lucia to the police station, Milt and I talked for a minute. My job was finished, so he said he'd give me a ride to the police station, where I could get my truck and he could begin questioning his murder suspect. I called Jim Ralsen after getting in Milt's car with him.

"I'll get your gun back to you tomorrow," I promised. "We caught Jerry's killer tonight. I'm sorry that I put you through so much."

"I'll hand one thing to you, Dallas," he said, sounding profoundly relieved. "You are good at your job. I just wish I still had you working for me."

"After what I put you through?" I said.

"Hey, I'd take you back in a heartbeat," he said. "I know now that you are someone I can trust completely."

"Tell you what, Jim," I said, kicking myself as I said it, "I will be busy tomorrow wrapping this thing up for my client, but if you'd like, maybe I can come back and help out for a day or two."

"You'd do that?" he asked.

"Only if it's okay with you."

"It's a deal," he said. "By the end of the week, maybe I can get some more help hired."

I called Alex next. She answered, saying, "We are still bored, Dallas. And it's getting late. I think Grandma would like to go to bed pretty soon."

"Would she like to sleep in her own house?" I asked.

Alex squealed. "Dallas, you did it? You did it!"

"Can I talk to my client now?" I asked. "I need to report to her."

"First, was it Jake?" she asked.

"No, it was his girlfriend," I responded. "I need to tell Ellen."

Ellen was packed and ready to go by the time I got to her hotel. The sweet little woman hugged me and reminded me and her granddaughter that the Lord had led her to me. She was both overjoyed at having a killer brought to justice and more sad than ever over the loss of an errant but much-loved grandson.

Alex timidly hugged me, and then she said, "I'm sorry I ever doubted you. I wish I could make it up to you."

"You can," I said.

"How?" she asked.

"Just one little kiss will do," I told her with a grin. I got that kiss, and I have to admit, I enjoyed it. It represented the good side of Alex Grady, a side I hadn't seen a lot of during the time I'd known her.

I drove Alex and Ellen back to the other hotel in my truck. "What are you looking for?" Alex asked as we rode.

"That's a good question," I said, feeling foolish. "I've had people tailing me so much for the past few days that I'm in the habit of watching behind me."

"Are you going to keep working for Hank Pierce?" she asked.

"That's the plan," I said.

"Then you better keep that habit," she said with a grin. "You never know when you might need it again."

After Alex and Ellen had loaded their things in the little lime green VW Beetle, Ellen said, "I'll see you in a little while, won't I?"

"Sure," I said. "I'd like that."

I watched them drive off, and then I went back to my room. Sophie was waiting outside my door, her suitcase at her feet. "Come on in," I said. "I still have to pack. Mrs. Grady is expecting me to stay at her place tonight."

It took me all of three minutes to pack. It took longer to drive to Sophie's house. She was unnaturally quiet all the way. When we got there, I looked up and down the street before parking my truck in front of her house instead of in the back. There were no black sports cars, no black vans, no white Cavaliers, and no silver Camaros. I helped Sophie out of the truck and up to her front door.

"You can come in if you'd like," she said, fussing with a strand of that gorgeous, long black hair of hers.

I wanted to, but I said, "I better not. I'm really tired, and I can still feel the effects of Kade's boots. I look forward to a long night of uninterrupted rest."

Her eyes fell. I touched her chin and gently lifted her head. For a moment, we just looked at each other. Her eyes were misty. I didn't ask her for a kiss the way I had Alex. I got one anyway. She opened the door, started to step through, then suddenly turned back and threw her arms around me. "Oh, Dallas, I'm going to miss you so much," she said. And I got another kiss, but it was not a little one. It left me feeling dizzy.

"Will I ever see you again?"

"After that," I said, "you better believe it." But I was still torn. I had come to know two young women. And I liked both of them. I hoped to get to know them better. I'd just have to see what happened.

Driving back to Mrs. Grady's home, my home for now, I was both elated that the killer had been caught and lonesome for the companionship I had enjoyed the past few days.

I didn't sleep as well that night as I'd hoped to. I went to see Hank the next morning. He was only slightly improved. Shirley, his faithful companion, was at his side. "How did you do last night?" he asked.

"It's over," I said. "And I'm still alive."

He smiled and said weakly, "In our line of work, it's never over, so get used to it."

EPILOGUE

LUCIA ROOT WAS CONVICTED OF two murders. It took several days of work, but Detective Richards, someone I knew I'd work with a lot in the future, eventually found out why Lucia had killed her own cousin. Kelsey had guessed that she'd killed Jerry. At first, he was helping her by trying to scare me off the case by threatening Mrs. Grady, by trying to abduct her, and by threatening me. But after I'd broken his wrist, the foolish man had become both angry and greedy, and he'd told Lucia that unless she paid him a lot more for his efforts, he would drop a few hints to the cops in Duchesne. Blackmail had been his undoing.

Hank Pierce never fully recovered, so he retired a few months later, turning his business over to me on financial terms he was sure I could meet. For a while I struggled, and had it not been for his willingness to let me consult him from time to time and to let his wife act as my office manager, I might have never succeeded. As it was, I soon had more work than I could handle, so I hired an assistant, or I guess I should say I got a partner. We call our agency Rowen and Rowen Investigations.

My partner only works part time since she also spends time being a wife and homemaker. Alexandra Grady and I are still friends. Sophie and Alex are still friends. I dated both Sophie and Alex for a short time. But it was Alex who pointed out to me that she and I would always have friction if we were too close. And no one has as yet replaced Ellen Grady as my favorite client.

As for Sophie, she is the best half of Rowen and Rowen Investigations. She's also the best half of Mr. and Mrs. Dallas Rowen. She has become to me what Shirley is to Hank. I am both loved and the luckiest guy on earth.

about THE AUTHOR

CLAIR M. POULSON RETIRED AFTER twenty years in law enforcement. During his career, he served in the US Army Military Police, the Utah Highway Patrol, and the Duchesne County Sheriff's Department, where he was first a deputy and then the county sheriff. He currently serves as a justice court judge for Duchesne County, a position he has held for more than twenty years. His career of over forty years working in the criminal justice system has provided a wealth of material from which he draws in writing his books.

Clair has served on numerous boards and committees over the years. Among them are the Utah Judicial Council; an FBI advisory board; the Peace Officers Standards and Training Council; the Utah Justice Court Board of Judges; the Utah Sheriff's Association, where he served as president; and the Utah Commission on Criminal and Juvenile Justice.

Other interests include activity in the Church, assisting his oldest son in operating their grocery store, ranching with his oldest son and other family members, growing hay and pastures, and raising horses, cattle, llamas, goats, and fallow deer.

He has published around twenty novels, most of them bestsellers.

Clair and his wife, Ruth, live in Duchesne and are the parents of five married children. They have twenty-three grandchildren.